MISS FELLINGHAM'S REBELLION

A Regency Romance

LYNN MESSINA

potatoworks press · greenwich village

Love Takes Root series

Anything can happen in Regency London, as five headstrong and passionate women defy propriety and find love with powerful lords as determined as they are.

Love Takes Root series

Beatrice Hyde-Clare mysteries

Book One: A Brazen Curiosity

Book Two: A Scandalous Deception

Book Three: An Infamous Betrayal

Book Four: A Nefarious Engagement

Book Five: A Treacherous Performance

Book Six: A Sinister Establishment

Book Seven: A Boldly Daring Scheme

Book Eight: A Ghastly Spectacle

Chapter One

✦

Nobody *who was* there at the inception of Miss Fellingham's rebellion had any idea that such an event was likely to happen. Not her mother, certainly, who relied on her eldest daughter's good sense in the absence of her own. Not her father, who had said not a fortnight before, after a particularly tearful outburst from his second daughter, Evelyn, that nothing did him credit like Catherine's calm nature. Not her brother, whose repeated pratfalls into disgrace and folly required his clever sister's machinations. Not even Evelyn, whose exalted status in the household relied heavily on her older sister's lack of interest in the social whirl, had the smallest clue. No, the only person who might have had an inkling was Melissa, the baby of the family at the age of thirteen. She, however, was not present in the breakfast parlor at that time but rather obliviously ensconced in the schoolroom conjugating French verbs.

The day started ordinarily enough, with the usual grumblings about the poor quality of the meal.

"I just don't see why Cook can't make chocolate the way Aunt Louisa's cook does," Evelyn said, her pretty heart-shaped mouth turning down at the corners as she thought of the lovely morning confections her Aunt Louisa provided, of which she was being deprived. "How difficult can it be?"

"Dear Evelyn," her mama comforted, taking a seat at the table and nodding to Hawkins to serve her eggs. "We must be patient. Cook has the rheumatic complaint."

"I don't see what that signifies," said Evelyn, who had no patience for any excuses but her own. "We are discussing the chocolate, not her health. Certainly, I deserve a decent portion of chocolate in the morning. Do I really ask for so much?"

"Yes, brat, you do," said her brother, Frederick, who, at nineteen, was one year her senior. "In fact, you are always asking for something. Weren't we just talking yesterday at intolerable length about the ostrich-plumed hat you *had* to have?" He took the seat across from Evelyn and made a flourish with his serviette. Seeing that he was dressed simply in skintight yellow pantaloons and a white lawn shirt, his mama suspected he was going for a round at Gentleman Jackson's rooms, an activity she found extremely distasteful and unbred.

"Pooh," Evelyn dismissed airily. "That's different. Madame Claude's ostrich-plumed bonnets are all the crack, and I will look like the veriest quiz if I go around in last season's fashions. I simply must have one. What I need and what I want are two vastly different things."

"Damn me!" a voice ejaculated from the head of the table. Sir Vincent, the patriarch of the Fellingham clan, stuck his head up from behind the morning paper, which he had been reading quietly for more than half an hour. "I say, m'dear, these eggs are atrocious. Why have I been given a plate of runny eggs?"

"Because Cook has the rheumatic complaint," Evelyn

answered pertly, earning a look from her mama, who wasn't the least bit entertained by her wit.

"What's that you say?" Sir Vincent asked. He was a solid man of medium height, with square shoulders, slanted nose and thunderous black eyes that glared frequently in the general direction of his wife, a petite woman with a sensibility as delicate as her beauty. Together, they made an odd pair, completely unsuited in looks and temperament, and most people, including their children, wondered how they'd ever made a match of it. "Speak up, girl. What's this about rumors?"

"Not rumors, Sir Vincent, but rheumatism. I am sure I have mentioned the problem to you before. I daresay you're not the least interested now, for you never are. Pray return to your reading and don't worry about us. We shall muddle through as always." Lady Fellingham raised a serviette to her lips and dabbed gently.

"How can you say that, Mama?" Evelyn asked, appalled. "I assure you, it is of the utmost importance. This chocola—"

"Brat, stop teasing your mother," Frederick interrupted.

"Me?" Evelyn all but screeched, her pretty heart-shaped lips not quite so pretty as they curled into a snarl. "How can you say that? Mama—"

"For God's sake, Liza," said Fellingham, folding his paper and laying it down on the table. This was most certainly not what he had in mind when he decided to have breakfast at his house instead of his club. "Can't you keep your brood of heathens quiet for one meal?"

At that, the room erupted in argument, as Liza defended her brood of heathens and said pagans decried their papa's unjust characterization.

"The eggs are runny because Frederick came in last night at four in the morning and had Caruthers wake up Cook to provide him with an early-morning snack. This is her act of

3

reprisal, which seems to me fairly warranted, as Freddy fell asleep at the table before the collation was served. As for the chocolate, it is always weak. Had Cook slept seven hours straight, something that is clearly a most cherished goal, the chocolate would still be weak. I suggest, Evelyn, that unless you're prepared to visit Aunt Louisa's kitchens and receive instruction as to how to make the drink yourself, you learn to like your chocolate weak."

The four other occupants of the room ceased their chattering and turned to stare at the utterer of these most extraordinary sentences.

Miss Catherine Fellingham sat at the far end of the table, wearing the same white cotton morning dress that she always wore and reading the morning paper as she always did. Perusing the news to avoid idle conversation with her family was her father's trick and one she had adopted six years before when every morning was filled with hopeless chatter about this ball or that rout she had attended the night before. During her first season, Mama bombarded her with ceaseless questions: Did she talk to Lord Bessborough? Did she dance with Viscount Eddington? Did Mr. Yardley take her into dinner? Their expectations were so high and her success so low, that she retreated from the social whirl as soon as she could—and from her family, as well.

She still attended parties, of course, acting as escort to Evelyn, who was just out this season. And sometimes she enjoyed herself. Only last night, for example, they had seen Kean in a wonderful performance of *Hamlet.* Of course, Evelyn, not surprisingly, hadn't been able to sit still, so busy was she examining the residents of the other boxes. But Catherine was able to ignore her sister. Catherine had the questionable ability to ignore every member of her family, except Melissa. She enjoyed being with her youngest sister, who had a quick, agile brain. She didn't miss much and thought of more than only eligible *partis* and ostrich plumes.

Not that Catherine herself was one hundred percent immune to the allure of eligible *partis* and ostrich plumes. She sometimes longed to wear beautiful gowns and elaborate coifs and chatter sparklingly with handsome beaux who found her enchanting. But her first season had taught her well: Awkward, tall women who can barely rub two words together do not win accolades such as *enchanting*. Indeed, they do not win any accolades at all because nobody knows they are there. Never mind the engaging gold eyes that could sparkle with keen intelligence when something caught her fancy or the rosebud cheeks that blushed charmingly just before she uttered some teasing reply. These things were not observed during her first season because they were not in evidence. The *ton* had made Catherine too nervous to be clever or even pretty. She was, instead, an indecently tall lump (five foot ten!) that stood on the edge of the dance floor, at once terrified that nobody would talk to her and terrified that someone would. More often than not, the former happened, but every so often a kind gentleman would try to strike up a conversation and she would stammer helplessly, gutted by a shyness she couldn't have imagined as an eager young girl in Glossop.

Six years later, she was still overwhelmed by the beau monde, particularly handsome noblemen who she assumed were looking down on her, though, of course, they frequently had to look *up* to do it. She had acquired, at least, a modicum of poise in the interval as well as a subtle sense of humor, but despite these improvements, she remained too self-effacing to make an impression.

Of course, the four family members who contemplated her now, wide-eyed and amazed, were inclined to agree with this assessment. They were used to Catherine's strange flights of fancy—why else would they let her do something so masculine as read the morning paper at the breakfast table?—but they had never before heard her speak in that tone. Her mother stared at her, wondering if her eldest daughter had just raised her voice.

"Have you told her yet?" Freddy asked, eating his eggs, which tasted just fine to him. He preferred his eggs with a little bit of run in them.

Catherine, her spleen comfortably vented, was on the verge of returning to an article on the Coinage Act, but she paused at this. "Tell me what?"

"Oh, pooh," Evelyn cried, "does she really have to know?"

Sir Vincent, who had been on the verge of asking the same thing, turned to his wife. "Really, m'dear, was it necessary to blurt it to everyone?"

"Tell me what?" Catherine said again.

Liza Fellingham surveyed the breakfast room. Only her immediate family and Hawkins were present. "Everyone? Surely my children are not everyone. Besides, I have said nothing on the subject to Melissa."

At this exchange, Catherine's concern grew. There was very little her mother endeavored to hide from Melissa—or anyone. She had always been too free in her manners. "Tell me what?"

Sir Vincent harrumphed and turned to his daughter. He folded up the paper, abandoning with some regret all hope of finishing it in quiet and resolving never to attempt a meal in his own home again. "It seems your mother has gotten herself into a little fix. Nothing to raise the roof over."

"Me? Sir Vincent," cried the accused, alarmed by the blame being laid at her slippered feet. "If it weren't for your gaming debts—"

Sensing that one of her parents' ugly rows was about to erupt, Catherine interrupted. "Hawkins," she said firmly, "we're going to retire to the drawing room. We'll have our tea there."

"The drawing room?" asked Evelyn, surprised. "But I haven't finished my chocolate yet. I don't want to go to the drawing room."

"Yes, you do, brat," her brother assured her, pulling her chair out. "Besides, weren't you not a moment ago complaining about the inferior quality of your chocolate? Come on."

Evelyn pouted some more but complied, getting to her feet with practiced grace. Her father made a similar show of disgust before yielding. All four followed Catherine into the drawing room, which her mother had redecorated in the latest Oriental fashion, following the lead of Prinny. Although it had been more than a year, the dragon-adorned furniture, Chinese red wallpaper and beech tables carved to resemble bamboo still made her cringe. Fortunately, Lady Fellingham had been unable to gain Sir Vincent's consent to redo the entire town house in the similar style.

They all sat down, save Sir Vincent, who chose to lean against the mantelpiece, his elbow resting next to a lacquered pagoda. He was still a youngish man, and his posture and demeanor were ingratiating. Catherine loved her father, although she often lost patience with him for the way he cavalierly treated the family's fortune and the contemptuous manner with which he sometimes treated her mother. Of course, Catherine realized that her mother was not much better, intentionally bothering her husband with trivial matters that she knew he took little interest in in order to put his nose out of joint. They were a quarrelsome pair and often loud. She had gotten in the habit of leaving the room when she sensed things were about to get uncomfortable. She hated arguments, raised voices and ugly disagreements, so she let Evelyn have her way when she pouted and Frederick her help when he asked. It was so much easier than having a scene. And now they seemed intent on dragging her into their nonsense. She trembled at the thought of what her nonsensical mother could have done now, especially if she was acting out of petulance at her husband's losses. If he could just leave off playing faro, the entire family would be a lot more comfortable. But nobody had ever listened to her when she talked sense, so Catherine had simply stopped talking altogether.

"Well, then," she said after Hawkins brought in the tea and closed the door quietly behind him, "we are assembled privately. What disastrous news need you impart?"

"Disastrous?" scoffed her sister. "It's nothing of consequence. A tempest in a teapot, really."

"That ain't true, brat, and you know it." Freddy said, accepting a cup from his mother before scowling at his sister. "You don't understand what has happened."

"Heathens!" Sir Vincent bellowed. "Enough squabbling. Liza, tell your daughter what you've done now."

Lady Fellingham, of course, would have preferred to argue some more over her husband's uncomplimentary description, which was insulting to both her children and herself, but what little sense she had demanded that she stay focused on the more pressing topic at hand. "As dear Evie says, it is just an insignificant snarl. It's like this, you see. You know my dear school friend Arabella Wellesly?"

"Of course," answered Catherine, "Lord Wellington's cousin."

"Exactly!" her mother exclaimed. "There, you see, darling, that wasn't so difficult." She folded her hands in her lap and smiled blithely.

"But, Mama, you haven't told me anything."

"Oh, yes. Well, my dear school friend Arabella married Courtland," she explained. "It was a beautiful wedding at St.

8

George's. Anybody who was anybody was in attendance, even Prinny, who was sporting an infamous waistcoat that was several sizes too small. I remember remarking—"

"Courtland reports to the Duke of Raeburn," threw in Freddy, who thought that detail was more important than what the regent had worn to a party more than twenty years before.

"I know who Courtland is as well as to whom he reports," said Catherine, wondering just how long this would take. Her mother was notorious for her digressions, especially on occasions like this one, when she was reluctant to get to the heart of the matter.

"Yes, well, you see, Arabella and I are very close. We are bosom friends, you see, and we discuss everything. She knows all about our family life just as I know all about hers," she said, somewhat anxiously as her three middle fingers tapped the cushion on which she sat, a nervous habit she adopted whenever presented with an unpleasant confession.

Catherine could not imagine where all this information was leading. "And?"

"Well, she is really a wonderful, caring person, full of sentiment and quite sympathetic to my suffering," Lady Fellingham explained.

Catherine looked around her at the opulent room, with its lavish designs, lush fabrics and extravagant details. "Suffering, Mama?"

For a moment her ladyship looked embarrassed, then she straightened her spine and looked her oldest daughter in the eye. "Yes, my dear, suffering. And dearest Arabella came up with a wonderful scheme to end my, uh, suffering."

"I'm sorry, Mama, but you are going to have to elaborate. What do you mean by suffering?" Catherine asked.

Liza blushed in earnest. "I'd hate to talk about it."

"Surely, Mama, you can tell me anything you can tell Lady Courtland," she said reasonably.

As much as she wanted to deny the logic of this statement, her ladyship could not, and she expelled a loud sigh before confessing, "Money problems. Your father—"

"Damn me, m'dear," interrupted Sir Vincent, "but this is your sin, not mine. Acquit me of any wrongdoing."

"How can I?" she cried. "Your wretched gambling has gotten us into this straitened circumstance in the first place."

"Your mother has been selling commissions in the king's army for a price," Sir Vincent declared, heedless of his wife's feelings.

"Fellingham!" Liza exclaimed in outrage. "To come out with it like that!" She stole a peek at her daughter. "He makes it sound so sordid, Catherine, and really it wasn't anything of the sort. These boys wanted to advance their careers, and my dear friend Arabella wanted to help them and me. You know what it's like...." Lady Fellingham trailed off as she watched her daughter leave the room. "Catherine, dear, where are you going? Frederick, where can your sister be going?"

Catherine wasn't going anywhere, although she was not inclined to tell her mother that, for she was far too angry to speak. After she shut the drawing room door behind her, she escaped into one of the large leather wingback chairs in her father's study. Since none of her relations involved themselves much in the more serious pursuits of life, Catherine often spent many hours alone in the quiet room, hiding from her family and reading the latest novel from the lending library.

Safely ensconced in the comfortable chair, Catherine told herself to calm down. A small part of her wondered why she was so upset. Her mother was always getting into scrapes, and this one was probably no worse. But that kind of cool logic didn't fly with her this morning, for she knew better. Even if her family didn't understand the ramifications of her mother's most recent transgression, she, at least, did. Something like this was worse than a scandal; it was a crime. Imagine! Meddling with commissions! My God, she thought, her head pounding as the reality of the situation set in, her mother was a national security risk. Surely the 10th Hussars would march in there at any second in their sparkling blue uniforms and take her away. And where would they take her? Where do prisoners of the Crown go? Newgate? Certainly that was worse than the debtors' prison her father seemed determined to send them all to.

Her mother was right, of course: The true cause of the problem was Sir Vincent and his careless ways. Even if they squeaked through this jam with only a few scratches, there would always be another one, for her father could not be stopped from depleting the family's coffers and her mother could not be stopped from trying to avert the coffers' depletion. What was she to do? Things could not go on like this for very much longer. Either her mother would do something even more extraordinary to put them beyond the pale or her father would have them rusticating permanently in Dorset.

Or would he? The truth of the matter was that Catherine had no idea of the true state of the family's finances. She knew they were fixed well enough but just how well was a mystery. Her mother refused to speak of money with her, claiming the discussion of all things material other than clothes and hats was unbred. She herself had never made a push to understand the nature of things. She knew they had enough money to send Freddy to Oxford and to buy Evelyn crepe dresses. Beyond that, she never gave it much thought. Were they dangerously close to Dun territory or was it all in her mother's head?

The only thing to do, she realized, in the absence of complete information was to gather more. To do that, she would have to convince her mother to share the ledgers.

Then, when she had a proper understanding of how matters actually stood, she could settle on the best way to proceed. If the situation wasn't as dire as Lady Fellingham thought, she would ease her anxieties by calmly showing her the tallies. If her predictions were on the mark, she would suggest simple economies to slim the budget. Catherine absolutely refused to believe there was nothing she could do. If there were no corners left to cut or no reasoning with her mother, then she would learn how to play faro herself and instruct her father on how to improve his game. Imagining herself in a gaming hell taking lessons from the dealer on how to wager so amused her that she began to laugh. After a few minutes, her mirth slowed to a giggle, and she stood up from the familiar leather chair. Before she could implement any plan, she had to extract her family from their current debacle, a task she hoped wouldn't be impossible.

When Catherine returned to the drawing room, Hawkins was clearing the tea, placing cups on the serving tray next to the silver teapot.

"Well, there you are, girl," her mother exclaimed, waving her handkerchief at her. "Where have you been? Has anyone told you that it is rude to walk out of a room like that? Have I not raised you with more manners than that ridiculous display demonstrated?"

Catherine didn't think that given the circumstances her conduct was a subject worthy of critique and ignored her mother's comments. She waited until Hawkins had left the room before proceeding. "Where has my father gone?" she asked upon seeing that he was the only one who was not still in the room.

"Gone," said her mother.

"Gone where?" Catherine ignored the way her mother had thrown herself onto the divan in the simulation of a faint.

"Just gone."

Catherine turned to Freddy. "Where did he go?"

"To his club, I imagine. He spends most mornings there."

"What does it matter?" whined Evelyn, who stood up in a fit of anger. "I want to go shopping. Mama, you promised we could go to the milliner on Bond Street today so I could buy one of Madame Claude's dashing bonnets."

"I'm afraid, Evelyn, that you don't quite understand the severity of the situation. Your mother was selling commissions in the king's army." Catherine said this slowly and distinctly as if clear articulation were all that stood between her selfish sister and comprehension.

Evelyn laid her head on her palm and looked very bored. "Yes, yes, I know all that. I still don't see why you have to be such a sad Sadie about it. It was a bad thing to do and she won't do it anymore, will you, Mama. Now, why can't we go buy hats?"

Catherine closed her eyes and counted silently to ten. "Mayhap it hasn't occurred to you yet that you can't go to balls if your mother is in Newgate."

"Really, Catherine, doing it a bit brown," Freddy ejaculated. "I mean, we're not completely sunk, are we?"

"I don't know, Freddy, but we can't run the risk. We have to scotch this immediately."

"Not go to balls?" Evelyn squeaked, all appearance of ennui chased from her countenance. "That can't be right, Mama. I'll still be able to go to balls no matter what happens, no?"

But Lady Fellingham was in no condition to give her daughter the assurances she sought. "Oh, Cathy, you don't think it's as bad as all that, do you?" Visibly pale, she stood up and walked across the room to her daughter. "What would *I* do in jail? Will they make me wear chains?"

When she saw how distressed her mother was, Catherine regretted her strong words. She did want to teach her mother a lesson, of course, but not at the expense of her peace of mind. As misguided as she was, her mother had only been trying to help. As soon as Catherine got her hands on the household accounts, she would make sure that there would be no more Cheltenham tragedies enacted in the Oriental drawing room. "We must do our best never to find out."

"Oh, dearest Mama." Evelyn rushed to her mother and held out her hands, the horror of it all finally sinking in. "Will they let you bring a maid?"

Lady Fellingham rested her daughter's blond curls on her bosom. "I don't know, dear child, I simply do not know."

Catherine turned away from the scene and caught Freddy's eye. They both started laughing at the affecting nonsense.

"I don't see what is so funny," Evelyn said. "Your mother is going to Newgate and I"—here her voice broke—"I will never be able to go to a ball ever again. Surely this is the darkest hour ever."

"Don't throw your dancing slippers away yet, brat," Freddy said, trying to control his laughter. "I'm sure everything will be all right."

Catherine's amusement soon abated as well, although her eyes continued to sparkle. "Right, let's all sit down and talk about this reasonably."

Evelyn led her mother to the settee and gently sat down next to her, keeping her hands tightly clasped in hers.

"All right then, Mama, tell me how this was done," Catherine ordered.

"How what was done, dear?"

Closing her eyes for a moment, Catherine prayed for patience. "How did you and Lady Courtland succeed in meddling with the lists?"

"Oh. Lady Courtland is very clever, and she came up with the scheme. It was quite simple, my dear. Surely you know how all those dear boys—mostly second sons, of course—want to be majors in the foot guards. But there are so few openings, especially now in peacetime, and some of those dear boys have to wait for *years* on those horrid lists. Arabella's scheme allowed them to bypass the queue, in exchange for a small fee." Having confessed all, she leaned her head back against the cushions and sighed.

Her eldest daughter looked on in wonder. "You took bribes."

Lady Fellingham lifted her head. "Bribes?" She considered it for several seconds before saying, "No, I don't think they were bribes. *Bribe* is such a harsh word, and Arabella and I were only providing a public-spirited service."

Catherine didn't have the wherewithal to debate the issue. "And?"

Blue eyes stared out blankly. "And what, dear?"

"What happened after you received your compensation for your public-spirited service?"

"I brought the money home and paid the servants' wages."

Catherine told herself to remain patient. "No, I mean what happened with the names?"

Lady Fellingham giggled nervously. "Oh, that. Arabella got hold of her husband's lists of pending commissions and added a few names before he submitted them to the Duke of York for his signature."

"Devil it," exclaimed Freddy, who had been listening intently, "you mean Lord Courtland knew nothing of this? What sort of bufflehead is he?"

"Freddy, you will not talk like that in my drawing room," his mother said. "Save that vulgar cant for your club."

To Catherine's amusement, Freddy both blushed and scowled. "Really, Mama, my brother makes a good point. How could Lord Courtland not know of this scheme?"

"I would never be so unbred as to presume what Lord Courtland does or doesn't know," she said without a hint of irony. "He didn't interfere, and I respected him for that."

"Very well," Catherine said. She knew that answer was the best she would get. "Who else knows about this?"

"Only the men who paid our mother for their commissions," Freddy answered.

"How many are we talking about?"

"Oh, dear, how do I know?" quivered her mother. "It all happened so quickly, and dear Arabella kept track of the minor details."

"How many, Mama?"

Lady Fellingham removed her fingers from Evelyn's grasp and ran a pale hand over her brow. "Oh, maybe ten, fifteen on the outside. We've only just hit upon the scheme." Then she added with a spark of rebellion in her. "And, really, I don't see why it shouldn't have continued to work. It is a very good idea."

Several rejoinders flew through Catherine's mind, but it was beginning to dawn on her that nothing she could say would convince her mother of how greatly she'd sinned. "How did we find out?"

"One of Freddy's friends—Pershing, Parsnip or something," her ladyship said bitterly. "The damn fool told him all."

"I think we have much to thank this friend for," Catherine said. "It isn't often that something good happens as a result of Freddy."

"I say, Catherine, cut line," insisted her brother, much offended. "I haven't gotten us into this fix."

"You're right, Freddy," she conceded. "I apologize for the injustice I do you."

"What fix is that?" her mother asked. "Arabella and I shall stop immediately, and nobody need be any the wiser. There, I have solved the problem. I'll simply send a note to that effect to my friend, and we will consider the matter closed."

Catherine, who knew that anything pertaining to her mother was rarely simple, did not think this was the best remedy and insisted that they go visit Arabella, Lady Courtland at once to make sure the message was not only delivered but received.

"At this hour?" Lady Fellingham asked, appalled. "Selling commissions in the king's army might not be up to your standards, but I assure you, my dear, making indecently early house calls isn't up to mine! We will not be so shabby."

"I find your scruples admirable, Mama, if a little misaligned. We shall go presently, for the confidential nature of our business is best served if we visit before proper calling hours," Catherine said.

Just then the doors to the drawing room opened to admit Sir Vincent, who was in the act of placing his beaver on his head. "Well, I'm off to my club. Ah, Catherine has returned. I hope, m'dear, that you've come up with a suitable solution to this mess, as I feel it has already wasted enough of my time. Please be advised, though, that I am here if you need any guidance." With that promise, he tipped his hat and turned to leave the room as quickly as possible.

"Rest assured, Papa, my mother and I will visit Arabella immediately to put a stop to this nonsense," Catherine announced coolly, with a sideways glance at her mother, who had yet to accept her fate and was even then marshaling another argument as to why they shouldn't leave just yet.

"Very good," he said, happy that a course had been decided on and that it didn't involve him.

"I thank you for your kind offer to go with me, Catherine," her mother said in a tone that conveyed much annoyance and very little gratitude. "But having gotten us into this 'mess,' as your father so inelegantly puts it, I think it's only right that I go to Arabella's on my own."

Catherine could easily imagine her mother doing exactly that: She would go to Arabella's town house and leave as soon as she arrived—without even knocking on the door. "And it's very kind of you to want to spare me, Mama, but I must insist on seeing this matter through to ensure that it's properly resolved."

Lady Fellingham scrunched up her nose, as if smelling something particularly unpleasant. "I really don't think—"

"Damnation, Liza," said Sir Vincent with some heat, "let the chit go if she wants to. We need someone to keep tabs on you and if she's volunteering for the task, I say let her."

"Really, Sir Vincent, you talk such nonsense," Lady Fellingham tittered, her anxious fingers at risk of rubbing a hole in the brocade. "Fine, dear, if you would like to come. But I shall need to change first, as shall you."

Catherine knew well her mother's penchant for putting off distasteful things and had no intention of indulging it. "Of course. But I must warn you that if you linger too long over your toilette, I shall be forced to go without you."

"Right, then," interjected Sir Vincent before he could be drawn back into the conversation with a look or a question. "As I said, must be going. Meeting Beaufort at the club, so I will take my leave of you now. M'dear." He bowed to his wife, turned on his heels and was gone before anyone could bid him adieu.

"Mama, I would like to come with you to lend you my support," said Evelyn, who had been sitting on the settee quietly contemplating a future without balls, "but I think it is best if I go upstairs and lie down. I am feeling quite fatigued."

"I understand, my dear," assured her mother. "You are of a delicate disposition just like your mama. Go rest." She leaned down and kissed her daughter on her cheek. "A little rest will revive you. You need to be beautiful for Lady Sefton's ball tonight."

"Lady Sefton's ball?" Catherine wondered aloud. "Are we still going to that?"

"What can she mean?" asked Evelyn nervously, the pitch of her voice unpleasantly high. "Why shouldn't we go? If Mama is going to Newgate prison and I won't be able to go to any more balls, then shouldn't we go to all the ones we can while we are still eligible?"

"Your mama is not going to Newgate," Lady Fellingham insisted with little conviction and a forced smile. "And of course we are going to Lady Sefton's ball. We bought that lovely ivory muslin for just this occasion. Now, dear, you go have a rest, and your sister and I will sort this whole thing out. Don't tease yourself about it one more minute."

Evelyn sent Catherine a smug look and kissed her mother on the cheek before quitting the drawing room.

"Freddy," Catherine instructed, "please tell Caruthers to have the carriage brought around immediately. Mother and I shall be changed presently, and it's best that we get this unpleasantness out of the way as quickly as possible."

"Really, Catherine, if that's the attitude you are going to take, then I think it's best that you stay right here. Arabella doesn't need you upsetting her so on the morning of Lady Sefton's ball," she announced, calling for her maid to help her dress.

Feeling drained, Catherine watched her mother leave the drawing room after Freddy, wondering what nonsense they would get up to next. Her family's proclivity for histrionics was why she didn't get involved in their day-to-day dramas. It was so much easier to read the paper as if nobody else was there and to simply walk out of the room when pretending became too difficult.

Chapter Two

***

Getting *Lady Fellingham* to Arabella Courtland's residence in Mount Street was not nearly as challenging as getting her out of the carriage once she arrived there.

"Come, Mama, you can't sit in that curricle all day with your back stiff and straight like that. The neighbors are going to start talking," Catherine said, as her mother continued to refuse Higgins's offer of help. "Why, look, there's the Duke of Trent. Shall I wave hello to him? Perhaps he and I could have a little talk while you are deciding whether to come out." In truth, she had no idea who the gentleman across the street was—she mentioned the duke only because he had recently made a scandalous marriage and his was the name on everyone's lips—but she raised her hand in enthusiastic greeting.

"Don't you dare," exclaimed her mother, who turned pink at the very thought of her daughter embarrassing her like that in front of such an esteemed personage. "I was merely gathering my wits. I am ready now. Please, Higgins, I'm ready to accept your hand."

When her ladyship's dainty feet were on the ground, she

accepted her daughter's proffered elbow with great reluctance. "I don't know why you're trying to start a scandal, dear, but I do wish you wouldn't. Think of your sister, please, if only for a moment. How is she going to find a husband if her family is in disgrace?"

Catherine couldn't find a reasonable answer to this unjust accusation, so she remained silent as they climbed the steps leading to the town house. Once at the door, Eliza grazed it lightly with her gloved knuckles. Her daughter watched this ridiculous display, which, of course, drew no response, for several moments. Then she knocked firmly herself. The door opened immediately.

"There, Mama, you just need to exert yourself a little," Catherine said as she turned to confront the dour-faced man who had answered her knock. "Hello. Please tell Lady Courtland that Lady Fellingham and her daughter Catherine are here to see her."

"Lady Courtland is not in right now," the servant drawled sternly from his considerable height. "Perhaps you would like to leave a card."

Lady Fellingham practically cheered upon hearing this news. "Oh, how fortuitous...ah, I mean, what a disappointment. I was so looking forward to having a coze with her this morning." She looked down at her shoes to hide her smile from her daughter. "Well, dear, we did try. Give the good man your card and let us be on our way."

Seeing her mother's poorly hid smirk, she said, "Nonsense, Mama. I won't have you disappointed. I think it would be best if we wait for Lady Courtland." Catherine turned to the butler. "She hasn't gone too— I'm afraid I don't know your name."

"It's Perth, milady." He stared unblinkingly down at her.

"Very good. She hasn't gone too far, has she, Perth?"

"I'm afraid I don't know, milady." His tone, if possible,

grew even more chilly at the inquisition, and Catherine, who had always been a self-effacing girl, felt wholly intimidated by his disapproving demeanor. She could think of no worse person to practice one's assertiveness on than a Mayfair butler, but she had no choice.

"It wouldn't do any harm for us to sit in the drawing room, would it, Perth?" she asked, with an overly bright smile.

"Milady, I think Lady Courtland would rather—"

"Lovely." Catherine brushed past the butler, who stepped back in surprise at the rough handling. "This way, Mama. Perth thinks we should wait in the drawing room."

The dour butler looked quite taken aback by this turn of events, and Catherine thought she detected a change in his manner. Although Perth remained well within the boundaries of civility, Catherine felt he was struggling with his temper. Doubtless, he'd never dealt with such a pushy young lady before, which made her sympathetic to his situation, for she had never been a pushy young lady before and found the experience very unpleasant. If only the fate of her family's fortunes didn't rest on the forthcoming interview with Lady Courtland, then she could have left like the shy and retiring miss she was as soon as Perth had said her ladyship was not at home. But Catherine had had a hard enough time getting her mother there once; she doubted she could do it a second time.

After several moments, Perth's face assumed its previous stony expression and he showed them the way to the drawing room. Catherine made herself comfortable on the settee as her mother stood awkwardly by the door. After a few moments of looking like a canary trapped by a cat, Lady Fellingham sat down across from Catherine.

Perth watched them take their seats and left, closing the doors quietly behind him. Then, not a second later, he opened the doors again, his professional dignity sadly overcoming his peevishness. "Would miladies care for some tea?"

Catherine was prepared to defer to her mother on this account, but since she gave no indication of her preference either way, Catherine acquiesced. "That would be lovely, Perth."

He nodded and left.

"Tea will calm your nerves, Mama."

"Nothing could calm my nerves now. Oh, this is so very wretched and well beyond the bounds of propriety." Lady Fellingham looked around the empty room, rubbing her fingers on the arm of the brocade sofa as if trying to remove a stain. It was a nervous habit of hers. "We really should go home."

Catherine felt a tinge of regret and wondered if she was doing the right thing. She hated seeing her mother so distraught, but something had to be done. She moved closer to the anxious woman and offered a comforting hand. "Look, you know what Shakespeare says. We shall do this quickly."

Eliza Fellingham didn't have a clue what Shakespeare had to say about intruding on one's friends before respectable visiting hours, but she was sure that if he advocated for such vulgar behavior, his plays should not be performed for the edification of young ladies.

They sat in silence for several minutes before the door opened. Catherine expected to see Perth carrying a silver teapot but was confronted with Lady Courtland herself.

"Darling Liza," she said, her hands extended in warmth to her old school friend, "whatever can the matter be?"

Eliza rose, met her friend halfway across the room and squeezed her hands. "Oh, it's just so horrible. I am sorry to bother you like this, only Catherine would insist."

Arabella's intent, dark-blue eyes surveyed Catherine steadily for several long seconds. Catherine felt disconcerted by the attention and concentrated on not fidgeting. The woman examining her so carefully was petite and delicate-looking with fluffy blond hair and perfect features. She might have been well past the first blush of youth, but she was still an Incomparable.

Thoroughly intimidated by the cool appraisal, Catherine mustered all her courage and introduced herself. "Hello, Lady Courtland. I'm Catherine Fellingham, Lady Fellingham's daughter. I don't believe we've met." She curtseyed politely but soon found herself enveloped in a warm hug.

"Of course I know you. When we last met you were but a little slip of a girl. I daresay you don't remember me." She placed Catherine at arm's length. "It's been so many years. Let me look at you now." After some moments of examination, she said, "What unusual eyes you have. I've never seen that shade of gold before. How charming for you, Liza, to have such a lovely daughter."

Despite the fact that it was Lady Courtland who had gotten her family into their present fix, Catherine found herself warming to her hostess. It wasn't often that she was admired by a stranger, even if it was mere courtesy.

"Now, let's do talk and get to the bottom of what has my friend so agitated." She took a seat on the sofa. "Here, Liza, sit next to me. Perhaps I should— Ah, there you are Perth. And with tea. Perfect. You anticipate my every desire yet again."

The butler placed the tray in front of Lady Courtland and bowed.

"Right, Liza," she said after she filled all the teacups, "why don't you tell me what has you so unsettled?"

"It's our plan," Lady Fellingham said hesitantly.

Arabella raised an eyebrow over her teacup. "Our plan?"

"Yes, our excellent plan has met with my family's disapproval," she explained with a censorious look at her daughter.

"Catherine insisted that I come directly here and put an end to the whole thing."

"I see." Arabella placed her cup on the table.

"It's just that Fellingham thinks that if it ever got out, it would cause quite a scandal," her ladyship elaborated. "Of course I told him he was being ridiculous. How would it ever get out? But then it was through one of Freddy's friends that he heard of it, so mayhap it's not quite as ridiculous as it had previously seemed." She fidgeted in her seat. "Not that that's a reason to abandon such a worthwhile endeavor but merely a warning to be more cautious. Catherine, however, is involved now, so we might as well give up on it. She will never let us continue."

Arabella looked at Catherine. "Yes, I can see that Miss Fellingham is an estimable young lady."

"Lady Courtland," said the estimable young lady, not sure if she was being maligned or mocked, "I and my family are worried about the damage this would do to our name if anyone should discover Mama and your scheme. I'm afraid that would put us beyond the pale socially and risk the wrath of the Duke of Raeburn, who, I'm sure from all I've read about him, would not appreciate such interference."

"You have read about the Duke of Raeburn?" her ladyship asked.

"Of course," answered Catherine.

"May I ask where?"

Catherine was annoyed by this line of questioning, which diverted her from her course, and sought to bring the conversation back to the relevant matter. "In a political journal, I believe, though I can't recall which one. My concern is for my sister Evelyn, for what chance of finding a good husband would she have if we are in disgrace? Please believe that we are fully cognizant of the honor you do us by trying to help Mama. I know she relies on your good judgment. Perhaps you can convince her that stopping the scheme is all for the best."

"Your daughter makes an interesting argument, Liza," she said as she considered Catherine over the rim of her teacup for an extended moment.

"She does?" asked Eliza, taken aback.

"Yes, she does. You have three daughters, two of marriageable age. Perhaps we should devote our attentions to getting them married," she explained. "If one of them married a wealthy gentleman, we would have no further need for excellent schemes."

Lady Fellingham smiled brightly and let out the breath she had been holding. She had been afraid that Arabella would take offense at Catherine's frank speech. "Oh, dear friend, you must know that that is my fondest wish, one that I have harbored these many years. I am sure that Evelyn would be very appreciative of any plan you conceive that would advance her on the marriage mart. She is a biddable girl with very pleasing manners, and I think she has a superb chance of making a brilliant match."

"And Catherine?" asked Arabella.

"Catherine?" Liza echoed blankly. "I don't know. I suppose Catherine also believes that Evelyn should make a brilliant match."

Her ladyship shook her head. "No, dear. I mean, do you think she would accept my guidance?"

"In what?"

"Finding a husband."

"Whatever for?" Lady Fellingham asked, still confounded.

"So she can get married."

"But Catherine is an old maid," exclaimed the girl's fond mother.

"Liza!" exclaimed Arabella. "I'm shocked. How can you talk about your daughter like that?"

Catherine, who had been listening to this conversation with only absentminded interest, broke out into a hearty—and what her mother would call unbred—laugh. "Please don't tease yourself about my feelings. At the advanced age of four-and-twenty, I've been quite on the shelf for some years, and my family has never made any attempt to put a pleasant face on it. I am a spinster."

"Ridiculous," Arabella dismissed. "You are young and pretty. We will see you engaged by the end of the season."

"But, Arabella, Catherine has had *six* seasons and she has never quite *taken*," Lady Fellingham explained, a little embarrassed for her daughter now that she had said it aloud. Six years was a long time. She was not entirely unsympathetic to Catherine's feelings, only it did seem to her as if her daughter had never really *tried* to take.

"Pooh," she scoffed, taking in Catherine's bright eyes, her lustrous brown hair and her statuesque figure. "Handsome young men are always interested in pretty girls with conversation. Don't worry, Liza, I'll take care of it."

Catherine's amusement faded as she thought of this formidable woman taking an active hand in her life. "I appreciate your offer of help, Lady Courtland, but my mother is right. I simply never took. Men don't like tall women."

She waved a dismissive hand. "Short men don't like tall women and why should they? They would look patently absurd standing next to a woman who had six inches on them, but I know for a fact that tall men like tall women. Now, don't you worry about it a minute more. I'll take care of everything."

And indeed it seemed to Catherine as if she were already devising one of her excellent schemes. The thought unnerved her and made her not a little anxious. "Lady Courtland, I don't think—"

"My dear, you simply must call me Arabella," she said.

"Oh, what a lovely surprise this has turned out to be. I had no idea why you had come to call so early in the day, and I will admit when I came in I was a little cross," she confessed. "But now I am delighted. We needed a new project, anyway, Eliza. The other plan was beginning to bore me."

Catherine felt as if the meeting had spiraled out of her control. Realizing there was nothing she could say at the moment to change her new friend's mind, she changed the subject, something she still had control of. "So the plan of selling commissions in the king's army..."

"What plan?" Arabella asked innocently.

"Thank you, Lady Cour—"

"Uh-uh."

"Arabella." Catherine smiled. "Well, since our business here is done, we shall leave you in peace. I'm sure you have other things you'd rather be doing." Catherine got to her feet and offered her mother an arm. Lady Fellingham stood as well.

"Nonsense," said her gracious host. "This has been a perfect diversion."

"Arabella, will we be seeing you at Lady Sefton's ball tonight?" Eliza asked as they approached the drawing room doors. Now that they were leaving, she was actually reluctant to go. The visit had gone far more pleasantly than she had ever imagined, and now she wanted to talk about her friend's plans for Evelyn. Imagine—Evelyn married to a wealthy young lord! It was everything Lady Fellingham wanted for her dearest daughter.

"I hadn't planned on going, but I'm willing to reconsider. Will you and Catherine be there?" she asked.

"Yes," Lady Fellingham said, "and Evelyn, of course."

Arabella nodded consideringly. "Perhaps I'll see you there."

"Wonderful!" Lady Fellingham kissed her dear friend on

the cheek and stepped outside. When she heard the door close behind her, she turned to her daughter. "There, you see, Catherine. When you are dealing with true quality, there's never anything to worry about. Was my friend Arabella not the most gracious thing? Really, I don't understand you, making such a big deal of all this. I believe in the end that Evelyn was right. It was nothing more than a tempest in a teapot."

When they returned to the house in Mayfair, Catherine disappeared into the study. She picked up the book she had been reading, *Childe Harold's Pilgrimage*. She had read it before, of course. It was one of her favorite poems, but for some reason she was unable to concentrate this afternoon. So much had happened in such a short span of time, and now, suddenly, passing the day in the comfortable room where she passed all her days felt confining.

She told herself not to be ridiculous. She loved the solemnity of the space—the rich woods, the dark paneling, the heavy curtains—and the encompassing quiet. Nobody ever bothered her in the study, and she was free to read whatever she wanted: gothics, scandalous novels, radical political tracts. She had the entire world in this single room and had never chafed before at the confines.

Yet today her mind kept wandering beyond its walls to the social world that had rejected her years before.

It was all Lady Courtland's fault, with her lavish compliments and promises to have her engaged by the end of the season. Catherine knew better than to fall for Spanish coin. Her looks were passable enough, for she didn't have a horrendously hooked nose or spots, but she was hardly of the first stare. No amount of curling and dabbing could give her the wonderfully pert features of her sister Evelyn. As for her conversation, it was a mercurial thing, tending to dry up in social situations consisting of more than two people.

No, she would not be engaged by the end of this season or the next.

But knowing the truth did little to improve her attentiveness, and twenty minutes later, she conceded it was futile and closed the book. For a long while, she stared out the window at passing carriages, wondering how to alleviate this inexplicable and unprecedented restlessness. She needed to do something, to be active and engaged, rather than quiet and calm. Then she hit on a perfectly scandalous idea and went to find Melissa.

Melissa, sitting on the edge of her seat, pressed her nose against the window.

"Sit back, Melissa. It's only London. You've seen it all before," Catherine said dampingly.

Melissa obeyed as she protested her sister's unfair request. "But I haven't, Cathy, not like this," she insisted. "Never from a hired hack before."

"The type of conveyance does not alter the scenery," she was assured.

"Oh, but it does. London looks much more exciting this way." She heard her sister laugh. "The buildings are not quite so imposing from the seat of our boring old carriage drawn by boring old Higgins."

"Higgins is no more than thirty," Catherine said, in defense of their coachman.

"I don't mean that kind of old. I mean the other kind of old."

Catherine had no idea what her sister was talking about. "There is only one kind of old, puss." She glanced out the window and saw the British Museum. "We are here."

Melissa squealed in delight and pressed her nose to the window again. "Is that it? That giant white building with the beautiful columns? Oh, it is gorgeous." She turned to her sister and took her hand. "I will never forget this, Cathy, as long as I live."

Catherine laughed at her sister's histrionics. Clearly Evelyn wasn't the only one in the family with a theatrical bent. "Don't be so dramatic. It is just a visit to a museum."

"But it's a museum that I have wanted to visit for the whole of my entire life." She was lost in thought for a moment. Then she turned to her sister, concern etched into her face. "What are we going to tell Mama? She's going to be furious when she finds out you've taken me here. You know she thinks the Elgin Marbles are indecent."

"Let me worry about our mother," she told her, although Catherine actually wasn't concerned at all. She didn't know what she would say, but for the moment she didn't care. She was almost as excited as Melissa. She, too, had been wanting to see the Elgin Marbles for a while, ever since she'd first read about them in the papers more than two years before. "Just enjoy yourself while we're here."

The hack stopped, and the two Misses Fellingham climbed down. Once inside the doors of the great building, they were met by a young man, who encouraged them to wander around freely. "If you have any questions, please do not hesitate to ask."

Catherine barely had time to thank him before Melissa dragged her off to the hall with the marbles, which she found almost by instinct. They were contained in a large room with a high ceiling.

"These marbles are called metopes," explained Melissa, unprompted. "This series is from the south side of the Parthenon and depicts the Lapiths fighting the centaurs, the half-human, half-horse creatures of ancient mythology. As you can see from this one"—she gestured to a sculpture in which a centaur was dealing a blow to the head of the Lapith while receiving one to his stomach—"the two are engaged in hand-to-hand combat. Here a centaur is carrying off a Lapith woman. You may have noticed that the central nine carvings are out of step with the others as they are not part of the battle scenes. There is some controversy about what these have to do specifically with the centaurs. Someone—I can't recall who—has suggested that these marbles derive from the well-known story of the Centauromachy in which the centaurs disrupt a wedding. Perhaps these women are preparing for the wedding. Another theory argues that an Attic myth is being represented. Yet another claims to see episodes in Daedalus' life. Personally, I think..."

Melissa rattled on, uninterrupted and unaware that her sister no longer listened. Indeed, Catherine had crossed the room to examine the sculpture of a reclining Dionysus from one of the pediments.

After enjoying the exhibit in silent contemplation for a while, she returned to her sister's side.

"Aren't they marvelous?" asked Melissa, her nose inches away from the hoof of a centaur. "Isn't the skill of the sculptor superb? Just look at the musculature on these. And on the pediment. Did you see those garments on Athena? They don't seem carved out of marble at all. Oh," she cried, surprising Catherine with the anguish she could pack into the lone syllable, "think of the great sculptures that have been lost. These here are the best preserved. Just imagine how wonderful the others must have been. Oh, to have seen them before they were ruined by war and decay."

Catherine nodded. She had thought the same thing, though she hadn't expressed it with quite so much vigor.

"Just think," Melissa continued, "these are from five centuries before Christ. They are more than twenty-three hundred years old. They are twenty-three hundred years old and I am 13. That's"—here she broke off to do the mathematical equation in her head—"a hundred and seventy six times as old as I am."

Catherine was about to compliment her sister on her calculation, the accuracy of which she was thoroughly unprepared to confirm, when an unexpected male voice intruded.

"Actually, it's one hundred seventy-six point nine two if you want to be precise."

Catherine saw that the voice belonged to a tall man who was just then striding carelessly into the room. Dressed rather casually in fawn-colored breeches and a blue morning coat, he was, nevertheless, adorned in the height of fashion. Hessians shinier than a new penny, coat labored over by Wesson—these were the things that Freddy always aspired to but never quite achieved. His hair was cut a little longer than fashionable, but that only added to his appeal. As he drew closer, Catherine noticed that he had a straight nose, a firm jaw and eyes of a startlingly clear green. In all, he was a very handsome man of approximately thirty years of age, exactly the sort of gentleman who had intimidated her into speechlessness during her first season. They were not in a ballroom now, but she felt the familiar anxiety overtake her and clearly articulated thought began to fly from her head, leaving a blank slate in their wake. Her palms started to sweat as she dumbly watched his approach, infuriated that after all these years she could still be overwhelmed by a handsome face.

But it wasn't her first season and she was no longer a green girl. Indeed, just this morning she had stared down a dour-faced, disapproving Mayfair butler.

Remember that, she ordered herself.

Melissa, unaffected by the man or his attractive countenance, exclaimed excitedly, "Oh, sir, are you good with sums, too? Nobody else in my family can do them."

"I am tolerably clever with numbers," he said, coming to stop in front of them. He bowed slightly to Catherine, who could do nothing in return except lower her head. Inside her chest, her heart was racing. She tried desperately to calm her nerves.

"Then what is sixteen thousand four hundred divided by six-and-twenty?" Melissa asked.

After a moment's hesitation he said, "Six hundred and thirty point eight."

"And twenty-nine hundred times thirteen hundred?"

It was only the realization that Melissa was capable of throwing numbers at their fellow visitor all day long that shook Catherine from her stupor. "I...uh, think"—she coughed to clear her throat and evaded the startled gaze of Melissa, who had never heard her erudite sister stammer before—"that the...um, gentleman has better things to do than mathematical equations."

At this statement, Melissa blushed and mumbled an apology.

The gentleman assured her it was quite all right. "I like showing off my humble ability. Nobody among my acquaintance is impressed by it."

"Nobody among my acquaintance is impressed by it either," confessed Melissa with delight, the redness fading fast from her cheeks.

The man laughed and turned to Catherine. "Please accept my apologies for interrupting your visit."

"Not at all," she mumbled, and hearing the weak tone of her voice, she thought again of Perth's disapproving scowl and resolved to do better. "You haven't interrupted anything, and we are happy to share the marbles with other visitors."

"This is our first time," Melissa blurted out, giddily. "My mother finds them indecent and has forbidden our attendance."

"I'm not surprised," said the gentleman, looking pointedly at the sculptures of unclothed men. "I imagine many mamas do not want their innocent, young daughters to lay eyes on men so intimately exposed."

Thinking of her mother, Catherine realized that her ladyship would be appalled by the idea of Melissa holding a conversation with a complete stranger, even a well-dressed one who was obviously gentry. No doubt she would expect Catherine to put an end to it. Ordinarily, she would, but right now she didn't feel like it. There was something about the man and his demeanor that made her feel oddly comfortable in his presence. In particular, she liked the way he listened to what Melissa had to say and how he took her ideas seriously with none of the patient condescension elders frequently showed toward children.

"It's not that," Catherine said calmly.

The gentleman looked at her, and she was momentarily thrown by his frank gaze. "No?"

"It's Lord Elgin's nose, I'm afraid," she said.

"His nose?"

"Mother thinks it's indecent of him to have lost his nose to a severe ague," she explained. Her face revealed not a hint of amusement but her eyes gleamed with humor.

Catherine could tell that the gentleman was trying to hold back a smile—perhaps he wasn't sure if she was teasing him—but he failed miserably. He broke out into a wide grin, exposing even, white teeth.

"And I think it is horribly unfair to hold it against him," stated Melissa, who had been deprived the pleasure of the Elgin Marbles for precisely that reason. "I'm sure he didn't mean to lose his nose like that."

The gentleman laughed. "No," he agreed. "I imagine losing his nose was a trifle inconvenient for him."

Catherine chuckled and her gold eyes twinkled. "But it is impossible to convince Mama of that. She is determined to believe that he lost his nose as a personal affront to her."

"Was she acquainted with him?" he asked.

"No, of course not," she said, smiling brightly, for the question was both reasonable and logical. "But what does that have to do with it, Mister—"

"Julian, please." He executed a leg. "I must insist upon informality among scholars."

"Julian, then," she said—and then did something entirely out of character: She held out her hand for a proper handshake. She couldn't quite say why she did it, other than she was at the British Museum on the day she stared down Lady Courtland's butler after finding out her mother could be brought up on charges of treason. It all seemed of a piece—one absurdity piled on top of another—and she could do nothing but take it to its logical conclusion. "And I am Catherine. This is my sister Melissa. We are pleased to meet you."

Julian looked momentarily taken aback by her proffered hand, and Catherine's smile faded as she realized the logical conclusion to any misadventure was her inevitable humiliation. But just as she was about to withdraw her hand with an awkwardly mumbled apology he took it and gave it a firm shake. At his touch, Catherine felt as giddy as Melissa.

"Is this your first visit?" Melissa asked, after he shook her hand as well.

"No, I've been here many times before," he said. "In fact, I was instrumental in bringing the marbles here. I worked as a liaison between Elgin and the government."

"Oh, no," cried Catherine, genuinely crestfallen at this intelligence. "Here we were, having such a pleasant conversation, and now I discover we are on opposite sides of the issue."

Julian smiled. "Ah, you believe they should have remained in Greece."

"They are the cultural and religious heritage of the Greek people," chimed Melissa.

"*Et tu?*" he asked, laughing.

"My doing, I'm afraid," Catherine confessed. "She is my sister, and I've had years to provide her with the right opinions."

"But surely if they were in Greece you might have never had the pleasure of seeing them at all," he argued reasonably.

Catherine assured him that she was well aware of that. "But I am not so selfish that I would have an entire nation deprived of its heritage so that I might enjoy it in a proper climate."

Julian nodded. "And what of our goal to preserve them? Look at the wretched state they are already in."

Catherine examined the marbles, which were riddled with cracks and missing fragments. "I don't know," she said. "I might hope to look this good when I am two thousand three hundred years old."

Melissa giggled.

"A valid point," he conceded, "but, I assure you, they're much better off here. The Greek government does not have the resources to preserve them. Here they will remain in the best possible condition."

"Yes," Catherine agreed, warming to the topic. "They will remain in the best possible condition until some classical scholar decides that the marbles' gray hue should be snowy white like other Greek statues and uses some potion that damages them irrevocably."

Julian laughed. "If that is your greatest concern, rest easy, m'dear. I can assure you that will never happen."

Catherine smiled and thought that she would rather stand there for fifteen minutes talking to this man whom she just met in the dusty confines of the British Museum than attend a hundred balls. If they had been at a ball, this man wouldn't have noticed her and she would not have had the presence of mind to talk to him, much less tease him and take him to task for his opinions. She wanted to stay there forever, it felt so good to have a normal conversation with a handsome man, but she knew her mother would be angry enough and that she should not provoke her further.

"I am very much afraid, sir, that Melissa and I have to be going," she said with genuine regret.

"Why must we?" whined her sister. "We just got here."

"Under no circumstances can an hour be considered just getting here," Catherine assured her before turning to face Julian. "It was very nice talking with you. And while I don't approve of the fact that the marbles are here, I very much enjoyed seeing them."

He smiled. "Please, let me walk you to your carriage."

"Oh...ah, you don't have to," she said, falling back into a slight stammer.

"But I want to," he insisted, looking steadily into her eyes. "It would be my pleasure."

She found something disconcerting about his penetrating gaze. "Oh. That's all right, then. Melissa?" She broke her eyes free from his and realized that her sister had wandered over to the statue of Athena. "Are you ready to go?"

Melissa said yes but so despondently that Catherine rashly promised to bring her back sometime soon.

Outside, Julian asked after their carriage. "Oh, we came in a hack. If you could hail one, I'd greatly appreciate it."

He did just as she instructed, and while he was helping her into the carriage, he asked Catherine her direction.

"Belgravia, please."

Catherine waited until he had supplied the driver with the necessary information before saying one final goodbye. "It has been a pleasure," she said with the utmost sincerity.

"The pleasure was all mine," he insisted.

"Adieu, then."

"Au revoir."

The hack pulled away, and Melissa waved at Julian through the window. Catherine watched, saddened by the thought that she would never see him again. She had been very tempted to ask his surname but restrained herself with effort. She'd had to remind herself that this had been an interlude, merely another unexpected moment in a day that had turned out to be full of unexpected moments. Tomorrow, life would return to normal. Tomorrow, a handsome, funny, smart gentleman like Julian wouldn't notice a tall, awkward woman who hid in the corner rather than stammer nonsensically.

But, oh, it was nice to have today.

Chapter Three

❧❧❧

The *he party was* late getting off to the ball because Lady Fellingham's relentless chastisement of her daughter left her ladyship little time to prepare.

"I don't know what has come over you today," her mother said as Betsy placed jewels in her hair at evenly spaced intervals. She couldn't talk without bobbing her head left and right, and the poor maid was trying to get as many pins in place as she could between nods. "As far as I can remember, you were fine yesterday. What did you do with yourself yesterday?" She made a show of trying to remember. "La, I have no idea. See?"

Catherine was seated in her mother's dressing room in her ball gown, a drab confection of pink satin that ill-fitted her age. "No, Mama, I don't see."

"What I mean, Catherine, is that what you do with your day is your business. I have never bothered you to be more like other ladies of the *ton*. You spend hours in your father's study, and I don't say a thing. What does she do in there, I think to myself. How can she spend so many hours in there, I ask your father. Why doesn't she have beaux like Evelyn, I question the good Lord. But I never bother you. No, I leave you be. But now you've come out of the study to chastise me, embarrass my friend Arabella and corrupt your sister. It is unacceptable, Catherine." She nodded her head fiercely, thwarting Betsy's endeavors.

"The Elgin Marbles are not corruptive," she said with a deep sigh. They'd had this argument several times before. "They're engrossing antiquities."

Lady Fellingham snorted, an undignified sound that made her maid giggle. "It is so like a man without a nose to have brought back so-called engrossing antiquities."

"They are also educational, Mama."

"One gets an education in a schoolroom, not traipsing around museums with indecent slabs of marble scattered about."

"But—"

"No more, Catherine," her mother ordered, turning her head around entirely and thoroughly undoing her maid's most recent efforts. Hair came tumbling over her left shoulder. "I have made my position clear, and I don't want to discuss this again." She faced the mirror and contemplated her appearance. She fingered the fallen strands. "What's this?" she asked. "Betsy, I thought I told you to put my hair up. Really, woman, what have you been doing this whole time? Now we are likely to be late."

The family arrived at the Sefton ball a little before eleven. They were without Sir Vincent, of course. He would most likely follow after losing a handsome sum at the gaming tables.

"Oh, isn't this lovely?" cried Evelyn upon entering the ornate room, which was lavishly decorated with hundreds of vases of delicate roses. "Do say we can have a ball, Mama. You know I would enjoy it so."

"Can't have a ball without a ballroom, brat," reminded

Freddy, who was busily surveying the room for cronies. "Ah, there's Pearson. Excuse me." Freddy bowed.

"Selfish boy," cried his mother. "To walk away without offering to get us punch." She patted delicately at her brow and looked at all the people. "My, this is quite a crush."

Evelyn was also examining the room's inhabitants. "I don't see Deverill."

At the mention of Deverill, Catherine cringed. Of late, her sister could do little but rhapsodize over the many accomplishments of the peerless Lord Deverill. He was more handsome than any other lord, he danced more beautifully than any other lord, he conversed more interestingly than any other lord, he dressed more elegantly than any other lord, he had a better seat on a horse than any other lord, he opened doors with more grace than any other lord. The list of encomiums heaped on his head grew daily, with Freddy, that ignorant puppy, tossing in the odd compliment. If Catherine hadn't known better, she'd think that Freddy was smitten with him, too, so full of admiration was he for the gentleman's skill at boxing.

She had never met the indomitable Lord Deverill, but the more she heard about him the less she wanted to. He sounded absolutely appalling in his perfection, and she didn't doubt that he was too stuffed with his own consequence to exert himself on anyone's behalf.

"Don't worry, dear. It is a little early yet for the gentlemen of fashion to have arrived. Give it some time," her mother advised.

"Oh, I know. But he said he would be here. You recall he stood up with me last week at the Huffington fête. Ah, I see Vickering coming this way," she said not unenthusiastically. "He is a poor substitute for Lord Deverill, but I suppose he will do as well as anyone."

"How you talk," said her mother. "Why, I have it on good authority that he has a generous income. Though I've not heard the exact figure bandied about, I can assure you, my dear, that he is not a *poor* substitute."

"Good evening, ladies," Vickering said, bowing over Lady Fellingham's hand while taking in Evelyn's flowing white dress and her à la Greek hairdo. "Miss Fellingham, you look enchanting," he said to the younger daughter. "I would be forever in your debt, dear Lady Fellingham, if you would allow me the honor of dancing this set with your beautiful daughter."

Eliza Fellingham nodded her ascent and twittered happily as the couple walked onto the dance floor just as the orchestra started up a minuet. "Doesn't she look beautiful, Catherine?"

Catherine agreed readily with her mother, although she wasn't quite sure what the question had been. She was too engrossed in observing Freddy and his companion, a tall boy whose face was half hidden by a lavishly tied cravat. His clothes, though tailored well, didn't seem to fit him quite right. He appeared gawky and fairly uncomfortable in his finery. Catherine knew exactly how he felt and found this sense of empathy endeared him to her. "Mama, that fellow Freddy is talking to. Is that the friend of Freddy's who told us about your excellent plan? Preston?"

Fearing another long discussion on the distasteful matter, Lady Fellingham glanced fleetingly in her son's direction. "Yes, that is he. Preston. Pearson. Something like that," she answered distractedly. Where was her dear friend Arabella? "Ah, there we are." She had finally found a familiar face. "Come along, Catherine. I see Lady Lawson by the punch bowl. We shall say hello and get ourselves a nice refreshment."

Catherine didn't want to chat with Lady Lawson by the punch bowl. She had spent too many hours listening to Lady Fellingham and her friend gossip about the marriage mart to blindly follow. They were both mean and spiteful when it came to the success of any daughter who was not their own. The horrible things they said made Catherine cringe, and rather than going where her mother led, she walked across the room to the other side, where Freddy was talking with his friend.

"Ah, Catherine," he said when he saw her approaching. "I would like you to meet my good friend Gerard Pearson."

"It's a pleasure to meet you, Mr. Pearson," she said with a smile as he bowed over her hand. "Freddy introduces us to so few of his friends."

"That's cause I don't want them mooning over Evelyn," Freddy explained. "But you're all right."

Catherine knew that Freddy didn't realize how discourteous this sounded, and she laughed. She was used to such shabby treatment from her family. Gerard Pearson, however, was not. "I am sure that this Miss Fellingham is as much a danger to the hearts of your friends as the other Miss Fellingham."

"You haven't seen the other Miss Fellingham," Freddy said.

His friend began to blush and stammer. "Still, your sister here is quite...um—"

"Please, Mr. Pearson, don't let Freddy's teasing discomfort you. He has no appreciation for the gallantry you have demonstrated."

"Gallantry?" echoed Freddy, seemingly bewildered by the idea.

Catherine sent him a withering look. "Yes, gallantry."

"Miss Fellingham," Pearson said, still faintly red from his blush, "would you do me the honor of this dance?"

Catherine didn't know who was more surprised—she or Freddy.

"Gerard, you don't have to do the pretty just because she's my sister and all," the insensitive boy said without thinking.

The blush returned in full force. "But I would like to dance with her."

Freddy didn't say anything more, but he continued to look confused by this unprecedented and seemingly inexplicable development.

Catherine decided there was nothing for her to do but ignore her brother's impolite outburst. Poor Pearson looked as though he was going to explode any second from the sheer embarrassment of it all. Often on the brink herself, Catherine easily understood. "I would be delighted," she said, taking his arm.

Once out on the dance floor, Catherine concentrated on the proper steps, ever mindful of her partner's feet.

"You are a lovely dancer," he said.

She wanted to beg him to leave off on the unnecessary compliments, but instead she thanked him and smiled. When she felt that she had the steps down, she looked up at her partner. "Mr. Pearson, I am fully aware of the service you've done my family."

For a moment he looked confused, but his expression quickly cleared. "Freddy's my friend, you know. Wouldn't want anything to happen to his family."

"Still, we are all in your debt," she insisted.

"Don't be absurd. I just did what anyone would have done."

Catherine thought of all the commissions her mother managed to sell before she finally put an end to her excellent scheme. "I am not so sure about that, Mr. Pearson."

"So then it has been taken care of?" he asked obliquely.

She nodded abruptly. "To the best of my ability, yes."

"Good."

"And you, sir, have plans to enter the army then?"

"Yes. I am waiting for my colors." Then, as if to assure her that nothing was amiss, he added. "Really waiting, the proper way. I would never accept such a bargain. For one thing, my older brother, Morgan, would thrash me for behaving so disrespectfully."

"I am very glad to hear that. Not that you would get thrashed," she immediately corrected, "but that you're following protocol."

Pearson smiled. "I assure you, I thought nothing else."

They danced the rest of the set in silence, and Catherine enjoyed herself. As she usually stayed close to her mother during balls, she rarely partook of them fully.

"That was lovely, Mr. Pearson," she said as he returned her to her mother, who was comfortably ensconced along the far wall with the other chaperones. "Thank you."

"Nothing to it. I enjoyed myself." They were standing next to her mother now, and Pearson lingered awkwardly. He coughed once, clearing his throat. "I...uh, don't suppose you would like to go for a drive with me tomorrow in the park."

Catherine smiled widely at the offer, which she found gracious despite its negative assumptions. "I'd be delighted."

"You would?" he asked, surprise getting the better of him before he recalled his composure. "I mean, lovely. Shall we say four-thirty?"

"Yes, let's."

Pearson bowed and walked away, slightly flushed from his success.

"There you are, Catherine dear," her mother said. "Where did you go off to? Well, it doesn't matter. Lady Lawson and I were just talking about how Lorena Burton is shamelessly throwing herself at Sir Quarles, and I was saying how her sister was exactly the same way before she landed Marsters.

She had her come-out the same year as yours. Don't you remember her? Always a very forward child. The entire family's that way. Why, I remember when her mother had her debut...."

As comment from her was neither expected nor necessary, Catherine stopped listening and surveyed the ballroom. Her mother and her cronies rarely paid any attention to her and she passed most balls like this—tucked quietly along the wall, watching the dancers. Tonight, however, she didn't feel quite so contented with the usual arrangement. Though she could hardly explain it, she felt an odd sort of excitement, as if anything could happen—as if, she admitted reluctantly to herself, she could turn at any moment and find herself face to face with the gentleman from the museum.

It wasn't only that sense of anticipation that made her feel different; it was also the confidence she'd shown in talking to him. She felt certain that it hinted at something auspicious for her—that she might finally, after all these years, be coming out of her shell. The idea made her happy, and she knew she should test her newfound social ease by striking up a conversation with a gentleman. It was a terrifying thought, but she wouldn't let that stop her.

She was looking for the right person to approach—someone known to be friendly and not too intimidating, perhaps a gentleman past the first blush of youth whom she'd met before—when a woman's voice caught her attention.

"My dear," she said excitedly. "I have hit upon the veriest scheme and you simply must help me with it. I shall wither and die of boredom if you don't."

It took Catherine only a moment to recognize the dulcet tones of her mother's friend Arabella Courtland.

Next, her partner spoke: "You realize, Bella, that you are always making dire threats about your health, and yet I have never seen anything but a pretty blush in your cheeks and a calculating gleam in your eye. If you aren't careful, I should begin to suspect that you're a confirmed crier of wolf."

That voice, thought Catherine, whipping her head around to try to get a glance of the speaker. It sounded like the man she'd met at the museum. Could it be? She thought it was unlikely, even impossible, and yet no two men could have that same beautiful baritone.

"Pooh, Deverill," Lady Courtland said dismissively. "You do me an injustice. I have never been quite this bored before. I assure you, I am plunging great depths this time. You must promise to help me."

Deverill? The man at the museum was Deverill, the horrible, wretched man her sister could not stop enthusing about? The insufferably perfect man who didn't have a single fault? She could scarcely believe it.

"I cannot do that before you divulge what is required of me," he responded smoothly.

But Lady Courtland was having none of it. "No, you must give me your word before I reveal all."

Catherine, who was taller than most women and many men, immediately began to stretch her neck to get a glimpse of the pair, but the ballroom was so crowded with guests that one could barely breathe much less survey the space successfully. They were to her left, that much she could tell, but when she looked in that direction she didn't see them. Were they around the bend? The room had several alcoves that were ideal for tête-à-têtes.

"Bella, darling, you can't believe I'd behave so rashly," he said, sounding every bit the nonpareil Evelyn had described: knowing, sophisticated, worldly. He was not at all the funny, friendly, approachable man she'd met at the museum, and Catherine could not quell her disappointment.

"Of course you would." Her ladyship's tone was assured

and confident. "You forget. I know you well. Most likely, you are as bored as I."

There was a moment of silence as the gentleman considered this. "Since you are right on that mark, I will reward you with my word that I will help you with your newest scheme whatever it may be."

"La, I knew you would," she cried triumphantly.

Much to Catherine's annoyance, there were other voices intruding and she had to fight to stay focused on the conversation. The gentleman directly to Catherine's right was talking loudly about his latest acquisition at Tattersall's, and a lady in a white crepe gown had a cackling laugh that was so loud it almost drowned out the orchestra.

"Stop crowing," Deverill ordered, "and tell me what I must do."

"My dear friend's daughter is the veriest quiz," she announced matter-of-factly, "and I want you to bring her into fashion."

Instantly, Catherine froze, her heart suddenly pounding as she realized Lady Courtland was talking about her.

No, she thought, ordering herself to calm down. It couldn't be her. It had to be another dear friend's daughter.

"It's not like you to be cruel, Bella," Deverill observed.

It wasn't her because she couldn't be described that way—she wasn't a quiz, was she?

"I'm not being cruel. Far from it," Arabella insisted. "I want to launch her. I want her to have a dazzling season."

Even if she was a quiz, she couldn't possibly be the veriest. Surely, there was at least one quiz among all of London society who was a tiny bit more very than she.

"But if she is the veriest quiz..."

Despite her attempts to exonerate herself, Catherine knew they were talking about her. It couldn't be anyone else—she fit the description too well—and hearing Julian, the wonderful man from the museum, call her the veriest quiz hurt like a little pin pricking her heart.

"She has countenance," Arabella announced.

Deverill's laugh was cynical. "That's precisely the thing one says when a woman doesn't have countenance."

Lady Courtland conceded the truth of this statement but insisted that this time it was actually true. "Trust me. She's unusual. Not in your line, of course, but definitely an original."

Catherine, her feet glued to the spot despite how strongly she longed to run away, took little comfort in her claim to countenance. Countenance didn't mean much if one was a quiz.

"Countenance doesn't hold water when one is a quiz," Deverill said, in perfect echo of her thoughts.

"Regardless," Arabella said, "you've promised to help me."

He sighed resignedly. "Very well, what would you have me do?"

"Be attentive—dance with her, take her riding in the park, look engrossed when she speaks. You don't need me to tell you how to do the pretty. If you lavish attention on her, I guarantee the *ton* will follow."

"Who's the chit?" he asked.

"Fellingham's daughter," she said.

The crepe-covered woman laughed and Catherine silently cursed her piercing cackle.

"Her?" Deverill's surprise was evident. "But she's a diamond of the first water. You don't need my help. Half the bucks are already dangling after her."

"Not that daughter, the other one," Arabella explained.

"He has another one?"

"Two, in fact, but we are discussing the eldest."

"The eldest? Have I ever met her?" he asked.

"I should say so. She had her come out more than six years ago."

"Good God," he said, sounding properly appalled. "You want me to bring into fashion a woman who has been out for *six* years? I might be a leader of the *ton,* but I am not a magician. Even I cannot make gold out of dross."

There was so much horror in his voice, so much conviction that the task was impossible, that Catherine felt tears form in the back of her throat. She knew she was beyond the pale, had known it for years, but it was still jarring to hear someone else say it. The comfortable truths of one's life sounded bewildering and stark when uttered by an unseen stranger in a crowded ballroom.

How dare Lady Courtland do this to her—bandy about her name at a crowded affair where anyone in the world could hear. Had she no sense of propriety or even humanity? Humiliating conversations like this one belonged in the privacy of a drawing room.

"I have every faith in your consequence, my friend," Arabella assured him, not the least bit perturbed by his attitude.

"To what end are we playing this game, Bella?"

"It is not a game," she said. "I sincerely hope to see her engaged by the end of the season."

"You have a kind heart, but no man marries an ape leader long on the shelf. Tell me, is she pretty?"

"Pretty?" Lady Courtland repeated thoughtfully. "She could be, of course, if she did the right things."

"My dear Bella, if she is not an Incomparable, there's no point to this exercise. Surely you realize that only superior looks could compensate for her advanced age," Deverill said reasonably.

"There are other men among the *ton* who are not so unyielding in their requirements as you. Of course, I know she would never do for someone like you. You need a woman who is a great beauty."

"Dash it, Bella, I'm not that bad."

The lady emitted a trilling laugh of genuine humor. "Save the whiskers for your mama, Deverill. You can't so easily hoodwink me. I know you too well for the spoiled aesthete you are."

"If you think so little of me, I fail to see why you want my help at all," Deverill said, sounding miffed.

As distraught as she was, Miss Fellingham couldn't help smiling at the annoyance in his voice. The irony of poor Lord Deverill taking offense at an unflattering opinion of his character was too good to resist.

"Deverill, you know that I hold you in the highest esteem," Arabella insisted. "It is simply that I have no illusions. Surely you appreciate that I see you clearly?"

The woman in white crepe laughed again, drowning out his response, and it was all Catherine could do not to walk over and clamp her hand over the lady's mouth.

"Yes, but that is neither here nor there, my dear," Lady Courtland explained. "As I said, she has countenance. I assure you, that's enough. You need only to make sure that other men notice her. She will do the rest. Of that I am certain."

"I am afraid, my dear, that you give us men too much credit."

"And I am afraid, my dear, that you give Catherine too little."

"Catherine, Catherine."

Shocked, Catherine looked up, convinced for a moment that her victims had discovered she was eavesdropping on them, but she realized almost immediately that it was her mother calling. Taking a few seconds to compose herself, she wiped delicately at her eyes to make sure they were dry and breathed in deeply. Then she plastered a wide, fake smile on her face.

"Yes, Mama?" she said.

"I asked you what you thought of Margaret Dumplemeyer's dress. I think it is entirely the wrong color for her. With her orange hair, she shouldn't be wearing red. She should be wearing...hmm, I don't know what color goes with orange hair. Green, perhaps?"

"She doesn't have orange hair," Catherine muttered under her breath in defense of the beautiful redhead who had as many beaux as her sister.

"What's that you say? Do speak up, girl," her mama ordered.

"Please excuse me, I need some air." Then, without waiting for her mother to comment, she strolled across the room to the balcony, which, although less crowded than the ballroom, was not quite the haven she was looking for. She found a deserted corner and looked out at a garden that was all aglow with hundreds of translucent candles. How beautiful, she thought, before closing her eyes.

She had to regain her composure. Nothing tragic had happened, she told herself. Nobody had been hurt, nobody mortally wounded. Only a few unkind words had been spoken, and they were not even words she had never heard before. She had already known she was an ape leader—not the veriest quiz, of course, but an ape leader nonetheless. Evelyn was always reminding her of her failure to wed, and her mother, who most probably loved her, frequently called her a spinster to her face.

No, nothing tragic had happened.

Yet she couldn't convince herself that there wasn't something heartrendingly sad about hearing those words from *his* lips.

Catherine thought back to earlier that day, to the gentle

smile he had worn as he wished her au revoir. What a fool she had been, thinking that maybe he wanted to see her again, too. He! Julian Haverford, Marquess of Deverill, one of the richest, handsomest, most sought-after peers in all of England, who could have any woman he wanted. Any fashionable Incomparable. Any diamond of the first water. It was laughable, really, to imagine him paying court to a drab mouse like her, to the veriest quiz, to a spinster firmly on the shelf.

It was so absurd it could make you cry, she thought, feeling the tears well up. Well, she wouldn't. She would not cry over something that never existed.

She took another breath and waited for the tears to pass. It required only five minutes. There, she thought, patting her eyes dry, *now* I must look like the veriest quiz.

The idea made her smile, despite her sadness, and she considered returning to the ballroom. Not quite yet, however, because her eyes were probably frightfully red from the tears. She would give herself another few minutes. The balcony was dark and comforting, and she would have stayed there all night if she could.

She couldn't, of course, and contemplated what she would do when she returned to the ballroom. She wanted to find Lady Courtland and hold her to account for the awful things she had said and done, but despite the confidence she mustered to confront her butler, she knew she would never muster enough confidence to confront the lady herself. No, she would, in fact, make it a practice to avoid her whenever possible. Deverill, too. She would not be their little project.

When Catherine felt as though a suitable interval had passed, she decided it was time to go back in. She took in a deep, steadying breath, pulled her shoulders back, raised her chin and—

"You look ready to do battle," the Marquess of Deverill said to her in a conversational tone that knocked the wind out of her and forced her to clutch the handrail for support. He saw this and apologized. "I didn't mean to frighten you."

She muttered a reply, but it was spoken so softly he couldn't hear. When he asked her to repeat it, she said more strongly, "You didn't frighten me."

To her utter surprise, Catherine felt oddly calm. She didn't know why, but now that she was confronted with him, her nerves had quieted. Perhaps because the worst was already over. She had been hurt so badly tonight that nothing else could touch her.

Hearing her voice, Deverill looked at her strangely before a delighted smile broke across his face. "We've met before, haven't we?"

Seeing that smile, Catherine marveled at how well he played the game. He actually seemed happy to see her—her, the veriest quiz!

"Earlier today at the museum, wasn't it?" he continued. "I'd hope we'd meet again. I enjoyed talking with you and your sister. An interesting child, quite precocious. You should bring her back to see the mummy exhibit. Unless your mother doesn't approve of mummies. If I recall correctly, they don't have noses either."

When Catherine didn't respond to this joke, he said, "I'm sorry. I don't mean to distress you by making light of your situation. Did you get a terrible scold upon returning?"

His concern sounded so genuine that Catherine felt compelled to answer. "Nothing too horrible. Fortunately, Mama was more concerned with the curl of her hair than the corruption of her child. I was repentant for five minutes or so, then it passed."

He laughed and it was the same deep baritone as earlier that day, the one that made her heart skip a beat then as it did now. Why was it, she thought, that there in the moon-light, away from the crowd, he seemed nice and friendly and not at all cruel? But he was the same man who called her an ape leader and demanded perfection in a wife. She had to remember that.

"Ah, do you hear that?" He gestured to the open doors. "They are striking up the waltz. My dear," he said bowing deeply, "much to my pleasure, I see no one else has come to claim you. May I have the honor of this dance?"

Catherine stared numbly at him for several seconds. *The waltz!* Any girl who nurtured the merest sliver of hope in her heart had learned the waltz. Even Catherine, whose sliver could be said to be slighter than most, had practiced the dance when she was alone in her father's study. She knew she couldn't trust him. She knew his motives weren't pure, but for the moment she didn't care. All she cared about was the chance to float around the dance floor in the arms of this tall graceful man who had laughed at her sallies and looked upon her kindly earlier that day. She would hate him again later.

"Yes," she said, accepting his proffered arm even as she cursed herself for being so weak.

Their dance started awkwardly, with Catherine not quite sure where to put her hands. She had never actually waltzed with another human being and was momentarily disconcerted by how solid he felt. But within seconds, she adjusted and settled into the rhythm of the music. She even closed her eyes and relied on Deverill to guide her safely.

He didn't talk and neither did she. Catherine was too caught up in the sensation of soaring to indulge in something as mundane as speech.

But then it was over. The musicians stopped playing, and the couples ceased twirling around the ballroom.

"You are a lovely dancer, m'dear," Deverill said, leading her off the floor as couples assembled for the next set. "Here, why don't I get us some punch?"

Catherine nodded and watched him disappear into the

crowd, completely unaware of the strange looks she was getting from members of the *ton* who had heretofore never noticed her existence. But she did notice one thing in particular: Lady Courtland's satisfied expression.

Mortified by how easily Lord Deverill's effortless grace and handsome face had overcome her resolve, Catherine left the spot. She would not be there when he returned with punch. Instead, she would be back at her mother's side, listening to the chaperones gossip as if fascinated by the wit of their bon mots. If Deverill tried to find her, she did not know, as she kept her eyes firmly fixed on Lady Fellingham's face until it was time to leave.

For Evelyn the ball had been a disastrous experience, thanks mostly to the fact that her dowdy sister Catherine had danced the waltz with the eminently eligible Lord Deverill. She herself had never danced the waltz with Deverill. A minuet or two, of course. Perhaps a quadrille. But not the waltz.

Evelyn had never considered her sister competition for a gentleman's favor, and that she had to do so now offended her. During the course of the carriage ride home, she made certain the other occupants knew it.

"I don't understand it," Evelyn said for what might possibly have been the sixth time. "Why in the world would he want to dance with *her*? I cannot credit it with any sense."

Catherine, who had passed the journey in relative silence in an attempt to take the high road, decided that she'd been maligned enough. "Evelyn, cease your endless prattle now or I will forcefully eject you from the carriage. Do you understand?"

"Mama, I do believe that Catherine has just threatened my life. Did you hear that?" Evelyn cried.

Lady Fellingham, who had enjoyed herself so much at the party that she was thoroughly exhausted now, smiled sleepily at her pretty daughter. "Evelyn dear, you have no cause to tease yourself over Deverill's defection. Gentlemen from good families were tripping all over each other tonight to fill up your dance card. Deverill is the first man to show an interest in Catherine in, well, years. I don't know why he chose to dance with your sister. Indeed, he did not apply to me for permission, and I am already somewhat put out with your sister for waltzing without my approval. Nevertheless, I don't think we should question her good fortune. Clearly, the Lord works in inexplicable ways and it is not up to us to decipher them."

"But he was my beau, Mama, mine," Evelyn whined, so distraught at this frightening turn of events that she stomped her foot on the carriage floor. "You know Deverill was my beau. Catherine hasn't had a beau in six years, and I don't think it's fair that she be allowed to steal one of mine."

"That is precisely why your sister should proceed unencumbered by us in this courtship," said her mother, closing her eyes and leaning her head against the cushions. "Evelyn, your beauty obligates you to act graciously in this matter."

"Courtship?" she screeched. "One dance does not a courtship make." She turned to her sister. "The richest, most handsome peer of the realm who courts great beauties and Incomparables is not courting *you*. He...he probably lost a bet and was forced to dance with you. Or it was a dare from one of his friends. You know what fashionable gentlemen are like. They have their jokes."

"You know, brat," said her brother Freddy, who had planned at the onset to remain silent rather than get involved in the petty ways of women but decided with this last jibe that the time had come to choose sides, "you can be a really mean person sometimes and I am devilishly glad that an out-and-outer like Deverill has the sense to pursue someone like

Catherine rather than a spoilt cat like you. Now cease your screeching and allow us to ride home in silence."

Evelyn was so angered by this slight that tears welled up in her eyes. "Mama, tell Freddy he can't talk to me like that."

"Freddy, gently bred daughters of peers do not screech," his mother instructed calmly. "Apologize to your sister."

Evelyn smiled smugly at her brother, who made a face at her in return and refused to say he was sorry.

It was a very long ride home indeed.

Chapter Four

When *Catherine came* down for breakfast the next morning, the parlor was empty, and a place setting had been laid out for her along with the morning paper. The staff knew quite well that after a ball, Catherine was the only family member who ever made it down for breakfast—the rest were sad layabouts who needed hours to recover after a night's dissipation. This well-documented pattern explained why Catherine and Hawkins, who was pouring coffee at the time, were entirely shocked to see her mother enter the room.

Lady Fellingham was attired in a Devonshire brown walking gown, just the sort she always wore for shopping expeditions with Evelyn. Catherine watched as her mother took the seat adjacent to hers and felt a tinge of fear at what this might mean. Nobody ever sat next to Catherine in the morning. They always left her at the far end of the table with her newspaper.

"Hawkins," said Lady Fellingham, sinking deeply into her seat, "I'll have some juice please and an assortment of whatever you have there on the sideboard. What's Catherine eating?"

"Kippers, my lady."

"Then make sure I have some kippers, too," she ordered pleasantly before turning her smile on Catherine.

Examining her mother's happy expression, Catherine felt an awful sinking feeling in the pit of her stomach that she had not experienced in almost six years. She was positively terrified of what would come next.

"Mama, I was sure you would still be abed after an exhausting evening like last night's," she said, only briefly glancing up from the newspaper.

"Pooh, don't be silly, my dear." She accepted the glass of juice from Hawkins, took a reviving sip and said, "How could I sleep on a glorious morning like this?"

"Glorious?" Catherine asked, her alarm growing. There was nothing particularly glorious about the day. Outside clouds covered the sun, threatening rain.

"Yes. Isn't it exciting?" Lady Fellingham asked.

"Exciting, Mama?"

"Yes, exciting. Your triumph last night has made me so happy I could weep."

"My triumph?" Catherine squeaked.

"Really, Catherine, why are you parroting me like that?" her mother asked impatiently as she removed the newspaper from her daughter's grasp. One could not have a proper coze with a newspaper on the table. She handed it to Hawkins. "You never used to be a stupid child."

"I haven't any triumphs," she said, watching the paper disappear with a mixture of regret, fear and confusion.

"Don't be modest, dear. Deverill is quite the catch. You couldn't do any better. And I couldn't be more proud."

Appalled at the egregious misunderstanding of the situation, she stammered, "But, Mama, he isn't...I haven't...we are not—"

"Don't worry about Evelyn," she said whilst buttering toast. "I know she was horribly upset last night, but she is young. She will recover from this disappointment. Besides, I don't think she was truly besotted with Deverill. He's handsome and well-to-do and full of consequence, and she was momentarily dazzled. But he has a certain gravitas that would not suit her. Whereas you, my dear, you are not as flighty as your sister. You don't jump from one beau to the next. If you have set your cap for Deverill, then by all means, you shall have him. You realize, my dear, that I only want what's best for you, and there's none better than Deverill. I imagine his income dwarfs ours several times over. Oh, how lovely, to never have to worry about your father's gambling debts ever again." Lady Fellingham reached a hand over and gently patted her stunned daughter's cheek. "Dear child, you have made me so happy."

As her mother stared at her teary-eyed, Catherine wondered what was the best way to deal with this wretched situation. She could not let her mother go on daydreaming in such a fanciful fashion, and yet how could she explain that Evelyn had been right, that Deverill had indeed been put up to it by her very dear friend Lady Courtland, that she herself was nothing but a project for a bored gentlewoman. She was too humiliated to admit the truth, even to her mother, but she knew she must lower her ladyship's expectation of impossible future events.

"Really, Mama, you should not get so excited. It was just one dance."

Much to Catherine's surprise, her mother smiled understandingly. "You might not believe this, but I remember what it is like to be young. And despite your advanced years, you *are* still youngish. I know you are feeling uncertain now. You don't want to get hurt. Yes, darling, it was just one dance, but oh, what a dance it was. The waltz! I know. I've never approved of it before and were Evelyn to start twirling around a dance floor held indecently in the arms of a man, I would box her ears, but you are more mature. And you dance so beautifully."

"I do?" she whispered, unable to remember the last time her mother complimented her on anything but her good sense.

"Indeed," she said before gobbling down a forkful of ham. "And that's why you and I are going directly to Bond Street to buy you some new dresses. The one you wore last night was horribly out of fashion. We can't have the Marquess of Deverill squiring you around in anything that isn't of the first stare." Lady Fellingham waved her fork in the air. "Upon consideration, Catherine, it occurs to me that I can't remember the last time you and I went shopping together. What have you been wearing these last six years?"

"But I'm not—" she protested, trying to assure her mother that the Marquess of Deverill would *not* be squiring her around, but she did it with only half a heart, and when her mother interrupted, she didn't really mind.

"I think we shall go to Madam Bonnard. She has made some excellent dresses of late for Evelyn. She has a very good sense of style, and simply everyone frequents her," Lady Fellingham said. "She's the height of fashion. You can't wear white like Evelyn, but I think some nice pastels will look very well on you. I've always thought you looked best in pastels. But I'm sure I've told you that before."

As Catherine sat there clutching her fork, she felt as though she were being seduced by some dark demon. It had been years and years since anyone cared if her dresses were the height of fashion—since her first season, in fact. When it had become clear that her eldest daughter wasn't going to take, Lady Fellingham lost interest in her. The casual indifference with which her mother treated her hurt Catherine, of course, but it also gave her the freedom to do the things she enjoyed, like reading and going to museums and taking long strolls in the park.

Now it was all starting again, and Catherine could feel herself getting caught up in the excitement. She knew she should tread carefully, but she couldn't help wondering if this time it could be different. She was older and, as her mother liked to remind her, more mature. Surely she could handle herself better and not be so overwhelmed and bewildered by the social whirl. Lady Courtland believed Deverill's attentions alone would make her fashionable. What if it was true? How would the beau monde appear when she looked at it from the top, rather than from the bottom? Perhaps the very act of being popular would make her feel popular, which could have the beneficial effect of putting her at ease and letting some of her personality shine through. Under those circumstances, she might very well meet a man she could love.

Love was not an emotion she allowed herself to think about very often, for she knew it to be elusive and hard to sustain. Her own parents' marriage was a mystery to her, and she could understand nothing of it except that it was a prime example of how spending a lifetime with the wrong person was worse than spending it alone. For this reason, she'd never really minded her unattached state.

Having thought the matter through, Catherine decided that a few new dresses would be just the thing. Only they reminded her of another plan she meant to implement. "I would like some new gowns. Thank you," she said. Then after a moment of silence she plunged ahead. "Mama, it occurs to me that perhaps you would like some help with the books."

Lady Fellingham, in the process of bringing a kipper to

her lips, looked quite puzzled by this statement. She stared at her daughter blankly.

"Perhaps you would not be forced to come up with any more...um, excellent plans if you have help with the family finances," she explained.

For a moment Catherine feared that she had angered her mother beyond repair, for her face turned such a deep shade of red. But then she said, "Aren't you a good daughter? I appreciate the offer, of course, but I can manage tolerably well on my own."

"I'm only thinking of you, dearest Mama," she said tactfully. "It is a burden you carry alone and I would be glad in any way to help alleviate it."

Lady Fellingham's cheeks slowly returned to their normal shade, and she seemed to be considering the offer with real interest. "Perhaps you can help," she admitted, laying down her fork. "It is an awful burden being the only one who knows how expensive candles are and how it tortures me to watch them burn down as if they were wood in the fireplace, which no one is giving away either."

Catherine nodded. "Good, why don't we look them over this afternoon after our shopping expedition?" And then, as soon as she said it, she realized she already had an appointment for the afternoon. "Or perhaps tomorrow morning. I am engaged to go riding in the park."

"With Deverill?" her mother asked, eyes bright with pleasure.

"No, Gerard Pearson. He's a friend of Freddy's."

"Pearson. Pearson," she repeated under her breath. "Isn't he the scoundrel who went running to Freddy with tales about his mama?"

"He was only trying to help us, I assure you," Catherine said.

"Very well. But just see to it that Deverill doesn't think

you've lost interest. Although," said her mama in her most scheming tone, "now that I consider it, it wouldn't hurt for Deverill to imagine he has competition. A nonesuch like he has probably had everything handed to him on a silver platter. You would do well…"

Lady Fellingham prattled happily on, advising Catherine on all manner of stealth in courtship, as her daughter stared longingly at the newspaper on the sideboard.

Catherine returned flush from the excitement of shopping and ran upstairs to change into her carriage dress for her appointment with Pearson. The expedition had been a success in all ways save one: At the modiste, she had caught a glimpse of a stunning redheaded Cyprian who was rumored to be a recent cast-off of Deverill's. Catherine hadn't expected to see her nor had she anticipated being so unsettled by the sight of the beautiful woman. It was a very good thing, Catherine decided, that she knew Deverill's real intentions and wasn't affected by his interest, for she would have been devastated to know that was the level of perfection he sought in a mate.

Climbing the stairs, she was relieved that she didn't see Evelyn. She wasn't ready to be in the same room with her yet because she was still feeling the sting of her barbs. *He probably lost a bet and was forced to dance with you. Or it was a dare from one of his friends. You know what fashionable gentlemen are like. They have their jokes.* It was too close to the truth for her to think about forgiving her sister.

She did see Melissa, however.

"Cathy," her sister called, coming into her room and throwing herself on the bed. "I've been waiting for hours for you to return. You must tell me all about it. Freddy said you waltzed." Melissa closed her eyes and tried to picture it. "Was it wonderful? Will you teach me to waltz?" she asked, jumping off the bed. "Right now. Can we waltz?"

Catherine rang for Betsy's help, laughing at her sister. "You know what Mother thinks of the waltz."

"It's unbred," they said in unison.

"But she let you do it," Melissa persisted.

"Because I am mature and as long as I have a beau, she doesn't care what I do."

"I know. I heard all about it from Freddy. How you stole one of Evelyn's *partis* and how she's being awfully mean about it. I don't care," Melissa insisted, "if her heart is in tatters as long as you are happy. Are you happy, Cathy?"

"Right now, puss, I am very happy. But you must be nicer about Evelyn," she advised. "She's younger than I and not so mature."

"As am I, and I am nice to you," Melissa pointed out pertly.

Catherine gave her sister a hug. "I know you are, dear."

After a moment, Melissa danced away. "I have to return to my lessons now or Biddy will come looking for me. I got to sneak out for only a moment." She walked to the door and stopped just short before turning around. "Do say we can go back to the museum soon? We were not there for nearly enough time and having seen a little of the marbles, I want to see more."

"I'll do what I can. Now back to your lessons."

She waved and left the room just as Betsy arrived.

Catherine was pleasantly surprised to discover that Gerard Pearson was a tolerable whipster.

"I am very impressed," she said as he competently evaded a carriage that seemed on an inevitable collision course with them.

Pearson blushed as he finished the maneuver. "I am not a four-in-the-hand like Deverill or Withering, but I muddle through well enough."

"I don't go riding often, you know, so this is a veritable treat for me," she assured him.

He smiled and directed the curricle safely around a large hole in the road. "I like coming to Hyde Park. My family's principal seat is in Kent, and when I am here, I miss the wide open spaces."

"We are from Dorset, but I know exactly what you mean. You don't feel quite so confined, do you? When you want to break out into a full gallop, you break out into a full gallop," she said on a wistful sigh.

"Yes, that's the very thing. Miss Fellingham, I should like to tell you— Oh, I say, is that woman in the blue hat waving at you?"

Catherine followed his gaze. "I do believe it is our hostess from last night, Lady Sefton. And she is with Lady Court-land." Upon seeing her, her stomach pinched in quite a painful way. Was she prepared to face her mother's friend yet? From the way the noblewoman was waving, the decision was clearly not hers to make.

"Catherine, dear," Lady Courtland said as she pulled her gig up to Pearson's. "What a lovely surprise. Lady Sefton," she said to the woman sitting next to her, "you do remember Miss Catherine Fellingham? She was in attendance last night. And this is Mr. Gerard Pearson."

After the introductions were completed, Catherine said, "Lady Sefton, I had a marvelous time at your ball last night."

Lady Sefton smiled kindly. "Fellingham, you say? Aren't you the chit who waltzed with Deverill?"

Catherine felt herself blushing. "I...uh...I," she stammered, wondering what she meant to say and how she would say it.

Lady Courtland came to her rescue. "Yes, indeed this is the same girl. She has the town all aflutter wondering where she came from. I assure you, Lady Maria, that she is the daughter of my dear friend Eliza Fellingham."

Lady Sefton nodded and addressed Catherine. "No need to blush, child, you dance charmingly." She examined her carefully. "I don't think I've seen you at Almack's."

"No, ma'am," said Catherine softly.

"I don't believe her mother has applied yet for vouchers for her and her younger daughter," Arabella said, clearly angling for the much-coveted entrée.

"That shouldn't be a problem," Lady Sefton assured her before addressing a newcomer. "Ah, look who's here."

Catherine turned around and cringed when she saw Lord Deverill approaching on a beautiful chestnut mare. He was dressed in snug leather riding breeches and a sloping tailcoat. When he noticed her, he smiled, seemingly delighted to see her. She smiled back, but it was a thin smile, and she didn't really mean it. She hadn't wanted to encounter him again so soon. The image of the beautiful courtesan she had seen at the modiste was still too fresh in her mind. She looked down at her worn afternoon dress and suddenly felt inadequate. For the first time in six years, she found herself longing to be beautiful so that a gentleman would pay her some attention. Catherine knew that if she had Evelyn's clear blue eyes, her heart-shaped lips and porcelain skin, Deverill would flirt shamelessly with her. After indulging these thoughts for several moments, she began to feel ashamed of herself. A woman was more than her appearance, Catherine thought. *She* was more than her appearance.

"Lord Deverill," continued the patroness, "I was just telling Miss Fellingham how much we look forward to seeing her at Almack's. Perhaps you would like to waltz with her there."

Catherine could have sworn that for a second Deverill looked much taken aback by the bold suggestion, but then he reined in his mount and the moment passed. Most likely, she decided, he was surprised that Lady Sefton would trap him so brazenly into yet another dance with her. He could not be pleased.

As Deverill answered Lady Sefton's query, he kept his eyes fixed on Catherine, making her feel warm with embarrassment. "I would be delighted to have another waltz with Miss Fellingham. Assuming," he added, a smile dancing across his handsome face, "of course, that Miss Fellingham would like to waltz with me."

All eyes turned to Catherine, who felt a tremendous urge to slide down in the curricle and hide from them, and from the imposing man on the chestnut mare in particular. But restraining herself, she maintained eye contact with him and said only, "Yes, of course."

Deverill sketched a bow in return. "I shall look forward to it, Miss Fellingham." After much contemplation of her, he finally looked away. "And I must thank Lady Sefton for arranging it so deftly." He kissed the hand of the lady in question. "I don't know when I would have danced with Miss Fellingham again if it weren't for your clever handling."

Lady Sefton laughed. "Doing a bit too brown, Lord Deverill. You are known for your clever handling of young ladies."

"Ah, but not ladies with as much countenance as Miss Fellingham here," he said, with a sidelong glance her way.

Hearing this, Catherine felt as if she had been punched in the stomach. All of a sudden, her head started to pound and she had trouble breathing. How could he be so cruel as to mock her like that?

Catherine regained her composure and examined the group to see if anyone had noticed her odd behavior. A quick glance at Arabella revealed that she wasn't following the conversational undercurrent as carefully as she could be.

Indeed, Lady Courtland looked delighted with this turn of events and completely oblivious to the derision Catherine had suffered at the hands of her friend. Lady Sefton was equally unaware, and Mr. Pearson seemed miffed at the impudence of the marquess in arranging a dance with her under his very nose.

Only Deverill appeared to notice something was amiss. His eyebrows furrowed and he seemed to be asking her with a look if she was well. She felt the heat rise in her cheeks again and looked away. Why must he be so perceptive?

"Lady Sefton," said Deverill, "Wednesday at Almack's seems so far away. Perhaps you can arrange for Miss Fellingham to come riding with me tomorrow?"

The patroness laughed, delighted by this ploy. "You are shameless," she said admiringly. "Well, girl, will you do Deverill the pleasure of your company tomorrow for a ride around the park?"

"I'm afraid my family does not keep stables in London. Alas, I must decline," she said with insincere regret, pleased that she had a legitimate reason to demure.

"Pooh," dismissed the interfering Arabella. "Deverill keeps a full stable and would be glad to provide you with a mount."

"It is true, Miss Fellingham," he said gently, as if taking care not to disturb her again. "I do have a full stable, and the truth is you would be doing me a favor. My horses do not get nearly enough exercise."

Catherine saw no gracious way out and, with an apologetic look at Pearson, agreed. "I'd enjoy that. Thank you."

Deverill's horse began to fidget, and he pulled the reins in tight. "I'm afraid I must be off. Gale here has no appreciation for the finer things in life. Lady Sefton, I must thank you for a very profitable afternoon. Is nine acceptable to you, Miss Fellingham? Yes? Good. Until then."

Catherine bid him adieu and the two ladies followed closely on his lead. Catherine and Mr. Pearson resumed their ride, but for her the enjoyment had gone out of the afternoon. She responded to Pearson's questions and even asked some of her own, but neither her mind nor her heart was in it. She was too busy thinking about other things—about what her mother would say when she found out Deverill was lending her a mount and dancing the waltz with her at Almack's, what spiteful words Evelyn would hurl when she knew, and how let down she would feel when this wretched adventure was over and she went back to spending her days in the study.

Catherine expected dinner that night to be a subdued affair—she planned to be on her best behavior and hoped that Evelyn would follow suit—and it would've been if Sir Vincent hadn't asked about Deverill.

"What's this I hear about my Cathy and that damned stiff neck Deverill?" he asked as he chewed some peas.

Evelyn made a pathetic little peep like a sparrow in pain.

Her father looked at her oddly for a moment and then continued. "They're talking about it like a cackle of damn hens down at White's."

Again Evelyn squeaked in anguish.

"Errant nonsense, I told them. Catherine with the Marquess of Deverill," he said with a muffled laugh, as if unable to decide whether to be amazed or amused by the idea. "A nonesuch like that interested in our Cathy! It defies logic. To be honest, it puts my mind at ease, for I cannot like the notion of having him in the family. Too high-minded."

When Evelyn let out yet another grief-stricken wail, her father threw down his fork and knife. They clattered loudly in his plate. "That's it. Eliza, what the devil is wrong with the chit?"

Evelyn stood up in her chair, tears crawling down her

cheeks. "I can't *take* it," she cried. "I just can't take it anymore. Why does no one care about me? Everyone's so happy for Catherine. Well, I'm not." She screeched and stomped her foot. "I'm not. Catherine doesn't deserve him. She's too old. She's too old," she said again and ran, crying, out of the room.

For a moment they all watched the door where she had passed through. Then Sir Vincent yelled, "Hawkins. Hawkins?"

"Yes, sir?"

"Where's my port?"

"Coming, sir."

Freddy and Melissa kept their eyes on their plates, and Catherine could tell they were holding in smiles. Catherine felt one tugging at her own lips. No, she thought, it wasn't right to laugh. But then Melissa let out a giggle and all was lost. Hawkins was carrying in the port as the three broke into laughter.

Sir Vincent took a reviving sip and considered the group of Bedlamites sitting around his table. "Would someone please tell me what's going on? What the devil was Evelyn prattling about?"

His question only made them laugh harder. Their mother gave them each a stern look to no avail. Their laughter was beyond chastisement.

Deciding it was best that she explain, Lady Fellingham said, "It's true, Sir Vincent. It seems that Deverill has taken a fancy to Catherine."

Catherine, hearing this and knowing the truth, laughed even harder. Tears started to stream down her cheeks.

"They did dance the waltz together last night at Lady Sefton's ball. Although you know I don't approve of the waltz, I thought they made a handsome pair, to be sure. And he is taking her riding tomorrow in the park, lending her a mount and everything. It is so exciting." Seeing no answering gleam of excitement anywhere in her husband's countenance, she continued. "However, Evelyn had counted him among her beaux and she is a teensy bit upset at the defection."

"A teensy bit?" said Freddy between bubbles of mirth. "She was a teensy bit upset when she couldn't get that sable-lined pelisse."

"Remember how she wouldn't eat for three weeks?" laughed Melissa. "Said she'd rather starve than face life without the pelisse."

"But then she had Betsy sneak her up meals when she thought nobody was looking," Freddy added with more than a little lingering amusement.

Their mother did her best to ignore their ill-timed humor. "Evelyn is full of sensibility. She feels things deeply. No doubt this will pass quickly."

"No doubt," echoed Freddy, who was beginning to get hold of himself.

Sir Vincent looked unsatisfied with this explanation and downed some more port in response. "I don't like Deverill dangling after Cathy."

"He's a gentleman."

"He's used to cavorting with high-fliers and dashers and Incomparables in their first blush of youth. What does he want with Cathy?"

Abruptly Catherine stopped laughing, as did her siblings. She looked at her father and thought again how easy it was for people to be carelessly cruel. "I don't know," she said, standing up and leaving the room in much the way Evelyn had, only she managed to take her dignity with her.

Chapter Five

The *following morning*, Catherine woke with a new resolve. She would not go riding with Deverill. She would not play her role in Lady Courtland"s drama. She would not be a pawn who was moved around the chessboard at another's will. It was humiliating, and although her confidence had taken several direct hits recently, she had enough self-respect left to find it unbearable. With these thoughts in mind, she dressed in a lavender walking dress and went downstairs to wait for Deverill.

She perched in the window of her father's study to watch for the marquess—discreetly to one side, of course, so her presence wasn't revealed to persons passing. Deverill arrived not fifteen minutes later, and as soon as she saw the horse she was meant to ride, her resolve began to weaken. It had been so long since she had been bestride and surely their stables in Dorset did not have anything as fine as the chestnut mare that was now occupying the street in front of her town house. Oh, what a beautiful creature.

Although she knew it wasn't at all the thing, Catherine opened the door before the marquess even knocked and immediately peered over his shoulder at the impressive specimen.

If Deverill found this behavior unusual, his greeting gave no indication. "Ah, Miss Fellingham, you look lovely this morning."

Catherine barely spared him a glance as she bid him good morning in return. Reconsidering the matter, she thought that perhaps it was best if she did go riding with him. For her scheme to work, she would have to be seen with Deverill, and a morning trot along Rotten Row was the perfect opportunity. Perhaps they would meet some of the marquess's friends, eligible men who did not find her the veriest quiz.

"Miss Fellingham, you are not wearing your habit," Deverill observed, still standing on the step, although Caruthers now loomed in the hallway, waiting to reinstate proper decorum. "Has there been a change of plans?"

"What?" Forcing herself to look away from the mare, Catherine turned to Deverill and had to concede that he was an impressive specimen, as well, in his white lawn shirt, buckskin breeches and Hessians. "Um, no, there hasn't," she said, quickly thinking of a reason for her inappropriate dress. "I merely had not expected you to arrive so early."

"We said nine, did we not?" he observed with a wry smile, amused at being upstaged by his own horse.

"Uh, yes," she agreed, feeling foolish. "I hadn't realized it was so late in the morning. Is it really nine already? My, where did the morning go? Please, take a seat in the drawing room while I change into my habit. I really can't believe it's already nine."

Hearing his cue, Caruthers stepped forward to lead Deverill to the appointed chamber in the appropriate fashion and offered him tea. Catherine tensed at this, imagining her mother coming down for her morning repast and finding the most eligible bachelor of the season comfortably ensconced in her own drawing room sipping tea. Such a development would send her into transports of delight so overwhelming, she might never recover.

Without waiting to hear Deverill's response, Catherine ran up the stairs, into her room and opened her wardrobe to look for her riding habit, which she had not worn since coming to London. Determined not to tarry a second longer than necessary, for she had told her mother Deverill was arriving a full hour later to avoid an awkward scene, she tossed several articles carelessly on her bed and groaned in frustration when her habit didn't magically appear.

"May I help you, miss?" asked Betsy, observing the ruckus with a patient expression.

Catherine gratefully sought her assistance in locating her riding habit. She longed to ask Betsy not to mention the episode to Lady Fellingham, but she knew as soon as the maid found the garment, she would run to her mistress to report the marquess's presence in the house. For this reason, she sought her help in putting on her habit and even requested that the maid retrieve her pelisse for her. By the time Betsy returned to the second floor, she and Deverill would be gone.

"Thank you, my lord, this is very kind of you," she admitted graciously a little while later as they entered Hyde Park, a groom following at a discreet distance. "It is my brother Freddy's dearest wish that we keep a stable in town, but I'm afraid it is simply too impractical to seriously consider."

"I thought we agreed on Julian," he said.

Surprised, she raised her eyes to his. "Yes, but that was before—" Her speech broke off as soon as she realized what she had been about to say.

"Before?" he prodded.

"Nothing, my lord," she said quietly, appalled by the

blunder she had very nearly made. Imagine—revealing her knowledge of his and Lady Courtland's scheme! Nothing would bring about the end of the game more quickly and, she realized in that instant, she very much wanted it to continue, at least until the end of the morning.

After examining her silently for a moment, he nodded. "Very well. But I would prefer it if you would call me Julian. Then I could call you Catherine without seeming too forward."

The absurdity of this statement made her laugh, for she had never met anyone more forward than he, and she felt some of the tension drain out of her shoulders. "I sincerely doubt, my lord, that you've ever worried about seeming too forward."

He smiled, perhaps conceding the truth. "And what about you?"

"Me?" she asked, at once surprised and amused by the notion. "I daresay nobody has ever thought me forward. Indeed, 'twould be very much the opposite."

"I doubt that," he said. "But I meant, do you wish you could keep a stable in London?"

"Ordinarily I would say no, since I think it's better not to ride at all if you have to keep to a sedate pace and can't gallop freely. However, this short ride has demonstrated to me how much I miss being atop a horse, and now I'm wondering if perhaps a little something is not better than nothing at all. You see," she said with unexpected earnestness, "I've always thought the reverse."

"A Spartan, Catherine?"

She examined him carefully to see if he was teasing her, for she felt certain he must be, but nothing in his gaze indicated amusement. Reassured, she said, "No, not really. I have just found that it is far easier to want nothing than to pine for everything."

"And what about the things you can't live without?" He looked at her curiously and waited for her answer.

"Hmm," she murmured consideringly, "I very much doubt that there is anything that I can't live without. Except, perhaps, gooseberry pie. But Cook bakes one for me every Sunday, so I don't have to pine for that."

"Nor shall you pine for a horse," he declared regally. "I shall leave word with my groom that my stables are at your disposal. Please make use of Daisy whenever you like."

Taken aback by his overwhelming generosity, she stuttered, "R-really, my lord, that...I, um, I am afraid that wouldn't be proper."

"Propriety be damned," he said forcefully. "And if there is anything else you're pining for, please let me know. Be assured I would help in any way I can."

Catherine stared at him, trying to reconcile this kindness with the cruelties he had uttered about her not two days before. Disturbed, she reminded herself that he was a bored nobleman looking for some game to play. She was naught but a project to him, a project he only took on at the instigation of a friend.

To save herself from folly, she changed the subject. They'd talked enough about her for one morning. "Lord Deverill, I am going to begin to wonder at your reputation as a flirt if you continue in this solemn vein. Come, let's talk of something lighter. Do tell me how you got involved with the Elgin Marbles. Some devil's bargain you made, perhaps?"

He laughed. "Not at all. My late father was a crony of Elgin's long before he went into diplomatic service in Greece. Elgin fell on hard times. He was in debt, as you know, and he lost his wife because his damned nose fell off—wretched business, that. I knew my father would have wanted me to help if I could. It wasn't my idea to sell them to the British government, but I supported it and helped facilitate the transaction."

"But the way he acquired them!" she pointed out emphatically. "How can one not disapprove? For a private citizen who was also a collector to use his position as special ambassador to the Levant is unconscionable. If he hadn't been there as a representative of the British Crown, the Turks would never have given him permission to dismantle the Parthenon Frieze in the first place."

At this charge, which was well founded and worthy of discussion, Deverill stared at her in amazement. "Remarkable," he said.

His gaze was intense, and she immediately began to wonder what she had done wrong. Was there a ridiculous speck of dirt on her nose? Had she grown another head without noticing it? Discomforted by the intensity, she demanded that he tell her what was remarkable.

"That you know all that," he explained. "Most of the ladies of my acquaintance know only where the modiste is on Bond Street."

"I'm afraid I should get very lost indeed if I tried to find Bond Street, let alone the modiste," she admitted.

"Don't be absurd, Catherine, nobody except the coachmen know where Bond Street is," he said, making her laugh again. "Come, explain to me how you are so knowledgeable in the news of the day."

"It's no great mystery, my lord. I simply make a practice of reading the dailies, which anyone can do. And I am quite a wretch about it, too," she confessed, "perusing the paper in the breakfast parlor while the others in my family eat and discuss the modiste on Bond Street."

"Ah, a bluestocking," he said.

There was a teasing quality to his tone, not a critical one, and she didn't feel the least bit offended or compelled to defend herself. "I prefer informed citizen."

He nodded slowly. "Let's see about that. The corn laws."

"Opposed," she said.

"Lord Liverpool."

"An undynamic prime minister. I am convinced I can do better."

"Crop rotation."

"An excellent idea and one that I've applied to my garden in Dorset. Viscount Townsend is a brilliant agriculturalist."

"Remarkable," he said again.

"Not really," she dismissed lightly. "It's expected that young ladies of my age and breeding know how to read. That's why our parents employ governesses when we are young."

"That is true," he conceded, "but they very rarely retain information or form opinions on the matters."

"Lord Deverill, I once again must express amazement at your reputation as an accomplished flirt," Catherine said. "Do you subject all ladies to your low opinion of our sex or am I the exception?"

He turned in his saddle and examined her carefully with his unusual green eyes. "You are, my dear Miss Fellingham, quite the exception."

Again he threw off her studied equilibrium with his words and deeds, proving that he was in fact the accomplished flirt he was reputed to be. "And what is your excuse?" she asked, grappling for a topic to keep the conversation going, anything so that he would stop looking at her like that.

"My excuse?"

"For being an informed citizen," she explained. "You will own, I trust, that the male half of society is not quite famous for its knowledge of political matters. Once, during my misspent youth, I attempted to converse with a gentleman—I believe he was an earl—by asking what he thought of the Treaty of the Dardanelles and he replied that the Dardanelles were a lovely couple and he was delighted they had worked out their differences."

Deverill laughed, as she hoped he would. "My excuse is very mundane. I've taken up my seat in the House of Lords."

At this, Catherine looked at him in surprise, for never in all her rhapsodizing over the unrivaled Marquess of Deverill had her sister mentioned an interest in politics. Knowing of it made her think better of him than the loan of any number of sweetgoers ever could. "You are to be congratulated, my lord. I understand from my father that the benches are too hard for the successful completion of any legislative business."

"Thank you," Deverill said with the utmost sincerity, though his eyes gleamed in a way that Catherine found entirely disconcerting. "They say the secret to parliamentary greatness is a stiff upper lip but I think it's a stiff upper back. If you can learn not to mind a creaky feeling between your shoulder blades, you can impose any number of protective tariffs."

"So you were in favor of the corn laws, then?" she asked, her tone only slightly censorious, for she was enjoying herself too much to disapprove fully.

He flashed her a smile. "You would think so, wouldn't you, given the deplorable role I played in the Elgin drama. But, in fact, I'm more liberal in my ideas than you would credit. As I said, I helped Lord Elgin out of a sense of obligation to my father, who, it should be noted, would have been appalled by my nay vote on the corn matter. He was a very good man, honest and fair with the tenants and generous and kind to the servants, but rather traditional in his beliefs. I fear my untraditional bent frequently frustrated him."

Despite the implied friction between father and son, it

was clear from his words that they had rubbed together well. "You still miss him very much," she observed.

He shifted his grip on the reins to one hand, turning slightly in his seat, and it seemed to Catherine as if he was about to reach for her with his other. She braced for contact, fearful of how it would affect her and uncertain of what it could mean, but then he straightened his shoulders and looked directly ahead at the bridle path, which was quiet. Only a few other riders were out, mostly grooms taking horses out for some exercise.

"Perceptivity, my dear Fellingham," he said softly, "is as rare among the *ton* as intelligent conversation. I imagine you learned that, as well, during your misspent youth."

Catherine had learned nothing of the sort, for she rarely made comments that one could classify as perceptive, and she felt self-conscious now as she wondered if she had put off the marquess with such a personal remark. He had spoken matter-of-factly about his father, and yet she had introduced a note of sentiment. Embarrassed, she looked down at her fingers holding the reins and felt her enjoyment in the morning fade. What she had liked most was the ease of conversation between them, and determined to restore them to solid footing, rather than retreat into her silent shell, she tried to think of harmless subjects to introduce. It could not be that difficult, for Evelyn did it all the time and she made it seem effortless, as if all she had to do was smile for clever nothings to fall from her lips.

Finally, she settled on the weather. She knew, of course, that it was the most insipid topic possible and the last resort of bores, but that was why it was ideal. She needed to brush up on her light conversational skills if she was going to take this time around.

"It's a beautiful day, is it not, my lord?" she asked.

He gave her a curious, sideways glance before agreeing.

"Why, yes, Catherine, it is. The sky is a deep cerulean and the clouds look alarmingly like fluffy, white bunny rabbits. Do you think it will rain tomorrow?"

Grateful that he took her cue, she responded, "My predictive skills are sadly lacking, but I would venture to guess yes, based on the fact that this is England and it rains frequently here. What think you about the temperature? Shall it grow seasonably warm any day soon?"

"I should imagine it will grow unseasonably hot just in time for Lady Rivington's ball," he returned with a smile. "I can do this endlessly, my dear. I've been conversing with *débutantes* and dowagers for what seems like centuries, although in fact I know the period can only be measured in years, and I am capable of holding any number of extended conversations on the weather or the modiste or the fireworks at Vauxhall Gardens. I'm familiar with all the polite courtesies expected of me and I am happy to follow them if that's what you'd prefer, but for my part, I'd much rather enjoy your company silently than partake in the insipidness that society would call lively conversation."

This speech, which Catherine listened to with growing wonder, unsettled her greatly, for she felt certain that somewhere buried in his words was the highest compliment she had ever been paid. Fearful of her own susceptibility, she reminded herself that he was only following Lady Courtland's orders.

Determined not to linger on the uneasy feelings he inspired—determined indeed to ignore them entirely—she looked at the marquess with a bold expression. "My lord, may we run?"

"Run, Catherine?"

She leaned into him as if revealing a great secret. "Gallop," she said, her eyes focusing on the path ahead. "I know it's not the thing, but it's early and so few people are here to disapprove. I feel confident that if the park authorities should take us to task, your consequence will pull us through. Is that very wrong of me?"

His eyes glowed for a moment, and Catherine was almost frightened by the look he gave her. She began to worry that she had again said something very wrong. Perhaps one did not talk of a marquess's consequence to a marquess. Her tone had been playful and she had meant no real harm. She was about to apologize when Deverill said, "I should like nothing better. Race you to the end of the path."

Catherine pulled in her legs, tightened her grip on the reins and took off in a full gallop after Deverill, who already had a sizable lead, thanks to the advantage of his horse's long legs. But Catherine was no novice at racing. She and Freddy used to ride hell for leather to the old barn every morning when they were children. She flattened herself against the horse's mane and talked gently into Daisy's ear. She had discovered early on that horses were much like people: They wanted only encouragement. "Come on, Daisy, we are so close. Thatta girl."

But Catherine didn't really care if she and Daisy won the race. All that mattered was that she was out here in Hyde Park on this beautiful morning under this deep cerulean sky littered with bunnylike clouds riding this chestnut mare at breakneck speed alongside Julian Haverford, Marquess of Deverill, one of the most sought-after peers of the realm. It might have been the happiest Miss Catherine Fellingham had ever been.

She arrived at the finish line a few seconds after Deverill. He, too, was out of breath—and smiling.

"Jolly good," he said when he was no longer quite so winded. "I have never seen Daisy move so quickly. I must admit, at the onset, I meant to do the gallant and ease up a bit so that you would feel as though it were a close race. But that, my dear, was genuinely a close race. Indeed, I've never pushed Gale so hard in the city before."

Flushing with pleasure at the compliment, she said, "I'm glad, my lord, that the season hasn't made me too rusty. It feels as though it's been years and years since I've ridden like that, but it has been only a few months."

"Then I sincerely hope that you will accept my offer to use Daisy whenever you want," he said. "As I mentioned previously, you would be doing me a favor since she doesn't get the exercise she needs."

Instead of instantly demurring again, she promised to think about it, and indeed she would. Her mind was already flooding with possibilities. To have a horse to ride whenever she wanted! Surely nothing could make her happier. And would she not meet more eligible men if she did? Perhaps that was what Deverill himself was thinking—her having her own mount would make her fashionable more quickly. "We shall see, my lord."

"Good. We should probably be getting back. As much as I'd prefer to spend the day in Hyde Park with you, I have some business matters to attend to this afternoon."

"Of course," she said, a little disappointed, even though she knew she had no cause to be. It had been a wonderful morning, and she herself had business to attend to, as well. Mama had promised to go over the household accounts with her after lunch.

"How is your sister Melissa?" he asked on the ride back.

"Very well, my lord," Catherine assured him. "Although far from sating her, our brief visit to the museum seems to have only whetted her appetite. She talks of nothing but seeing more of the marbles."

"Have you figured out a plan for returning?" he asked.

"Not quite. Mama was very cross with me for taking her once, so I do not know how I'll take her a second time. Of course, things are so much easier since I've started spending time—" She broke off, her cheeks turning a deep shade of red at the thought of what she almost confessed. She could just imagine the look on his face if she had finished the sentence. No doubt the marquess knew the truth—that any match-making mama worth her salt gave her daughter more latitude when an excellent connection was on the verge of being formed—but it, like a peer's consequence, was not discussed.

"Regardless, I do not know when we'll make a return trip," Catherine said as her embarrassment began to fade. "Melissa has already started the campaign but I'm not—"

Here Catherine broke off a second time, but now she looked at Deverill in a new, predatory light. "Although," she said consideringly, squinting her eyes in concentration, "we could go back if you offered to escort us."

"I, Miss Fellingham?" he said, looking at her with more hauteur than she'd ever seen on his countenance.

The look was daunting, but Catherine refused to be cowered by it. For one, it was an excellent way to gain her mother's approval of a return visit. Lady Fellingham would have suggested tea with the noseless Lord Elgin himself if she thought it would further her daughter's cause. For another, she thought it would do Deverill good to be maneuvered into a situation that was not to his liking. It was an occurrence that could not happen very often.

"Yes, of course. It is the perfect solution. Mama would never say no to you. You are far too important." There she went again, referencing his consequence. No matter, she thought, as she trooped gamely on. "Oh, what marvelous fun it shall be. I can just see her face now. She will say all manner of good things about the expedition, but privately she will be appalled." Catherine looked at her companion to gauge his compliance with her plan. "Will you do it, my lord? I assure you, my sister would be forever in your debt."

"It is not your sister's good opinion I wish to cultivate," he said pointedly with a look that Catherine was convinced had broken many a heart like hers.

But not hers, she resolved. Never hers.

"No, of course," she agreed calmly. "I would appreciate it as well."

"In that case, how can I refuse? When shall we go?"

"Tomorrow?" she suggested before reining in her enthusiasm and behaving with a modicum of decency. "No, you must name the day since we are forcing you to escort us."

His lips twitched. "I wouldn't quite say 'forcing.'"

"No, you wouldn't. You are decidedly too well-bred for that," she pointed out. "And here I am behaving like a veritable jade. I daresay, if I were more well-bred, I would release you from your promise and turn away, blushing over the entire affair. And yet I remain perfectly composed. Whatever's the matter with me? Now, Deverill, pick a day that is most agreeable with your calendar."

"Tomorrow is out of the question because I have some business that I must look into. However, I have no pressing engagements on the following day. How is that for you?"

"Perfect," she said, delighted with the scheme and with him. "Then it's a date. Tuesday, shall we say after luncheon?"

He nodded his head slightly in agreement, and they finished their ride in companionable silence. Catherine did not feel the need to chatter.

When he was taking his leave of her, he said, "Will you be in attendance at my Aunt Bedford's rout this evening?"

"I must confess, my lord, that I am in complete ignorance of your aunt's route," she said.

Deverill looked surprised. "How peculiar. I am sure she invited you."

Catherine wondered how he could know such a thing but chose not to dwell on her curiosity. "Not really peculiar, as my mama often forgets to mention things to me and then gets cross when I am not dressed at the appointed time," Catherine explained, her gold eyes glowing with humor. "It's not that they don't want my company; it is simply that they forget about me. I am very quiet, you see."

He laughed. "No, I haven't seen that, Miss Fellingham."

Catherine blushed profusely and muttered goodbye as Deverill kissed her hand, lingering with his lips a shade longer than was necessary.

Once inside the town house, she went to her room to change into a walking dress and to think about her ride with Deverill. As much as she wanted to take him up on his offer to provide her with a mount, she knew she would never do it. The gesture was by any account generous and kind, and that, of course, was the problem. Her mother would find the loan of a horse to be as good as a declaration, and Catherine would have to spend the rest of her life apologizing for letting such an eligible catch get away. It would become yet another failure for her to shoulder.

Deep in thought, she did not notice her mother in the hallway until she heard her squeal. "You are back! Why have you returned so quickly? Has the weather turned? Did you not invite the marquess in for tea? How ramshackle he must find us, though, I must say, arriving at nine for a ten o'clock appointment isn't entirely the height of courtesy either. Nevertheless, do invite him in for tea next time."

"Quickly, Mama?" she asked in wry amusement. "I was gone for almost two hours."

This reasonable response did little to quell her mother's anxiety. "How are you going to bring him up to scratch if you spend so little time with him?"

The accusatory note in her mother's voice, so much in evidence during her daughter's first season, quite destroyed Catherine's good humor and she had to bite back a sharp retort. Losing patience with her mother would serve no purpose and would only make the trip to the British Museum harder to arrange. Instead she asked, "Why didn't you tell me about the rout tonight?"

Lady Fellingham gaped at her in amazement and even dropped the bud vase she was holding. The little vessel bounced on the rug and landed at her feet. "Tell you?"

Catherine looked at the forlorn rose and water stain on the floor, then at her mother, baffled by her response, which seemed more overwrought than her usual histrionic reaction. "Yes, tell me," she said calmly.

"Because," her mother said, pausing for dramatic effect, "the last time you went to a rout, you assured me that you never wanted to hear about another one for as long as you lived."

Catherine flinched as she recalled telling her mother precisely that after a particularly unpleasant affair last season. The event had taken place on an unusually hot night, and there had been too many people pressed into the room than was either safe or sane. Additionally, the Dowager Duchess of Lennox stepped on her toe and a pink in a purple waistcoat spilled lemonade on her dress. In the carriage immediately after, she had vowed to never attend another such function.

Slightly embarrassed by the abrupt about-face, Catherine floundered for a graceful way of assuring her mother that she would like to go to this rout on this night without committing to going to other routs on other nights. As she did so, she noticed that the lady in question's eyes were suspiciously bright.

"Mama, whatever can the matter be?" she asked, instantly concerned. She had seen her parent cry before, of course, but only in the presence of Sir Vincent after he had lost a particularly large sum at gaming.

Lady Fellingham wiped the tears away before skillfully

skirting the bud vase to wrap her arms around her daughter. "It is nothing."

Unaccustomed to displays of maternal affection, Catherine stood stock-still and wondered if she should comfort her mother. Perhaps she should pat her gently on the shoulder. "But why are you crying?"

Eliza raised her head and straightened her shoulders, though her grip on Catherine remained firm. "I'm just so happy that you are finally showing some interest in the social whirl. This is the first time you've ever asked me about a social engagement. I assure you, my dear, this is a moment I have dreamed of since your debut six years ago. I knew you wouldn't take. You were always an unnaturally shy child. I saw the way you hated going to routs and balls."

"I ask about the theater all the time," Catherine pointed out.

"The theater? The theater?" she repeated, contempt dripping from every syllable. "My dear, nobody falls in love at the theater."

Catherine took a step back so she could look her mother in the eye. "I am not in love," she said with quiet force.

Lady Fellingham shrugged as if this fact were a mere trifle. "That's all right, give it time."

"And Deverill," she added just as firmly, "he's not in love with me."

"I know, dear. Men don't fall in love as easily as women," she intoned wisely, dabbing at her tears. "Don't tease yourself on that account. Deverill isn't a greenhead. He may cavort with women like the one we saw at the modiste, but he knows his responsibility to his name and consequence. When he marries, it will be to secure an heir, not because he's in love. Still, my dear, it doesn't hurt to have some affection toward one's husband. It makes marriage so much more palatable." There was a trace of bitterness in her voice, and

Catherine wondered if she was getting the wealth of her mother's experience.

The discussion of marriage, even one so unlikely to happen as hers, made Catherine feel oddly queasy. She knew Deverill didn't—and couldn't—love her, but the thought of entering into a union in which the affection was one-sided sounded miserable to her and she knew she would never do it, no matter what the provocation. She would much rather lead apes into hell than be the smitten wife of a man who married her only to beget heirs and to propagate the family name.

Unwilling to discuss it further, she turned away from her mother and leaned down to pick up the vase and the rose. "I have to go change my dress but after that I will be available to look over the accounts. Shall we meet in the study in twenty minutes?"

Lady Fellingham agreed and said it sounded like an excellent plan, but she didn't join her daughter in the study for another two hours. When she finally did, she found Catherine curled up in a large wingback chair fast asleep with a book on her lap.

"Really, my dear," she said, coming into the room, followed by one of the footmen. "I wish you wouldn't waste candles so."

She woke instantly at the sound of her mother's voice but was nevertheless disoriented for a moment or two. She stretched her legs and yawned, causing the book to tumble to the floor.

"Regis, put the accounts on the desk there," Lady Fellingham directed the servant, who was carrying the heavy volume, before returning her attention to her eldest daughter. "Why must you choose this room of all rooms? It gets so little natural daylight. The front parlor, with its lively shades of light blue, is much happier than this dreary room, with its daunting reds and cheerless browns." Her mother took the candle from next to Catherine and placed it on the heavy oak desk. Then she sat down. "I don't know why we must have a library *and* a study. Your Aunt Louise has only a library and, as I am sure you know, she's one of the most fashionable hostesses of the beau monde. Prinny attends all her parties. I wonder why your father insists on having both. He doesn't study anything except cards, and he never gets any better despite the attention he devotes to them."

Catherine picked up *A Vindication of the Rights of Women,* which was lying at her feet, and tucked it under the seat cushion so her mother would not read the title and lecture her on unbred females with indecent ideas. "I like the study," she said, pulling the chair up to the desk so she could look at the accounts along with her mother. "And the darkness doesn't bother me. I find it comforting."

"Yes, but you always were strange. Even as an infant. Your nursemaid—Adelaide or Adela, or was she Freddy's wet nurse? —had such a time with you, I couldn't bear to look in on the nursery."

Since she had heard this complaint before, it didn't upset her in the least. She just pulled her chair closer to the desk and rested her chin on her hands as she looked down at the garble of numbers. Without Melissa's genius for mathematics, she found the notations meant nothing to her. "So tell me what I am looking at."

Lady Fellingham took Catherine through the entire ledger, explaining which numbers referred to the salaries of the staff, which covered the cost of food, which went to clothing the family and so on.

As she listened, Catherine realized how little she knew about money matters. She was amazed to see that their maid Betsy received annually little more than Evelyn spent on a few dresses. Granted, Evelyn's gowns where made of the finest-quality muslin and heavily embellished with lace, bows and elaborate embroidery, but still...the equivalent of a whole year's salary? Because she read newspapers and journals regularly, she had expected to have a better grasp of these things and was surprised to discover how wrong she was.

"Why are some figures in black and others in red?" Catherine asked.

"The red ones have yet to be paid."

Some of the numbers in red were extremely large, and Catherine wondered at their ability to pay them. "Mama, this figure here is from eight months ago. When do we plan on paying it?"

Her mother leaned over. "Don't tease yourself over the candle maker."

"Why not?"

"Because he's a tradesman," she said sensibly, "and nobody pays the tradesmen. It's unbred, my dear."

Catherine very much suspected that this wasn't true—or if it was, the tradesmen very much wished it weren't—but she didn't want to argue with her parent about it. She simply resolved that as soon as she took over the accounts, the tradesmen would get paid in a timely fashion.

"And what is this figure here?" she asked of an extremely large amount that had her name next to it.

"Those are your new dresses that we purchased yesterday morning."

"My dresses?" she echoed, aghast. "But that's so much."

"Not just dresses, my dear, but kid boots and gloves and bonnets and hosiery and reticules and that beautiful pelisse that I insisted you get."

Catherine was horrified. She didn't need a wardrobe that cost more than the downstairs servants' salaries combined. It was indecent. "Then we shall cancel those orders right way. I am very glad that we had this talk, Mama. I wish you had made me aware of the situation sooner."

"My dear child, you are being absurd," Lady Fellingham told her, laughing happily at her daughter. It was unusual for Catherine to misunderstand something. "'Tis a paltry sum, really. Sir Vincent has been known to lose twice that on the turn of a card."

That such a significant amount could be called *paltry* staggered Catherine, and she understood now what a wretched fix they were in. "B-but that is so much money," she stammered finally. "How can this be?"

Her mother smiled, satisfied. "Why else would Arabella and I have come up with our excellent scheme? I assure you, dear, it was nothing short of completely necessary."

Catherine was beginning to see that. "Are there any economies we can practice?"

"We *could* use rushlights, of course, but I would feel so wretched about it. What happens when my sister Louise comes for tea? Louise would never use rushlights instead of candles. They're for servants. And we already are poor ones for entertaining. I've told Sir Vincent several times that we should host a rout or even a musicale. Something small and intimate for our closest friends. How I loved giving parties for my father. I was very good at it, in fact. I always knew exactly what to do. That's the rub, my dear, knowing when to do what. So many hostesses are paralyzed by decisions. Have the servants set the table or hang the decorations? I assure you, it is not easy." Lady Fellingham's eyes shone as she remembered. "But you'll see, my dear, when you are married to Deverill. His house in Grosvenor Square has a beautiful ballroom. They had an extravagant coming out for Deverill's sister years ago. Then you'll see how hard it is to coordinate a large, lavish affair. Perhaps you could throw a ball for your dear sister Evelyn."

With her mother lost in a dream world of future possibilities, she studied the books carefully, looking for a corner to cut. She knew her family's income was modest, and she could tell from the accounts that they owed money to many creditors. Not that they were in Dun territory, for they weren't at all. The monies they owed could be covered by next quarter's income. Unless, of course, they spent next quarter's allowance before it came.

It was a serious problem and one that she couldn't find any way out of. Since she clearly could not stop her father from gambling away the money, she would have to discover a way to augment their income. Surely the answer to the solution was to have more money coming in to the house than they had going out. But how to do that? Her mother, having arrived at the same conclusion, had come up with a money-making scheme that was completely unacceptable. Would she be able to do any better?

Chapter Six

A s *Catherine walked* in to the drawing room of Georgina, Lady Bedford, she conceded that despite who may or may not be present (Deverill, of course) she really did hate routs. They were always, to the supreme satisfaction of one's hostess, such devastating crushes. As soon as they arrived, she lost sight of Evelyn, who looked stunning in her primrose gown. The air of tragedy she had assumed upon seeing her sister waltzing with Deverill two evenings ago still clung to her, making her beauty seem almost delicate and ethereal. In many ways, Evelyn truly baffled her. She knew her sister was selfish and rarely thought of anyone but herself, and yet the recent events seemed to have wounded her more deeply than Catherine would have expected. Her sister couldn't be in love with Deverill, she assured herself. No, Evelyn was only miffed to have lost an accomplished flirt to a dowd such as herself. Wouldn't it be funny if she knew the truth, Catherine thought, well aware that it wouldn't be funny at all.

Catherine observed the crowd, keeping an eye out for Deverill and not seeing him. Although disappointed, she readily conceded that it was for the best. She needed to put her plan into action and wouldn't succeed in meeting other suitors if she was in the marquess's pocket all night. She knew she was in fine looks that evening, for the early ride in the park had put a lovely blush in her cheeks that no amount of examining the dismal financial accounts could dim, and she felt reasonably confident that she could find someone to talk to.

Since Freddy hadn't come with them this evening, she couldn't rely on him to introduce her. She would have to muddle through on her own. Surely she knew someone in this room. After all, she had been out for six years and had met scores, if not hundreds, of ladies and gentlemen in that time. To her dismay, she saw faces that were only vaguely familiar but none that she could actually put a name to, and just as she was beginning to despair, she spotted Mr. Pearson.

"Miss Fellingham," he said, bowing over her hand, "you look charming tonight."

"Thank you, Mr. Pearson." She curtsied in return. "I'm extremely pleased to have found you. I'm afraid I've lost my sister completely, and Freddy is not in attendance. You don't mind, do you, if I use you as a social crutch for a little while? I haven't been to such a crush in a long time, and I am a little overwhelmed."

Pearson didn't seem the least put off by her honesty. "By all means, my dear, lean on me. To return candor for candor, I must admit that I myself am a little surprised by the number of people who are here. I would offer to fetch you some punch, but I don't think I could make it to the table and back."

"That's all right. I am not yet parched." She considered Mr. Pearson for a moment and thought that he would be handsome one day when the spots on his face cleared up and he grew accustomed to his height. Of course, right now he was by far too young and too awkward to be a beau, but Catherine thought he made a very nice friend. "So, tell me, Mr. Pearson, without betraying any confidences, of course, stories of Freddy's scrapes. I know he must get into a lot of them. Otherwise, they wouldn't keep sending him down the way they do."

It was just the right thing to say because Pearson indeed had a fair number of stories to tell and just as he was embarking on a narrative about an incident with the bubbles in the schoolmaster's apartments, Deverill presented himself with a slight bow.

Catherine, who had kept one eye peeled for him, was surprised by his sudden appearance and realized, after greeting him in return, that Mr. Pearson was not known to him. She made the introduction and discovered that the marquess was acquainted with his brother, Morgan. After confirming that both Pearson and his brother were in good health, Deverill announced that he would like to introduce Catherine to his aunt, who was eager to meet her.

Catherine saw the young man's disappointment and promised him that she would return presently. He had been a good friend to her in her time of need and she would not desert him now.

As they made their way across the room, Deverill said, "He's but a puppy, you know."

Catherine laughed because the observation was so patently obvious there seemed no reason to make it. "Of course he is. He's my brother's age. Regardless, he's a charming companion and it is nice to have someone to talk to amid this crowd."

"I am here. You can talk to me now," he said, more autocratic than she had ever heard.

She couldn't quite tell from the quality of his voice whether he was teasing or not, though it seemed to her that it must be the former, for nobody could be that arrogant. "Perhaps I don't want to talk with you, Lord Deverill."

Rather than respond to that blatant lie, he simply smiled with satisfaction and guided her in the direction of his aunt.

"Why does your aunt want to meet me?" she asked.

"She listens to the gossips and has heard my name linked with yours," he explained, pressing his hand to the small of her back to indicate that she should turn left out of the room. "She wants to look you over and report back to my mother."

"Your mother, my lord?" she asked cautiously, determined not to get into a fix like this morning, where she showed too much interest in his family. Nevertheless, she was curious, as the idea of his mother knowing her name made her heart trip.

"Of course. She might bury herself in the country during the season, but she does keep abreast of every nine days' wonder to blow through town."

"Is that what I am?" she asked in a chilly tone because it hurt to hear herself described so, even though she knew that was exactly what Lady Courtland had meant for her to be. "A nine days' wonder?"

He examined her carefully, trying, she supposed, to make sense of her suddenly changed demeanor. But "a wonder, certainly," was all he said in the end.

They found his aunt standing in the hallway, greeting guests who were still arriving in great numbers. Deverill saw that she was in conversation with Lord Haskell, an elderly man, gray of face and hair with a beaklike nose, and waited patiently for the conversation to draw to a close. When it did, he said, "Aunt George, may I present Miss Catherine Fellingham?"

Despite her remarkable height, Catherine felt as though she were being looked down on by this petite woman who was so much grander than she. Deverill's aunt was a legendary figure on the London scene who had somehow managed to brazen out an adulterous scandal—*she* being the adulterer—dozens of years before. "It's an honor to meet you," she said in her quiet voice. She wasn't surprised when she was ordered to speak up.

"Miss Fellingham," the older woman said, "you are familiar to me. Who's your mother?"

"Eliza Fellingham. She was a Lewis before she married, ma'am."

Lady Bedford seemed displeased with this answer, as if Catherine were intentionally thwarting her. "No, that's not right." She thought for a moment before saying, "Your father, is he Sir Vincent?"

"Yes, ma'am."

"You have the look of him," Lady Bedford announced. "I can always tell a person's relations by looking at her face."

"An impressive skill, to be sure," Catherine said, an irrepressible tongue-in-cheek note marring her sincere admiration only slightly.

Noting the impertinent tone, Deverill's aunt lifted an eyebrow. "You are very like old Felly. He's quite a rascal."

Catherine thought of the man who occasionally joined the family for meals and who wanted only a peaceful house and exclusion from all Cheltenham tragedies enacted there, including the ones he himself authored with his antics. She didn't doubt old Felly got into quite a lot of mischief when free of the obligations of family. "I wouldn't know, ma'am," she said stiffly.

"Aunt," said Deverill, sensing Catherine's discomfort, "we should let you return to your guests."

She waved her hand dismissively. "Pray hold off on your escape until I'm done with my interview." Her sharp gaze examined Catherine. "What's this about your dangling after my nephew?"

Taken aback by the unexpectedly direct question, she found her earlier boldness deserted her and she kept her mouth closed for want of something to say. Her instinct was to deny the charge, but she knew the more one denied a rumor, the more everyone believed it. The clever thing to do would be to dismiss it with a joke, but she could think of no glib rejoinders.

Fortunately, Deverill replied before her silence became marked. "Whoever is feeding you your daily dose of gossip has left you sadly misinformed, Aunt. Miss Fellingham isn't dangling after me, much to my regret. Indeed, to arrange this meeting I had to drag her away from the side of another suitor. And, what's more, as soon as we leave you here, she's promised to return to him," he said, sounding more disappointed than necessary.

"More fool she," assured his aunt before returning her attention to arriving guests.

"I am sorry to have subjected you to that," he apologized as they negotiated their way through the stifling crowd. "I wish I could say that she means well, but I'm afraid it would be nothing but an outright lie. My aunt chooses to amuse only herself."

"It must run in the family," she murmured, thinking about his pact with Lady Courtland and how he had no true concern for her feelings.

Although he looked at her oddly, he said nothing, so she was unable to judge whether he heard her comment or not. She glanced around the room in order to locate Pearson and encountered the silky blond curls of her sister instead. "Tell me, Deverill, who is the gentleman talking with my sister Evelyn. I have never seen him before."

Deverill examined the tall, thin man with the wiry black hair before responding, "That is Mr. Oscar Finchly." He made a moue of disgust. "I would advise my sister to give him his congé if I were you. He's a rather unsavory character."

She had drawn a similar conclusion simply by looking at him, for he had a slippery appearance and his eyes beheld her sister with a disconcertingly avaricious gaze. She did not, however, want to judge anyone unfairly. Having been the victim of just such an injustice only days ago, she knew how hurtful that could be. "How so?"

Deverill was disinclined to go into details and merely said that Finchly played cards by a different set of rules.

"You mean he cheats?" asked Catherine, not content to be so discreet.

He shook his head. "Nobody has ever been able to prove anything. I will say only that there are other sins that have been laid at his door and beg you to leave it at that. Ah, there's Pearson now chatting with my cousin Constantine. Have you made his acquaintance? He's a very good chap, if a bit of a fop. "

Catherine thought that by calling his cousin "a bit of a fop," Deverill was understating the case by several degrees. Dressed in an elaborately decorated pink topcoat, the man gave new meaning to "pink of the *ton*," which he was—and then some. But he was easy to talk to despite collar points so well starched that he could barely move his head, and Catherine found him delightful company. When Deverill moved on to mingle with his aunt's guests, she barely missed him.

At the end of the evening, Catherine, who had been introduced to several interesting prospects, was in such a good mood that she tried to mend fences with Evelyn.

"I think that was a lovely party," she began. "Did you have a good time, Evelyn?"

"I had a fine time, Catherine," Evelyn said, sounding bored and refusing to look at her sister. "I didn't talk to

Deverill, of course, but I saw that you talked to him enough for the both of us."

"And I saw that you had a court of admirers around you." Catherine forged onward despite this unencouraging start.

Evelyn didn't answer.

"And Mr. Finchly..."

"What about Mr. Finchly?" her sister demanded when she trailed off.

Since it was clear to her that no fences were to be mended that night, she said, "He's not to Deverill's taste. According to him, Mr. Finchly is a scoundrel."

"In light of recent events, I don't put any stock in Lord Deverill's tastes," Evelyn assured her. "And I don't need him to tell me which of my suitors are proper."

"You're right," Catherine agreed. "However, I can't help wondering if—"

"Mr. Finchly?" muttered their mother, her eyes still shut. "Where have I heard that name? I know, Evelyn has complained about a horrid Mr. Finchly." Her mother's eyes opened enquiringly. "Is it the same one? You know, there was a Finchly who Arabella and I helped. A tall man with a thin face who lived in Upper Seymour Street, number 28, I believe. It must also be the same gentleman, for it would be absurd for there to be so many Mr. Finchlys running around London."

"Yes, that's the very one," said Evelyn since her mother had revealed her true feelings on the subject. "And I don't need Deverill to tell me who's suitable. I can decide for myself who is to my liking."

"Of course," Catherine said calmly, unsurprised by her sister's prickly response. "I have every faith in your powers of judgment. I was only trying to help, you see."

"If you really want to help," said her sister, falling into a pout again, "you can go back into your shell. Don't think I don't know about the shopping trip you took with Mama yesterday, the one I wasn't invited to share. Because I did know about it and I didn't want to go." She dissolved into tears again. "I didn't want to go at all."

Showing what Catherine thought was a surprising amount of insight, Lady Fellingham said, "I'm sorry, Evelyn. You were still abed, recovering from the ball the night before, and I didn't want to disturb you. I know how you need your beauty sleep because I was very much the same when I was your age. After a long night out, my sister Louise would be up running around the house doing assorted duties that I never quite understood, but I knew that I needed to sleep. If I didn't, I would have hideously ugly black circles under my eyes and there was no way to get rid of them, despite my abigail's insistence that placing cucumbers under the eyes would do just the trick. Louise didn't have that problem and if she did, it wouldn't have mattered because she wasn't the beauty of the family. Things are different when you are truly beautiful."

Having grown up in one such household where beauty had indeed elevated one daughter over the other, Catherine could attest that things were different when one was beautiful. Thank goodness Evelyn would be long since married when the time arrived to present Melissa, a passably pretty girl, of course, but not a diamond of the first water like Evelyn. Catherine felt very protective of her youngest sister and hoped that she had an easier time of it than she.

"I know, Mama," said Evelyn, thoroughly corrupted by a lifetime of such reasoning, "that's why I can't understand why Deverill is interested in Catherine over me."

"Because sometimes beauty isn't everything," her mother explained, almost sadly, it seemed to Catherine. "And in those cases there is nothing you can do, my dear, except put on a brave face and move on to the next Lord Deverill. There is always another, more handsome peer waiting in the wings."

Catherine closed her eyes and tried to sleep. The conversation had taken a ridiculous turn, and she didn't want to hear any more of it if she could help it. She'd always known how beautiful her mother had been when she was young—she had seen the miniature that Lady Fellingham always carried with her—but she had never quite understood what aging meant to a woman whose self-confidence was based entirely on something that would inevitably fade over time. Here in the carriage she had been given a glimpse, and it made her worry for Evelyn's future. For the first time in her life, Catherine allowed that it might be a far better thing to have countenance than beauty. She dozed with a smile on her face.

When Julian Haverford, Marquess of Deverill, showed up at her door a few days later to take her children to the British Museum, Lady Fellingham could have been knocked down with a feather, her shock was so great.

"The British Museum?" she said, watching as Caruthers took his hat and coat from him. "*The* British Museum?"

"Make no mistake," he said, "there is only one British Museum."

Lady Fellingham laughed distractedly. "Of course. There's only one. How silly of me. And how rude. Catherine," she said, not noticing that her daughter was fighting to hold in a fit of giggles, "don't just stand there staring, take Deverill into the drawing room. Caruthers? Caruthers? Where is that— Oh, there you are. We will have tea in the drawing room. Come, my dear Deverill, and let us talk about the...uh, British Museum."

Catherine entered the room and closed the door behind her. Her mother and Deverill were already seated. She sat down across from Deverill and studiously evaded his gaze lest she break out into delighted laughter.

"What are you going to see at the museum?" her mother asked, just as the servant brought in the tea. "Caruthers, could you please tell Melissa that she is wanted in the drawing room. Do make sure her hair looks all right before she comes down."

Caruthers's lip curled a little at the thought of this very unbutlerlike duty, but he acquiesced with a nod. When he was gone, Lady Fellingham turned to Deverill for confirmation. "You did say Melissa, did you not, my lord? Catherine, be a dear and pour Lord Deverill some tea."

"I did indeed, madam," he assured her.

"And you are quite sure you didn't mean Evelyn?" she asked, somewhat disconcerted by the unexpected situation.

"I am very sure. However, if Evelyn is a fan of antiquities, she is quite welcome to join our little expedition." He accepted the teacup from Catherine with a glint in his eye, but she refused to respond in kind for fear of losing her composure altogether.

"Evelyn a fan of antiquities?" Lady Fellingham laughed merrily before realizing that she might sound rude. "That is to say, no, she's not. But I am sure she will be very pleased to hear that she is invited."

"Isn't Evelyn napping, Mama?" Catherine said, afraid that they would have to take Evelyn on their trip. She could think of no quicker way to ruin an excursion to the British Museum than to have her fashionable sister dragging behind, complaining of dust and boredom.

"That's right," Eliza remembered. "It wouldn't do to disturb her."

"I didn't think so," her daughter agreed.

"But to return to Melissa. I am not sure I comprehend why you want to take her," said her devoted mother.

"I understand from Catherine that she is a student of antiquities," he said, rather disingenuously, "and I thought she might enjoy seeing the Elgin Marbles."

"The marbles!" she said crossly, tipping over her tea as her hand trembled with shock. "Oh, dear me, what a mess I've made. Catherine, pull the bell."

Catherine obeyed, but instead of sitting there just waiting for someone to respond as her mother did, she dabbed at the spill with a cloth.

The doors opened and in stepped a housemaid. "Yes, my lady?"

"Some tea has been spilt," Lady Fellingham said, her voice still a little weak. "Please bring fresh linens."

The housemaid curtsied and left. Eliza took a deep, steadying breath and said calmly, "You were talking about the marbles, my lord?"

"Yes, I thought that the Misses Fellingham might want a look at the marbles," he explained, with a sideways glance at Catherine, who kept her eyes focused on the carpet, so her mother wouldn't see her smile. "They've been a particular interest of mine since I helped my friend Lord Elgin secure the purchase of them by the government."

If this information also scandalized Lady Fellingham, she contained it entirely. Her fingers holding the teacup did not so much as quiver. She did, however, look at Deverill cautiously, as if no longer certain what to make of this handsome, rich and titled suitor. "I didn't know you counted Lord Elgin amongst your friends, my lord."

"Oh, yes," he said. "He and my father had a long-standing relationship."

"What happened to him...for a man to lose track of his nose like that—" She broke off here and shook her head mournfully. "He has my sympathy, of course."

"I will be pleased to pass along your regards," he said, the irony apparent to no one but Catherine.

"Thank you."

"As I was saying, I have been assured that your daughters have been only once before," he explained. "As once is not enough to absorb their magnificence, I thought to offer them my escort for a second visit."

"You thought?" asked Eliza with a suspicious glance in her daughter's direction.

Intercepting it, Deverill said, "Entirely my idea. In fact, Miss Fellingham was hesitant to say yes because she feared you wouldn't approve. I'm afraid I cajoled her into agreeing." He gave Catherine a fond look for the benefit of her skeptical parent. "I thought she should see the marbles again, and since I enjoy her company, I suggested that we go."

Catherine was so impressed with Deverill's performance that the need to clap well-nigh overcame her good sense, but she caught herself just in time. This, however, left her hands perched awkwardly in midair and she poured herself some more tea even though her cup was already half full.

"And taking Melissa?" Liza had yet to be convinced. She recalled Catherine's uncharacteristic behavior of the previous week and suspected she had something to do with Deverill's invitation.

"Miss Fellingham explained that she couldn't in all good conscience go when her sister Melissa was the real enthusiast," he explained reasonably.

"Did she? How thoughtful," said her fond parent through practically clenched teeth.

"So naturally I suggested that Melissa come along as well."

"How nice."

"Lady Fellingham, perhaps you'd like to join us?" Deverill offered graciously.

The teacup clattered on the saucer at the very suggestion. "Join you?" she managed, her voice faint.

The marquess nodded enthusiastically. "Yes, there's plenty of room in my carriage, and I would be delighted to give you a private tour of the marbles."

"A private...oh, dear...you are...I can't..." Eliza's face

contorted as she foundered for a proper reply to such an indecent yet generous proposal. Finally, she said, "Thank you very much, my lord, for your, uh, kind offer, but I already have a plan for this afternoon. I am going to visit with my dear friend Arabella."

"Deverill knows Lady Courtland quite well," threw in Catherine impulsively.

After looking at Catherine with confusion for a second, Deverill said, "Please send her my best."

"Mama," called Melissa as she ran down the steps, "why must I make sure my hair is pres— Oh, you're here," she said when she set eyes upon Lord Deverill. "I am so happy to see you, Julian."

Lady Fellingham looked at her youngest daughter sharply. "You've met Lord Deverill before?"

"Only briefly," answered Catherine, covering for her sister. Her mother would not like it if she found out her daughters had taken to conversing with gentlemen they were not yet acquainted with in public museums.

"I can't imagine when that was but regardless, you do not call gentlemen you barely know by their first name," she instructed. "Now, please say hello to Lord Deverill."

Melissa curtsied deeply, too deeply to her mother's way of thinking. "Good afternoon, Lord Deverill."

Deverill, who had stood upon her entrance, bowed in return.

"Why have I been summoned?" asked Melissa as she poured herself a cup of tea rather than wait for her sister to offer.

"Lord Deverill has been kind enough to invite you on a trip with your sister to the British Museum," she explained, wincing as she watched Melissa drip tea all over the table. She laid a linen over the spill.

Unaware of her sister's scheme, Melissa blushed with pleasure and smiled. "Have you really, sir?" He nodded. "Oh, thank you, Lord Deverill. It would be my supreme pleasure to go with you on this most worthy outing."

"Supreme?" her mother scoffed. "Child, how you do go on."

"I should like it above all things if we could drop our heads into the room with the Elgin Marbles whilst we are there," Melissa announced.

"No doubt you would, imp," remarked her sister affectionately.

"Of course you shall. You know how highly I regard the treasures from Egypt," Lady Fellingham said with a pointed glance at Deverill. "Why, just the other day I was explaining to Catherine that the marbles are engrossing and educational antiquities. I know that some people are prejudiced against them as well as against Lord Elgin, but I am more open-minded than most. I would never hold a man's physical condition—be it the kind most disagreeable to look upon—against him. As I always say, let he who's blameless cast the first stone."

"Do you always say that?" asked Melissa ingeniously. "I thought that was Papa whenever you take him to—"

"Clever girl, don't go around correcting your mama," her mother interrupted, not wishing to be embarrassed by her youngest child's candor.

"Perhaps we should get going," suggested Catherine, who was enjoying the scene far more than was decent. "We don't want to take up too much of Lord Deverill's time. No doubt he is a very busy man."

"I am entirely at your disposal, Miss Fellingham," Deverill said, rising to his feet as Catherine stood.

"Yay," cheered Melissa, clapping her hands excitedly. "Does that mean we can go to St. Paul's cathedral as well? And climb up onto the dome and look down on London

Town? I've always wanted to go there, but Mama insists that all those stairs are indecent. I don't mind the stairs; I swear I don't."

Lady Fellingham laughed nervously as her cheeks blushed becomingly. "Clever girl," she said again.

Chapter Seven

❦

Catherine caught Freddy just as he was leaving the town
house.

"Ah, there you are, dear," she said, entwining her
arm through his and spinning him around until he faced the
drawing room. "This way please." She pulled him inside and
closed the doors. "There, now we can talk."

"Don't have anything to talk to you about," he insisted,
sitting down and considering the situation. "At least, if I did,
I can't remember now so it couldn't have been very important," he said, relieved. "Well, I guess I should be off. I am
late for an appointment with Pearson."

"I have something I'd like to talk to you about. I promise,
this won't take a minute." She leaned her back against the
doors, effectively blocking his only avenue of escape.

"It better not," he mumbled, less than graciously, his sister
thought.

"Right, then. Freddy, I think the time has come for me to
learn how to gamble."

Freddy, in the process of examining his nails, jerked his
head up in shock. "What?"

Convinced that she now had his full attention and that he wasn't going to bolt, she abandoned her post and took a seat. "I have given this serious thought, and it occurs to me that I should know how to gamble."

Freddy jumped to his feet, outraged at the suggestion. "No sister of mine is going to be a ramshackle gambler." He even waved a finger at her in a disapproving way.

Catherine laughed. "I don't want to be a gambler, per se. I just want to learn how to gamble."

"Well, don't look at me." Freddy wasn't used to playing the levelheaded one, and it made him oddly uncomfortable. "Mother would have me strung up if she ever found out."

"Mama isn't going to find out. She never discovered that you went off to the races with Dalton instead of staying home sick in your bed," she reminded him. "What was wrong with you that time? A little whooping cough?"

"Don't be absurd. I had laryngitis. Whooping cough is for babies," he corrected before he realized something. "Hey, how do you know about that?"

"I know about everything that goes on in this house," she stated simply. "I know all about your many varied supposed diseases. I have much admired your creativity, which is why I thought you'd be the perfect person to teach me how to gamble and then take me to a hell."

"No, absolutely not! You can blackmail me all you want, but I am not taking my own sister to a gambling hell." His denial was accompanied by a curious and faith-inspiring improvement of his posture.

"I am not trying to blackmail you, silly." Although now that he had mentioned it, she had to admit it wasn't such a bad idea.

"Regardless, those were harmless pranks and if you want to tell Mama out of a vicious disregard for me, I can do nothing to stop you," Freddy said, standing very much on his honor indeed. Catherine had never seen him like this—he had always been little more than a lovable scamp—and she was happy to note that he had backbone.

"But this will be nothing but a prank as well, a harmless lark, I assure you." Catherine stood beside him and placed an arm around his shoulders. "Tonight Mama and Evelyn are going to a musicale at Lady Steven's. Could anything be more dreary?"

"Then don't go if you don't want to," he said reasonably.

Catherine decided that another approach was required and commenced begging. "Please, Freddy, please. This is very important to me and you would be the best of good brothers if you would just do this tiny little favor for me." She tried a pout, but she wasn't sure that she could do it right. Catherine was not used to cajoling anyone. Either there was nothing she wanted that she couldn't get for herself or she used reason and abandoned the project when that failed to prevail. No, as far as she could remember, this was the first time she actually put herself out trying to convince someone to see something her way, and she found it very undignified.

"Don't do that," he scolded. "You sound just like Evelyn asking for a new hat. It doesn't become you at all."

Catherine knew that, of course. "Then please say you'll do it and spare me the humiliation of debasing myself further. I assure you it doesn't come quite as naturally for me as it does our sister."

Freddy sighed heavily and sat down again. It seemed to his sister that all the fight had gone out of him. "But why?"

She took the seat next to him. "I told you. The time has come for me to learn how to gamble."

"But why must you learn?" If he was to capitulate, he would at least have all the information first.

"Because if Papa is going to send us all to the poorhouse, I want to at least know how. What is faro and how is it played?

Don't you see it's driving me crazy? He is holding our future in his hands, and I can do nothing at all about it."

Freddy agreed that this was true. Their father could gamble away their entire estate, and they were all completely powerless to stop it. But Freddy, being a gentleman, understood this in a way that Catherine could not. Their father had the right to gamble away everything he owned if he so chose. That was the point of being a gentleman. He tried explaining this to Catherine with carefully chosen words that he thought quite clearly represented the matter.

"What a bag of moonshine," she dismissed. "If that's the way you men think then it's no wonder Mama is at the end of her rope, selling commissions in the king's army to aspiring hopefuls." Catherine laughed as she thought about the situation. "You do realize, Freddy, that this interview has me more in sympathy with my mother right now than I ever have been in the four-and-twenty years previous?"

Freddy wasn't at all surprised that the ways of gentlemen were beyond his sister's comprehension. "Catherine, I really think you should just leave it alone."

"I can't," she said, deciding it was time to alter her argument once again. Perhaps threats would work. "If you won't help me I shall have to go somewhere else."

Thinking of his sister's limited social life, he laughed. "Go where?"

She tried to think of a name, any name. "I don't know. Perhaps Pearson will help me."

"No, he won't." He thought of his staid friend. "Pearson would never take an innocent young lady into a gambling hell. He's not a sapskull."

"Hardly young," she pointed out.

"Young enough. And you're still my sister," he said. "Pearson knows the meaning of honor. That's why he told us about Mama in the first place."

Catherine knew this was true and tried another tactic. "Very well, then, I will go on my own. If you would be so kind as to give me the direction of the nearest hell, you can be on your way. I should imagine you are very late for your appointment by now."

From the look on his face, it was clear that Freddy had forgotten entirely about it. "Devil it, Catherine, you cannot go to one of those places alone, and I'll be damned if I tell you where one is."

"That's all right." She waved her hand dismissively. "I can find one on my own. I shall simply hop into a hackney and order the driver to take me to the closest hell. I'm sure it won't be a problem. You can run along now," she said, giving him permission to go but not the least bit surprised when his feet stayed firmly planted to the rug. "It's really all right, Freddy. I realize now that it was wrong of me to ask you. A brother can't escort his sister to a gaming hell. It would be too infamous. How very clever you are to have seen that. I'll be much less conspicuous on my own. But do tell me what I should wear? Will a simple evening dress be too much?"

She could tell by the look on his face that she had finally hit upon a strategy that worked and wondered why she hadn't started with it. It was so much more dignified to manipulate her brother into helping than to beg for his assistance. Trying to hide her triumphant smile, Catherine looked at him patiently, waiting for his capitulation.

"Very well," Freddy said, sighing deeply. "Tell Mother you have the headache. She herself is afflicted with the complaint and would never doubt that you were in too much pain to listen to the Steven chit howl away at the piano."

"Do you promise?" she asked.

"I give you my word."

Catherine threw her arms around him and squeezed. "Oh,

you dear, dear brother. I will never forget this. You are the best of good men."

Freddy submitted to the indignity of the hug for a moment before shrugging free. "Enough of that," he insisted. "And I don't know why you are thanking me. Tonight's work could very well be our downfall. I shouldn't have agreed," he said, already regretting his momentary weakness.

"Pooh, Freddy. Don't be such a sad sack. We'll go in, play a couple of games of faro with the others and leave. That will be all and I will never bother you about gambling ever again," she assured him happily.

He didn't put much stock in this promise. "You are assuming, of course, that you don't have the sickness that Papa has. Some people start gambling, and they don't stop until they have ruined themselves."

Catherine dismissed his concerns with a wave of her hand. "You needn't be so dramatic, dear. Think whom you are talking to. I have never been susceptible to anything in my entire life. I'll be fine."

"The gambling sickness could be in your blood and you simply don't know it yet," he insisted.

"Bah. I don't believe such faradiddles. Surely if my blood were infected, I would have succumbed to some sort of impulse years ago. Don't worry, brother dear, if my plan goes sour, I will accept the consequences of my actions and not blame them on something so intangible as the blood." She consulted the clock resting on the mantle. "Do look at the time, darling. You are very late indeed for your appointment. You mustn't keep Mr. Pearson waiting. Please apologize to him for me."

As late as it was, he was reluctant to leave, for he wanted to stay and take back his word. That would be useless, of course. There was no swaying Catherine from a path once she had set her mind to it. But perhaps he could talk her out of it later after she'd had some hours to think about her proposed rash behavior.

Freddy put on his hat and left the town house, his happy mood much destroyed by his sister's pigheadedness.

Getting out of Lady Steven's musicale was easy work for Catherine. Evelyn didn't want her to come anyway and actually cheered when she was told the bad news. Her mother was only somewhat dismayed.

"No doubt it was your expedition to the museum yesterday. I knew I should never have given my consent." Her mother touched her hand to her daughter's head to see if she was running a temperature. She was not. "You poor dear, you must be exhausted. No doubt you aren't used to all this activity. Evelyn and I, of course, are accustomed to buzzing around like busy bees, but you, my dear, have never kept the same hectic pace as us. We would like to stay in more, but one has social duties that one cannot bow out of gracefully. Now get some rest and I'll check on you in the morning. I am sure you only need some extra sleep."

Catherine was already in bed, and she fluttered her eyes tiredly.

"La, look at you," her mother exclaimed, "barely able to keep your eyes open. Rest now. You must recover tomorrow for our expedition to Almack's. What would Lady Sefton say if we showed up without you?"

As her mother shut the door, Catherine wondered how upset Lady Fellingham would be if she pleaded the headache tomorrow night as well. She would not be nearly as understanding then. She didn't doubt that the kind lady would roll her out of bed, pour a medicinal draught down her throat and order her to put a brave face on it. The thought brought a smile to her lips, even as she acknowledged how much she was dreading the evening. She didn't want to go to Almack's, not because the patronesses were intimidating or the assembly rooms famously stifling but because she feared dancing with Deverill again. It was too risky. As confident as she had been that she could use him to her own ends, Catherine found herself being drawn deeper and deeper into a web of emotion that she couldn't control. The visit to the British Museum demonstrated to her just how susceptible she was to his charms. By all accounts, their trip had been a stunning success—and that, of course, was the problem. She had thoroughly enjoyed the outing. Deverill was an enthusiastic tour guide, able to speak with equal familiarity of the Rosetta stone and Egyptian mummies, and he listened to Melissa's lecture on the pediment statues with a patience that could only be described as endearing.

Catherine was desolate to admit to herself that she genuinely liked Julian Haverford, Marquess of Deverill.

It was, by and large, an unexpected development, and yet, looking back, she could see that it was entirely inevitable. The gentleman had so much to recommend him, from his sense of humor and amiable disposition to his clever conversation and beautiful green eyes, that an inexperienced girl like her had little chance of remaining indifferent. Indeed, she was as bad as Evelyn had been when it came to heaping encomiums on his head.

Practical as always, Catherine knew that she would simply have to halt her feelings for Deverill at liking. To form a *tendre* for him would be fatal. The true state of his emotions had always been known to her. He accompanied her and Melissa to the museum only because she had maneuvered him into it. He was committed to dancing with her tomorrow night only because Lady Sefton had backed him into a corner. He had waltzed with her the first time only because Lady Courtland had asked him to.

Catherine had too much respect for herself to become a besotted fool, and she resolved to redouble her efforts to meet eligible *partis*. Tomorrow night at Almack's, she would dance and converse and flirt with as many eligible men as possible, and perhaps Deverill, observing her success, would consider his promise to Lady Courtland fulfilled and leave her in peace.

Any satisfaction she might have felt at her resolution was undercut by a pervasive sadness that made her worry that her feelings could not be halted after all. But Miss Catherine Fellingham had no patience for mopey misses, which explained her almost continual annoyance with Evelyn, and she gave herself a stern lecture. You will get over this, she told herself firmly. In a week or two, you will look back on this and wonder how you could have been so melodramatic.

She recalled the young army officer whom she had formed an attachment to in her first season—a man she hadn't thought of in years—and took that as proof of her resilience. Now she couldn't even remember his face. But perhaps the difference was that she and the officer had barely known each other whereas she and Deverill had already spent so much time together. He had demonstrated that he could be kind and—

No, she decided, shaking her head, as if to clear it of all thought. She had mooned over Deverill enough for one day. Now she had more important matters to attend to, and she climbed out of bed, wondering what to wear to a gaming hell. Although Freddy had assured her that one of her evening gowns would be fine, she knew she also had to disguise herself. But how? She examined her wardrobe, grimacing in disgust as she looked at all the dowdy gowns in a row. She pushed them aside with increasing agitation. She would borrow one of Evelyn's only she would look ridiculous in her sister's petite gown. Why must she be a head taller than everyone in her family save for her brother?

Thinking about her ridiculous height, she realized the

only solution was to borrow clothes from Freddy, who, at an even six feet, was two inches taller than she. If she turned herself into a man, then her tall stature would not draw attention.

After a glance to confirm that the hallway was empty, Catherine strode quickly into Freddy's quarters and made a beeline for his dressing room. She knew enough about men's clothing to pick out suitable evening wear: doeskin breeches, stockings, waistcoat, linen shirt. Catherine encountered only three problems with her excellent plan. The first was how to hide her feminine curves. Even when she put the waistcoat on, one could still tell that she was quite obviously female. After a moment's thought, she began to dig around the room, looking for something she could use to flatten her chest and settling on a long neckcloth. That done, she confronted the problem of how to tie the cravat. She tried one of the simple confections she had seen gentlemen recently sporting, but she quickly learned that there was nothing simple about a cravat. Every time she thought she had accomplished a reasonable knot, it fell apart in her hands. In the end, she realized there was no way around it; she would have to ask Freddy for help.

The last problem was considerably harder to solve. Though her height might be commensurate with a man's, her feet were not. Freddy's shoes were at least two sizes too large for her, and when she walked her heel lifted out of the black pumps. This was going to be tricky, she realized, sitting on the bed and considering her options. She had come too far to let a silly thing like too large shoes stop her now. Finally, she decided the only solution was to stuff the toes with cotton. This improvisation made the shoes tighter, and they now stayed on when she walked. There, she thought, well satisfied with her solution.

It was only when she was ready to go downstairs and wait

for Freddy that she realized she had overlooked her hair, which was remarkable because it was right there, on top of her head. "Devil it," she said, annoyed.

Cutting it was not an option. Not only would her mother never talk to her again, but she also feared how it would look. What else could she do? She remembered her father's collection of wigs. Surely he had one that wasn't powdered and ancient looking. Catherine ran down the hallway, heedless of how ridiculous she would appear to the servants.

Once in her father's dressing room, she found exactly what she needed: a brown-haired wig. It was eons out of fashion. For one thing, the hair was too long, easily covering Catherine's ears. But it would do well enough. She brought it back to her room and began plaiting her hair very tightly. Then she gathered it at the back of her head with dozens of pins before putting the wig on.

She inspected the final product and decided she hadn't done such a bad job, after all. Surely nobody would recognize her now. In order to test her theory, she climbed quietly down the servant's staircase and out the back door. She then walked around to the front of the house and rang the bell. Caruthers answered.

"Please tell Mr. Fellingham that Mr.—" Catherine broke off as she realized that she hadn't come up with a name. She thought of her favorite book. "Harold is here. Mr. Jeffrey Harold."

If Caruthers thought anything was queer, his expression didn't show it. "Mr. Fellingham isn't at home, but we are expecting him any minute. Perhaps you would like to wait in the front parlor?"

Catherine accepted this offer and followed Caruthers to the front parlor. Once there, he directed her to take a seat and left. She didn't have to wait long because within ten minutes she heard Freddy saying, "A Mr. Harold, you say? I don't know any Harolds. Very well, Caruthers, I'll take care of it."

She was already standing by the time Freddy opened the doors. He examined the room's occupant, but there was no gleam of recognition. Her brother bowed stiffly. "I am afraid, sir, that I do not recall where we've met."

Catherine smiled widely and thought of something to say. She knew that she must disguise her voice as cleverly as she had her person. "It was at Lady Sefton's ball. Your friend Pearson introduced us." Much to her surprise, she discovered that a respectable baritone was readily available to her. She watched Freddy struggle to recognize her.

"Of course," he said, offering his hand, though he clearly had no recollection of meeting a Mr. Harold at Lady Sefton's or anywhere else. "How do you do?"

Catherine laughed happily as she shook his hand. "Freddy, you clunker, it's me."

He jumped back at the surprise and hardly seemed to believe his eyes for a second. "Catherine? My girl, you are a complete hand. You had me thoroughly taken in." His admiration for her accomplishment dimmed as he examined her outfit. "Wait a second. Are those my brand-new breeches? Devil it, girl, have you no respect for the sanctity of a man's dressing room?"

"Pooh respect, Freddy. I need your help with this." And she showed him the neckcloth. "I haven't the faintest clue on how to tie one of these. I thought I had done a decent facsimile of the mail coach, but it came undone before my eyes."

Freddy looked at the strip of fabric she held out. "I don't know how to tie those. Why do you think I have a valet?" But seeing her disappointed look, he tied the cravat into a simple knot that, although it wasn't the height of fashion, held together. "There," he said, standing back to admire his handiwork.

"What do you think?" Catherine said, turning around to give Freddy the complete view. "Do I look like a young buck out on the town?"

"Not bad at all." He nodded appreciatively. "I am impressed. And I think you have Caruthers fooled, though if you don't, he'd be the last one to let you know."

"See?" said Catherine. "This won't be so bad. We'll be in and out before anybody is the wiser."

"I am still not convinced, but I know better than to argue with you," he admitted. "I must change my clothes before we leave. Shall we say a half hour?"

Waiting a half hour seemed interminably long to Catherine, who wanted nothing more than to be on their way. But she realized that Freddy was doing her a great service and knew it went very much against the grain, so she nodded agreeably to his offer and sat down again. At one point, Caruthers came in to offer her tea, but she declined. She would much prefer that he fetch her book from the study, but she knew that to ask him such a thing would very much give up the game. And she didn't want to do that quite yet, for she hadn't even begun playing.

"This is not where Papa goes to gamble, of course," explained Freddy in the carriage ride over. "Most gentlemen prefer to play at their clubs, where they know and trust everyone."

"Is cheating a common thing?" Catherine asked.

"It could be, I imagine. But a gentleman doesn't cheat. His honor depends upon it. Great men have been destroyed by the suspicion alone."

"I wish rumor would destroy Mr. Finchly," she muttered.

"Who?" asked Freddy.

"Just a wretch who is dangling after Evelyn. I daresay she

can take care of it." Catherine looked out the window. She loved London at night. It glittered. "Now tell me about faro. Is it very difficult?"

Freddy, never really one to enjoy gambling, explained faro as he understood it until the carriage stopped. He climbed down and offered his sister a hand before he realized how odd that looked—his helping another man off a carriage.

"Now, Freddy," she said as they were about to go in, "don't worry about a thing. I can handle myself. Just stay close and we'll muddle through this." She tried to sound calm but in truth her heart was racing with excitement. She had never done anything as daring as this before and it felt good. Frightening, of course, but very good.

Once they were inside, Catherine began to relax. She examined the faces around her and realized that she knew some of the patrons. She had never held a long conversation with any of them, but they had been introduced at least once if not twice or three times. Mixing with the well-dressed members of the *haute ton* were elements of a less savory segment of society.

In truth, the gambling hell wasn't what Catherine had expected, for the room had a decided elegance to it, despite the fact that it erred on the side of ostentation, with its gilded mirrors, gold lamps and silver wallpaper.

The space wasn't filled with noise exactly but with the buzz of people talking quietly. She could see men and women standing around tables watching the activity with obsessively careful eyes. Catherine inched forward toward the action.

"That's faro," said Freddy in her ear, pointing to a green table with representations of cards painted on top. "That game there with the dice is called hazard. Papa plays hazard as well but not quite as much as faro. Hazard is a complete game of chance. Some claim there is an element of skill involved with faro."

"Really?" asked Catherine in her baritone. "Then perhaps there's hope for him yet."

When a waiter came around asking them if they'd like a drink, Catherine ordered a brandy because she didn't want to stand out. She would have preferred ratafia but suspected that wasn't all the crack in a gaming hell, particularly if one was a man.

The waiter brought their drinks, and Freddy cautioned her to be careful. "Brandy is slightly stronger than that female stuff you're used to drinking."

After one sip, Catherine announced brandy delightful and then gulped half the glass down.

"Hey, watch it," her brother ordered. "Can't have you getting foxed."

"Pooh," she dismissed. "Come, let's play faro. I have all my pin money from last quarter to lose. Of course, I might win something, too. If I do, I shall buy you a gift."

"Don't talk so loudly," ordered Freddy, looking around the room to see if anyone was suspicious yet. "Men don't buy men presents. Follow me, do what I do and, above all, don't draw attention to yourself."

Catherine followed instructions and pretty soon found herself playing faro. She didn't quite see what the fuss was about, nor did she think the game required any skill. As far as she could tell, all one did was speculate on what card the dealer would turn up next. A player won the hand when he guessed correctly. The thought of the entire family rotting in debtors' prison because her father couldn't make the correct guess angered Catherine. What a stupid game, she thought. But then on the next turn of the cards, she guessed right and won a small pile of guineas and felt a little tingle. Winning, she decided, was fun, and as she placed her bet for the next hand, she felt herself tensing as she watched the dealer turn over the cards. She wanted to win and was very excited when she did. The tidy stash in front of her grew. What a lovely game.

Freddy remained by her side for a time, playing against the same dealer but not doing quite so well as she. Then he left to try his luck at hazard, although he assured her he wouldn't be gone long. Catherine shrugged and while he was away, ordered another brandy.

She was finishing her second drink when the tide started to turn. Her guessing became erratic as she abandoned the system that had served her well for the first portion of the evening. She felt little beads of perspiration begin to trickle down the back of her neck. Winning was fun. What was happening now wasn't nearly as enjoyable.

And then she saw it. At first she didn't credit it. Surely it was just her eyes playing a trick on her. Or maybe it was the light. But then it happened a second time. It wasn't the light or her eyes; it was the dealer's sneaky fingers pulling from the bottom of the deck. In her deep baritone, she called the dealer a cheat. The room became silent, but Catherine didn't notice.

"You there," she said to an official-looking gentleman she had seen earlier, "please come here and talk to your dealer and let him know that cheating is not acceptable behavior." The man she gestured to walked slowly over to her table.

Before she knew it, Freddy was at her side. "Damn it, I leave you alone for one moment," he muttered angrily into her ear. "What have you done?"

"It will be all right," she assured him before turning to the boss. "Tell me, my good man, what shall you do about this?"

"I'm afraid, sir, that we're going to have to ask you to leave," the unhelpful gentleman said, his arms folded over his chest, his look intimidating.

"My good sir, if you think on it a moment, I am sure you will realize that you meant that you will ask *this* man to leave and not I." She pointed to the dealer. "He is the one dealing from the bottom of the deck, which I know for a fact is not the way the game is meant to be played. I am a fine, upstanding law-abiding citizen of the Crown who has come to your establishment in good faith." Catherine stood her ground, refusing to be intimidated.

The man in charge nodded his head and three large men surrounded Catherine and grabbed her arms. "There is no cheating going on here," he said. "Take him outside."

Catherine began to squirm violently in their grasps, despite the painful pressure they applied to her arms. "Let go of me, you brutes," she yelled, looking to Freddy, who had gone awfully pale at this development. Clearly, he didn't have the slightest clue what to do next. Catherine was about to protest again when a voice interceded.

"Marlowe, tell your men to let my nephew go." At Deverill's command, the three brutes freed Catherine so quickly, she lost her balance and had to steady herself against the green baize table. "He is new to London and not quite familiar with our ways. I'm sorry that he made a scene." The crowd, amazed by this turn of events, averted their eyes under Deverill's steady gaze. "However, he may have handled the situation poorly, but he made no mistake. I suggest you sack the dealer and watch over them all more carefully if you want to maintain a decent reputation."

Having said this, Deverill turned on his heels and walked to the door. Catherine and Freddy followed. Once outside, Catherine got a good look at Deverill, who seemed very angry indeed, but he didn't say anything until they were in his carriage. Catherine, mindful of the good turn he had just done them but equally horrified that he should discover her ruse, said in her deep baritone, "Thank you, sir, for your help. I am—"

"Not now, Catherine," he said through clenched teeth.

"Don't say a word." He turned on poor Freddy. "What were you thinking, you irresponsible pup, to bring your *sister* to a place like that?"

She leaned forward in her seat to defend her brother, using her regular voice now that the masquerade had ended. "Freddy had no choice," she said. "I made him do it."

"I said, not a word out of you." He pinned her with his eyes and dared her to speak again. Catherine sank back.

"You are right, sir," said Freddy. "It is my fault. I should not have given in no matter what argument she used. I have learned my lesson and will never do so again."

Deverill, seemingly satisfied that Freddy had learned a lesson, laughed. "That's all right, pup. I've known your sister for scarcely two weeks now, but I am quite familiar with her outrageous behavior. I daresay that I myself went to the British Museum under similar circumstances."

The rest of the journey passed in silence because that seemed to be the way the Marquess of Deverill wanted it. Catherine, who had quickly overcome her embarrassment at being found out, tried several times to defend herself, but Deverill kept shushing her with word or deed until she finally gave up and stared sullenly out the window. London was not as glittering on the ride home.

When the carriage arrived at the Fellinghams' London residence, Deverill requested a moment alone with Catherine. Freddy, not anticipating this, was unsure how to respond. He had already behaved improperly enough this evening and thought that their mother would certainly not approve of his leaving Catherine alone with a man like Deverill, suitor or not.

Catherine could tell what thoughts were running through her brother's mind because they were quite well reflected on his face. She knew that he was debating how to handle the situation. He couldn't very well just abandon her to Deverill's devices, but at the same time, he was still very much intimidated by the fashionable older peer who had just rescued them from an ugly scene. "It's all right, Freddy, I won't be a minute. And Deverill here promises to be the perfect gentleman."

Looking uncomfortable, Freddy stammered, "Of course you do, sir. Would never imagine you could be anything else. But perhaps I should stay. We have had a frightfully improper evening already, and I should hate for it to grow even more improper."

"Very good," said his sister, laughing, "you've done your duty as my brother. Your concern has been registered and duly noted. Now, please let me have a moment with Lord Deverill. I swear I won't be a minute."

Freddy hesitated for a moment more before giving Lord Deverill one final glance and climbing out of the conveyance. When he was gone, Catherine turned to Deverill. "Well, what is it?" she asked impatiently. "I imagine you want to take me to task for my improper behavior. Please, do make it quick. I don't want to worry Freddy and he has already been through enough this evening."

"And whose fault is that?" he asked haughtily with an accompanying eyebrow raise that Catherine imagined could intimidate all the young misses on the marriage mart. It did nothing for her.

"I expect you mean for me to say it is my fault." She let out a bored sigh. "It is not. If that dealer hadn't been cheating, I would have been in and out of there with no one any the wiser." Seeing the look on his face, she added. "Of course, I am not saying that we aren't appreciative of your help. Because we are. We are very thankful indeed that you were there to smooth matters over. I shudder to imagine what those brutes would have done to me and Freddy. Still, *my* behavior was circumspect."

Deverill, whose expression previous to this announcement had been positively stormy, broke out into amused laughter. His countenance lightened, and Catherine thought she detected dimples in his cheeks. Why, he's absolutely beautiful when he laughs, she realized, amazed that a man whose looks were already so close to perfection could improve so dramatically.

After a few moments, Deverill's outburst ended and he contemplated Catherine in a detached sort of way that made her uncomfortable. "You're extraordinary, Miss Fellingham."

Miss Fellingham, who had never been called extraordinary in the whole of her four-and-twenty years, blushed becomingly and lowered her eyes. It wouldn't do for a woman of her age to have her head turned by meaningless flattery. "Surely you exaggerate, Lord Deverill. I am extremely common. Indeed, there's nothing remarkable about me."

"Come, my dear, don't be so modest," he said, amusement still evident in his tone. "You are sitting alone with me in my carriage, disguised as a man, wearing a cravat that is tied in the most wondrous fashion, after an evening of playing faro in one of the worst gaming hells in London, which you were almost forcefully ejected from, claiming that your behavior is above reproach. You can't really think that there is nothing remarkable about you."

"Is there something wrong with my cravat?" she asked, looking down at the confection that she and Freddy had cobbled together. "What is wrong with my cravat?"

Deverill considered the starched white linen. "An invention of yours, I suppose. What do you call it? The Roman Ruin?"

Despite her ire, Catherine laughed at his witticism. "No, you wretch, it's the Windblown."

He smiled but seemed disinclined to linger over the light moment. "Regardless, your behavior tonight was unacceptable. Whatever were you thinking? And how could that hapless pup have agreed?"

"Leave Freddy out of this. I used all sorts of persuasion to get his consent and won't have you criticizing him. Tonight's work was all my doing," she said, taking full responsibility for the debacle before reiterating that it wasn't her fault. "If that oafish dealer hadn't tried to cheat me, neither you nor anybody else would have ever known the truth."

Deverill, who had been sitting across from her, took that moment to switch sides. The carriage swayed a little with the movement, and Catherine jumped in surprise. "You do me an injustice, my dear," he said softly, taking her hands. "I recognized you the minute you walked in wearing that ridiculous costume."

This intelligence so shocked Catherine that she gave up trying to devise a way to free her hands from his. "You lie, sir. My own brother did not recognize me and, several times more impressive, neither did my butler."

Deverill shrugged. "Mayhap I know you better than your own brother."

"Bah. I haven't known you for even a month." She withdrew her hands from his. "What gave me away? Was it the hair? I know this style is exceedingly out of fashion but still. ..."

"I don't know what it was." He examined her carefully. "Suffice to say, I simply knew it was you from the moment you walked in. There is a certain quality about you that gentlemen's breeches and a poorly tied cravat cannot hide, and you were with Freddy. It was an easy enough conclusion to arrive at."

"Leave off ridiculing my cravat," she ordered.

Deverill did not laugh as Catherine intended. Instead, he grew serious and said, "Come, tell me now why you have behaved so foolishly."

She didn't like the change in his demeanor. She liked him best when he was in a teasing mood and found his somber expression unsettled her. "I'm afraid, my lord, that must remain my secret. I cannot feel right discussing personal business with you."

"You shall, regardless of how personal it is," he insisted. "I lent you my assistance tonight. You must agree that gives me the right to know."

"Virtue is its own reward, not the receipt of information that does not concern one," Catherine said. She wished he would return to his side of the carriage. Having him so close, with his hands very nearly touching hers again, was playing havoc with her thoughts.

Deverill looked extremely annoyed with her, and Catherine shuddered as she wondered what he might do. It was all very well and good to assure Freddy that she would be safe alone with him, but with that expression on his face, she wasn't sure of anything. "Considering my involvement, it does concern me and we will sit here until you realize that."

Catherine stared at him in amazement. "I cannot believe, my lord, that you don't have more pressing business somewhere else."

"Other business, certainly. More pressing?" He shook his head dismissively. "I assure you, Catherine, that there is nothing more important than this conversation."

Her hackles up, Catherine folded her arms in front of her and stubbornly refused to confide. Several minutes into the standoff, she realized he would be true to his word and barked, "Fine. It is nothing significant, I assure you. Merely a trifle. I am dressed like this in the company of my brother because I wanted to learn how to play faro. There," she said like a petulant child, "may I go now?"

"Not yet. I figured that much out for myself. Before you leave, you must first explain *why* you wanted to learn faro."

He leaned back against the cushion, seemingly content to wait as long as necessary.

Catherine considered the obstinate set of his chin and wondered how she could have ever thought him attractive. He was too stubborn to be handsome. "It seemed to me that if my future is tied up in faro the only sensible thing I could do—and I have behaved sensibly this evening, despite what you think—was become acquainted with the game."

"Your father?" he asked gently.

She wasn't surprised that he knew—amongst the *ton,* her father's gaming debts were common knowledge—but she was still unwilling to discuss the matter with him. "Please do not concern yourself with it, Deverill. It is a trifle, I assure you." She reached for the door, deciding it was time she left. The quarters in the carriage were a little too close for her peace of mind. She needed to get away from Deverill. "Now, if that is all, I shall be going."

She went to open the latch, but Deverill forestalled her. With one hand he reached over and gently pulled her away from the door; with the other, he raised her chin until her eyes met his. In a husky voice she had never heard before, he whispered. "There's one more thing." Then he slowly lowered his lips to hers and kissed her gently.

Catherine, who saw him draw closer, couldn't figure out what was happening until his lips made contact with hers. Then she got it. Then she quite understood. The kiss was gentle and sweet and everything that Catherine, having never kissed a man before, thought a kiss should be. She closed her eyes and leaned into Deverill, who wrapped his arms around her.

How long the kiss lasted, Catherine didn't know. Time seemed to stop for a while, which she didn't mind at all. It was only when Deverill growled softly and increased the pressure on her lips that she became aware of the impropriety of the situation and her own indifference to it. She pulled away immediately, horrified by her passionate response. She had in a matter of moments been quite thoroughly and entirely swept away by a tide of feeling.

"My lord Deverill," she gasped, hoping the shock she felt would also cover her own culpability. "How dare you! And after assuring my brother that you would be the perfect gentleman."

"I did nothing of the sort. In fact, it was you who assured him." He grinned, unrepentant. "Let this stand as another example of your rash behavior."

Catherine moved her mouth several times but nothing came out. She was too amazed by his impertinence. "M-my r-rash behavior," she finally stammered. "Why, I want to—" She didn't know what she wanted to do, but she balled up her fists and waved them at him just in case something came to mind. She couldn't remember ever being this angry before, not even when she found out her mother was selling commissions in the king's army. Catherine realized she needed to get a grip on herself if she wanted to make a dignified exit, so she closed her eyes and counted to ten slowly. When she opened them again, her heartbeat had slowed somewhat, but Deverill still had that satisfied grin on his face, which overturned all her good work. She got angry again. "Lord Deverill, your behavior has been reprehensible and if I never see you again it would be far, far too soon." She put her hand on the door and opened it. The cool night air touched her face. "Good night and goodbye."

He laughed and followed her out. "Aren't you forgetting something?"

Catherine groaned and tried to remember that she was a gently bred lady. "Thank you for your help tonight."

"You're welcome, of course, but I didn't mean that," he said as he walked her to the door. He rapped on it and seconds before Caruthers came to answer he said, "Our waltz at Almack's tomorrow night. I am greatly looking forward to it." With that he bowed and left, and she went inside, wondering how she would explain her bizarre outfit to the butler.

Chapter Eight

B*y the time* Betsy came to help her dress for Almack's the next day, Catherine had already been through a violent range of emotions and was so exhausted that the thought of going to the assembly rooms and seeing the marquess made her want to hide under the bedcovers for the rest of her life.

At first she had been angry. How dare he think he could treat her like that, like an insignificant bit o' muslin! He was but a confirmed rake, for who else would mistreat her so? Harassing her physically had certainly not been in his original agreement with Lady Courtland. He was to court her and show interest in her, not try to seduce her. It was insupportable that her mother's friend had made her vulnerable to evil machinations such as these. Despite her advanced age, she was an inexperienced miss and could not begin to fathom the feelings Deverill aroused in her. The kiss had made her angry, yes, but it also made her head light and her heart pound and her blood rush. She had never imagined in all her wildest daydreams that anything, let alone a kiss, could be so powerful. Yet as giddy as it had made her feel, it saddened her as well, for she knew the experience to be a rare, wonderful thing. What if she never felt this way again? What if Deverill was the only man who could make her experience these sensations?

The idea was too terrible to contemplate.

It was a good thing she knew of his compact with Lady Courtland. She could only imagine how deeply embroiled her heart would be now if she were in complete ignorance of his game. As it was, the organ was more than a little bruised.

I must put an end to this, she thought, and the very idea of doing so made her Friday-faced. No matter what careless chatter her mother directed at her during nuncheon, she could not reciprocate. Her manner was so lifeless, she reminded herself of Evelyn, a prospect so troubling she decided to remedy her situation immediately by finding a new beau.

She began by taking out a sheet of paper and listing men she had recently met along with their strong points. The first name she wrote down was Lord Constantine. She recalled talking with him at Lady Bedford's rout. Since he had made her laugh, she wrote "funny" next to his name. She tried to think of other characteristics about him that she admired but nothing came to mind save his eye-catching pink topcoat. Determined to be positive in her outlook, she added "shopping" next to his name and thought they could purchase pink clothes together, for wasn't that what a happy marriage was made of: mutual interests?

Next on the list, she put Mr. Robert Radnor, a gentleman she had met while riding in Hyde Park with Pearson. He had even teeth, as she did—there, a point in common!—and freckles along the side of his nose. She tried to recall what they talked about but drew a blank, which was disappointing. Nevertheless, they shared excellent teeth and could no doubt form a strong bond over good dental hygiene.

She went on in this manner for forty-five minutes, and when she was finished, she had a long list of names but few genuine prospects. As nice as the men she had met of late were, few excited her interest or held her attention. In fact, all of them seemed fairly dull and faceless in comparison with Deverill.

But no! She could not compare them with Deverill. To make him the standard against which she measured other men would not be fair to them or to her.

Frustrated, Catherine tore up her list and started writing another one. She was determined this time to be more open-minded and less ridiculous.

And she wouldn't think of Deverill one single time.

During the carriage ride to Almack's, Catherine marveled at Evelyn's high spirits. Her excitement over the prospect of Almack's overcame her ill will toward her sister. She prattled on, discussing gloves, hats, shoes and ribbons, completely unconcerned by Catherine's half-hearted replies.

As they pulled onto King Street, Catherine's stomach did a flip at the thought of seeing Deverill again. He must not know, she thought, how much that kiss disturbed her. He was an accomplished flirt, and she would treat him as such by keeping the conversation light and trivial.

Catherine's resolve was firm and as she walked into Almack's there was a pleasant smile plastered on her face. She would have a good time tonight even if it killed her. A swift glance around the room confirmed it: He had not yet arrived. Catherine let out a sigh of relief. Despite her resolve, she was terribly nervous. She tried to still her jittering hands with little success and wondered if she should seek out lemonade as a distraction. From afar, she watched her mother and Evelyn do the pretty with Lady Jersey.

On her own, Catherine surveyed the room, looking for a friendly—or at least familiar—face. Unable to find Gerard

Pearson, her gaze settled on Marcus Lindsey, the Earl of Winter, a man she had been introduced to at Lady Bedford's rout. Despite the fact that he was standing alone and looking dangerously bored with the company, Catherine resolved to flirt with him. But first she had to think of a topic about which they could talk. She tried to recall what they had discussed last time. The theater, wasn't it?

Taking a deep breath, she threw back her shoulders and approached the gentleman with a nervous smile on her lips. "Lord Winter," she said, "how lovely to see you again."

He turned, looked at her quizzically—Catherine tensed for the moment when he disavowed all knowledge of her—and smiled in return. "Good evening, Miss Fellingham."

The relief she felt at being remembered was almost over-whelming, and she felt her smile widen as the tension left her shoulders. "I was just reading in the dailies a review of *Hamlet*. Have you seen Kean's performance?"

Lord Winter had not only seen Kean perform but also had so many thoughts on the subject that he rambled on for more than ten minutes. When the orchestra began playing up a minuet a few minutes later, she was genuinely pleased to join him on the dance floor.

Feeling satisfied with herself, Catherine decided her pluck deserved a reward so she went in search of the refreshments table. She found it with little trouble and contemplated the lemonade, which looked weak and warm. As she stared at it for several seconds, her euphoria began to wane and she real-ized that Deverill would be arriving soon. What should she say to him when he did? How should she act? Should she be abrupt? Stilted? Bored? Polite? Effusive? What would be the best guise to mask her disappointment?

"It's really not as bad as all that," said a woman next to her.

Catherine, catapulted out of her introspection by this

intrusion, turned white and jumped from the shock. How could this woman know what she was thinking? Was she a friend of Deverill's or Lady Courtland's? Had they been talking about her? And, damn it, it *was* as bad as all that.

"I've had it before," the dark-haired woman in a high-waisted blue gown explained. "The bizarre thing is that while you can barely taste the lemons at all, the concoction is oddly thick." She reached for the ladle and poured some of the drink into a glass to demonstrate. "See how it glops down in that strange way like gelatin?" Shrugging, she handed Catherine the lemonade. "But it has never caused anyone to expire so it really isn't too horrible." Thus saying, the woman filled a second glass, took a sip and made a face. "But perhaps I spoke too soon. I am suddenly feeling faint."

Catherine laughed, determined to put aside her problems for the moment and be social. "Thank you. I see what you mean by oddly thick. Perhaps I shall pass on the so-called refreshments for now." She placed the glass down on the table.

"Good thinking," said the other woman, abandoning the lemonade as well. "If you are going to be taking advice from me, perhaps we should be introduced. I'm Clarise Menton."

"Hello. I'm Catherine Fellingham," she said, charmed by Miss Menton's easy manner. "This is my first time here, and I appreciate the advice. Please feel free to share any other tips you have."

The other woman laughed happily. "Jolly good. I knew when I saw you staring at the lemonade in horrid fright that we would get along, and now I get to advise you in all manner of Almack's things. I've always wanted to be a mentor. Let us find some chairs and have a proper coze. I always trust anyone who distrusts the lemonade," she said, explaining her system of judgment.

Catherine followed Clarise, and the two of them sat down

near the dowagers. She was still anxious about Deverill but was prodigiously pleased to have made a friend. Of course, she didn't know Miss Menton very well, but there was something about her that she liked instantly. Perhaps it was her ready smile and her easy manner. She had large blue eyes that stood out in startling contrast to her milky white skin and jet-black hair, but she didn't have any of the intimidating qualities that Catherine had often seen in other beautiful women. For one thing, she seemed completely unaffected by her appearance. For another, she appeared genuinely interested in other people. This surprised Catherine because in her experience, beautiful people were interested in only themselves.

"Ah, so this is your first time here," observed Clarise. "What do you think so far?"

Catherine looked around the crowded assembly rooms at the overheated guests and thought of the routs she had been to, the ones where everyone smelled foul. "I am reserving judgment for the moment."

"Good for you," cheered her new friend, "but just between the two of us, this is as good as it gets. Wait another hour and it will get even more crowded. I am only here because I am bringing out my younger sister this year. As much as I detest making the social rounds, I know I have to do it for her." Seeing Catherine's look, she said, "Now I've shocked you, I suppose. Is it really so awful for someone to hate endless silly chatter and bad lemonade?"

Catherine considered her answer carefully. "No, of course not. I myself find it a little trying but that's because I'm... well, not suited for it. But I would think that an Incomparable like you could not *not* enjoy it."

"I think the enjoyment of social events is more a matter of temperament than appearance, don't you?" she asked, her clear blue eyes beguilingly honest.

"Yes," agreed Catherine, "I suppose it is." She had never thought about it quite that way before.

"My sister loves it. I hope she will make a match of it soon so that I may retreat into my quiet routine again. I haven't the heart to deny her anything. My parents died when Cecy was tragically young, and all she has is me and dear Aunt Loll, who barely knows her head from her heart." Leaning in closely, she whispered in Catherine's ear. "Dear Aunt Loll is more than a little senile, but we need some sort of chaperone to keep up the appearance of propriety. Cecilia and I have set up our own establishment rather than live with our awful cousin." She leaned back and considered Catherine carefully. "Have I shocked you again?"

"Not at all," Catherine assured her. "I am full of admiration. I would set up an establishment of my own if I could figure out a way to do it. I am a quiet person and much prefer solitude to a full house."

"Indeed!" cried her new friend in perfect sympathy.

After a while, their conversation turned to books and poetry. Just as Catherine was describing her favorite scene in *Childe Harold's Pilgrimage*, Clarise said, "Catherine, is there something you wish to tell me about Lord Deverill?"

Startled, Catherine looked at her oddly. "Uh, no. Why? Do you know him?"

"Not yet. But of course I know who he is, as does everyone," she said, looking over Catherine's shoulder. "I was just wondering, you see, what he had to do with you since he is coming just this way and I know it isn't because of the dowagers."

Catherine had known this moment would come. Still, now that it had arrived, she was ill prepared to deal with it. She turned slowly in her chair and instantly made eye contact with him. He was wearing a simple cutaway waistcoat in Devonshire brown that showed off his shoulders to perfection, making him look splendid. She also observed—and envied—his elaborate cravat, flawlessly tied. Catherine smiled weakly, and he grinned widely in return. Damn him, she thought, why did he have to be so blasted confident?

"Miss Fellingham," he said, reaching for her hand, which she had not thought to offer, and grazing her knuckles gently with his lips. "May I say you look delightful this evening."

Catherine, of course, wanted to tell him that he could not say anything of the sort, but she didn't want to appear rude in front of her new friend. To that end, she introduced them and watched Deverill carefully to see his reaction to the ravishing Miss Menton, who was much more to his speed than she. But he greeted her politely and with no more interest than one would expect. Indeed, he turned immediately back to Catherine and winked. "Ready for that dance now?" he asked, holding out his arm. Catherine took it. "Miss Menton, if you'll excuse us, we have an engagement."

Much to her disgust, Catherine's heart was beating wildly and she damned him for being able to affect her like this and herself for being susceptible. Why couldn't she be stronger?

No answer was forthcoming, and before she knew it she was back in Deverill's arms, gliding on air as the orchestra played the waltz. She kept her gaze fixed on his cravat, much as she had the last time they had danced. But she had barely known him them. Had that really only been two weeks ago? It seemed so much longer.

"Catherine, I do wish you would look at me," he said gently. "How can I admire your beautiful eyes if they are staring at my cravat. My valet tells me this style is called the Mathematical. Please note how the top layer curls underneath the bottom layer. Something to remember should you try wearing one again."

This reference to their recent conversation in the carriage had a terrible effect on Catherine, for at once she felt warm at the reminder of the shared history that a longstanding joke implied and cold at the reminder of the way he'd kissed her with ruthless disregard of her feelings.

For a long moment, she was incapable of speech, then she composed herself and looked up. "I am not sure a gentleman of my stamp would be seen sporting such a frilly confection. It's good enough for you, of course," she conceded graciously.

"That's much better," Deverill said, pulling her almost imperceptibly closer. "Do you know your eyes twinkle when you—"

"Don't, please," she said, a mask falling over her features. It was the satisfaction in his tone—the way he made it sound as if drawing a smile from her was his most-cherished goal—that made her realize she couldn't go on with this charade. She was already in too deep, for if she'd learned anything from his kiss it was that she never wanted it to end. But end it must. She was nothing to him but a project to alleviate his boredom.

"Don't what? Compliment you? I assure you, my dear Catherine, I can no more cease admiring you than I can halt my next breath," he said in a low voice that caused Catherine's heart to shudder and break. He had a way with words that left her helpless. "How such a prime specimen as you could have reached the advanced age of four-and-twenty without securing a husband, I will never understand."

At these words, Catherine missed a step and her heart leaped into her throat. Only a moment ago, she'd thought the charade had to end, and now, here, suddenly, was the end. For weeks she had known the moment was coming, but she had never imagined it would happen in the middle of the dance floor at Almack's, and yet it had.

So be it.

Ignoring the pain that had started in her heart and was now spreading through her body, she said with admirable calm, "I assure you, my lord, it takes a special talent to be an ape leader and the veriest quiz."

Deverill stiffened for a moment, then relaxed. "Come, now, Catherine, you know I am just teasing."

But Catherine, insecure and vulnerable, knew nothing of the sort. "Are you sure, my lord? Or is your little game starting to bore you?"

"Game?" he asked, his voice not quite as soft as it had been, nor the light in his eyes quite as bright. "What game?"

Admiring the skill with which he performed his part, Catherine said with scathing admiration, "Yes, you play a very good game indeed, my lord, but enough is enough. I am tired of being a project."

"Excuse me?" he asked.

"I said I am tired of being Lady Courtland and your project. Not that I am completely unsympathetic to the honor you have done me by condescending, against your inclination, to spend time with an ape leader like myself." As she heard herself speak, she was amazed how apathetic she sounded. She didn't feel apathetic. Her heart was about to pound out of her chest, and tears were starting to form in the back of her throat. She had to get out of there before she humiliated herself completely. "I trust your consequence hasn't suffered too much. Now, if you'll excuse me."

But Catherine had forgotten that she was on the dance floor in Deverill's arms and not in a drawing room, and as she tried to turn and walk away, she found herself clasped tightly in his grip. Deverill was pale now, and his eyes seemed to shine unnaturally bright, his earlier amiability nowhere in evidence. "Despite what you think of me," he said through clenched teeth, "I will not let you turn yourself—and me—into a spectacle. We will finish this dance, I will return you to your mother, and we will say good night like civilized people."

Catherine nodded, consenting to the scheme because she

realized he spoke the truth. She didn't need to be at the center of a scandal, not now while her feelings were in such turmoil.

"And then tomorrow, I will call on you and we will talk about this," he added quietly, having regained some of his composure, though she could tell from the way his fingers grasped her arms that he was not entirely calm.

Catherine stiffened and missed a step.

"Keep dancing," he growled into her ear. "And we *will* talk about this tomorrow."

We'll just see about that, she thought, knowing that she would not consent to see him tomorrow. She would tell Caruthers to deny him entrance, or, even better, she would be away from home when he called. She would go out shopping or walking or something completely distracting. Maybe she'd take a trip to the lending library and get that book by Francis Burney that Clarise had so highly recommended.

The rest of the dance was intolerable to Catherine, and several times she had to fight the urge to simply walk away and leave him alone then and there on the dance floor. But she was sensible to the kind of scandal it would create and wasn't brave enough to weather either it or her mother's wrath. There was nothing for it but to continue twirling around the floor in his arms.

Then, after what seemed like an eternity to Catherine, the music stopped and Deverill returned her to her mother. He greeted Lady Fellingham with a polite bow and some meaningless chatter before turning to Catherine to make his goodbye. "I will call tomorrow afternoon, Miss Fellingham, and we will talk then," he said forcefully.

Catherine, aware of her mother's keen interest in the conversation, bit back the rude reply that jumped to her lips. "I shall look forward to it, my lord," she assured him, with not an insignificant amount of irony that her mother, oblivious to undercurrents, didn't notice.

If the marquess detected it, he gave no indication. "Until tomorrow then," he said with a bow and disappeared into the crowd.

Whatever relief Catherine felt at seeing him leave was short-lived, for as soon as he was out of hearing, her mother cried out joyfully. "An interview with you, my dear, tomorrow! And he so serious! Why, that can only mean one thing." She took her hand-kerchief and wiped her forehead with it, as if overcome from the excitement, but Catherine knew it was merely the heat of the assembly rooms. "He's going to declare his intentions! How thrilling. To think, just a month ago we had no hope for you at all, and now the most sought-after peer in all of London wants to take you to wife. I must make sure that Sir Vincent is at home tomorrow so that Deverill can ask for your hand. Your prospective husband is a very proper sort of gentleman and knows how these things are done. I'm surprised that he hasn't asked to speak to Sir Vincent first. But then again, he's very modern in some of his ways. Take his interest in the marbles, for example."

Catherine knew that she should interrupt her mother. The longer the woman went on about Deverill's proposal, the more disappointed she would be when none was forthcoming. But she was too exhausted from her ordeal on the dance floor to try to talk sense into her mother, and besides, she thought with just a little bit of spite, it would be a much-needed lesson on counting one's chickens before they hatched.

She let her mother cherish her high hopes for several minutes and interrupted only when it became clear that listening to those lovely fantasies was more painful than telling her the truth.

"Mama, Lord Deverill has no intention of declaring himself. He is coming over tomorrow to show me...and

Melissa...his"—she thought quickly—"sketches of the marbles."

Lady Fellingham, in the act of dabbing her brow, abruptly froze. The look of stark disappointment that was so plainly etched in her face might have been comedic if it hadn't been so tragic. "Melissa, you say? He wants to see you and Melissa?" She spoke slowly and carefully and seemed a little bit unsure that her brain was working properly. "Both you *and* Melissa?"

"Yes, he told us about the drawings en route to the museum, and Melissa well-nigh begged him to show them to her," Catherine explained. There, she thought, that should put an end to her ridiculous fancy.

But Eliza Fellingham, just now recovering from the shock her daughter's intelligence caused, was even more inured to reality than her daughter supposed. "I understand, of course, but surely these drawings are merely a ruse. I've no doubt that after a few minutes of showing his interesting sketches to Melissa, he'll ask for a moment alone with you. It wouldn't do to leave you unchaperoned, of course. But if he did ask your father first, it would be quite proper to give you a few moments alone."

"Actually, I think it might very well be the other way around. Deverill will have a short coze with me for propriety's sake, then closet himself away with Melissa," she said crushingly. "You should have seen them, Mama, talking at length about the marbles as thick as thieves. He was quite fascinated by Melissa's ideas."

"Interfering child," her mother murmured.

"I think Deverill is a little shy about the quality of the craftsmanship," she continued, prevaricating as she went along, "and Melissa had to go to great lengths to convince him of her interest in the drawings over the skill of the artist."

"Nevertheless, I shall have Sir Vincent on hand," she insisted as she wondered what she could do to help bring about a proposal. She would, of course, never consent to anything superbly improper but perhaps leaving Catherine and Deverill alone in the drawing room for a shade longer than a moment might help matters along. "One never quite knows what's going to happen, does one?"

Catherine agreed with this statement and let the subject drop. If her mother was determined to hold on to some thin strand of hope, then who was she to deprive her of it? Instead, she said, "I fear that I am suffering from the headache. Do you mind terribly if we leave now?"

Eliza looked at her daughter and realized that she did not look well. "You poor dear, you must be exhausted from all the excitement, and we can't have you accepting a proposal with pale cheeks. That wouldn't be at all the thing. Where is Evelyn?" Her eyes swept the dance floor until she found her younger daughter's gleaming head. "Ah, there she is, dancing with Mr. Finchly. They make a lovely couple, don't they? We shall wait until this set is over and leave at once. Ah, there, the music has ended. Here they come now."

Catherine watched her sister approach and was surprised to see the cross look on her face. I wonder what caused that, she thought, recalling the happy girl in the carriage ride over.

"Mr. Finchly," Lady Fellingham said to the young man next to her daughter, "thank you for returning my dear child to me. We must take our leave now. I'm afraid Catherine isn't feeling quite the thing."

Evelyn's face instantly brightened at this communication. "Oh, pooh, what a disappointment. Do we really have to go?" she asked, pouting in the usual way but not imbuing her words the smallest drop of sincerity. "But I suppose we must if Catherine isn't feeling up to scratch. Goodbye, Mr. Finchly." She raised her hand as if to wave goodbye, but Finchly caught it in his grasp and gave it a lingering kiss. Evelyn pulled away. "Enough of that, Mr. Finchly, or people will talk."

"Let them talk," he said, laughing in a way that made Catherine cringe. "I am sorry we'll not be able to get that lemonade together."

"Oh, well," she said indifferently. "Mama, we shouldn't stand here like this. Poor Catherine looks as if she might faint."

Taking her cue, Catherine put a hand to her forehead and tried to look frail. "No, I'm sure I'll be fine," she said weakly.

"Of course, dear, we must get you home and into bed as soon as possible. You have a big day tomorrow. Goodbye, Mr. Finchly." Eliza put an arm around her daughter and led her to the entrance. "Come along, dear. Here, Evelyn, let me take Catherine's reticule. You shouldn't have to bother with it. What a lovely evening, wouldn't you agree, dears? Why, I had no idea Almack's could be so very wonderful. Did either of you try the lemonade? It was quite excellent."

Chapter Nine

T*he next morning* Catherine kept out of her mother's way, staying in bed later than usual. On her lap sat a book that she had been trying to read, but she couldn't concentrate. How could she concentrate when she needed to come up with a plan, something that would ensure that she would not be at home when Deverill arrived? What errand could she invent? She racked her brain for something she needed, but there was nothing to be done. Besides, she knew her mother would not let her walk out of the house any time that day. At least not until Deverill called to propose.

Propose—ha! What would her mother think if she knew the truth? Lady Fellingham probably wouldn't be surprised. If she'd thought about it logically instead of launching into transports, she would have known that Deverill's interest was too good to be true. In six years, nary a gentleman had paid a jot of attention to her eldest daughter, and now Deverill, the primest of the prime catches, was dangling after her. It was a lovely story, yes, but the stuff of fairy tale, not real life.

No doubt Deverill looked at her long career of failure and thought her inured to the appeal of a handsome beau. That was probably why he'd played with her expectations—because he assumed she was too old to have any.

It was funny, Catherine allowed, in a gallows humor sort of way, because she had assumed the same thing. It was humiliating and oddly exhilarating to realize an old maid such as she still nurtured hope. Perhaps one day, when she was over this demoralizing and perfectly absurd heartbreak, she would try to find another man who made her laugh as much as he.

For now, however, while the pain was fresh, she could not go through with the interview. If she couldn't calmly walk through the front door without getting caught, she would sneak through the back door or even a window like a thief. She would do whatever she had to to avoid seeing him again. Of course, she realized such a solution would work only for today. Deverill and she inhabited the same social sphere and would inevitably run into each other periodically. She couldn't very well climb out of windows in the middle of balls. But she had existed on a separate social plane from him prior to Lady Courtland's plan to rehabilitate her and she would simply return there.

Catherine slid out of bed and dressed without Betsy's help. As her plan was to steal away, it seemed wise to call as little attention to herself as possible. She put on a pink lawn walking dress and kid boots. She examined her appearance in the mirror and decided she looked passable, despite the headache that lingered from last night. She doubted it would go away until she was out of the house and safe from Lord Deverill's presence. Because she was still pale, she pinched some color into her cheeks and went to find Melissa. In order to minimize the ruckus her sneaking out would cause, she needed her sister's help.

Melissa was in the schoolroom as usual, practicing her French.

"Catherine!" her sister called happily.

"I don't want to interrupt, Biddy," she said to the governess. "I wanted only a quick word with Melissa."

"Please, go right ahead."

Melissa clapped her hands. "Yay! Are we going to the museum again?"

Catherine laughed. "No, imp, but I do have a favor to ask you. I don't have time to explain, but I need you to visit with Lord Deverill this afternoon. He's going to come by to see me, and I want you to see him instead. I'm not going to be here."

"Where will you be?"

"I don't know. The lending library, I suppose."

Of course Melissa wanted to know why. She'd always been a curious child and could sense something was afoot.

"That isn't important," she dismissed, loath to tell her the truth for a variety of reasons, the most important of which was she didn't want to confess her cowardly behavior. "What you must remember is that Deverill is here to show you the drawings he did. Remember, he promised."

"Does he draw? How wonderful. But Julian has never mentioned any drawings to me," Melissa added.

"I know he hasn't, darling, but you must tell Mama that he did or she will be very, very cross with me."

Melissa examined her sister with oddly penetrating eyes, which discomforted Catherine. After a long while she said, "It's not like you to ask me to lie so I must assume that this is very important to you. I am sorry that you feel you cannot trust me with the truth, but whatever it is, you know that you can rely on me. I'll tell Caruthers to inform me the very moment Julian arrives, and then I will bound downstairs like the veriest piece of baggage and ask him where his drawings are."

Catherine hugged her sister. "Thank you. And perhaps

one day I will tell you what this is all about. I assure you, you'll find it—and me—very silly."

"I could never do that," she promised earnestly.

"Don't be so sure, my darling. But I must go now. I'll see you later."

Catherine knew that the hour was growing late and that she must leave now before the servants started laying the luncheon table. She put on her pelisse and grabbed her reticule from her room before heading to the back staircase. In the hallway, she ran into Evelyn.

Seeing her sister dressed so, Evelyn said, "Catherine, where are you going? Mama says that Deverill is coming here this afternoon to propose to you. Should you not be here to receive him?"

"I will be back in plenty of time," she said confidently and moved to slip past. Catherine didn't think that Evelyn would realize anything was amiss, for she rarely showed enough interest in other people to give their motives proper consideration. However, this assumption proved false when her sister stepped to the side to block the passage.

"Is there something wrong, Catherine?" Evelyn asked.

"No, why do you ask?" She heard a noise behind her and turned around nervously, but nobody was there. Wonderful, she thought, standing in the hallway, all she needed now was for Mama to come up and ask her where she was going.

"You are heading toward the back stairs," Evelyn observed. "That's highly unusual."

It was, Catherine thought churlishly, inconceivably bad luck that her sister chose today of all days to become perceptive. For years, she'd walked around the house seeing nothing but her own nose and now suddenly she was noticing highly unusual behavior in others. "Nothing is wrong, I assure you. Now please let me pass."

Evelyn did not find this answer satisfactory and stood

firmly in her sister's way. "No. Come into my room. Let's talk."

Catherine wasn't given the opportunity to decline because Evelyn, with more force than her sister thought her capable of, grabbed her arm and well-nigh dragged her in the bedroom. "There is nothing wrong. Now I will be on my way."

Evelyn ran to the door and threw herself bodily against it. "Catherine, I am trying to be a good sister here. I suggest you make this easy for me or I might not make the attempt again."

Catherine laughed. Her sister looked earnest and cross at the same time. "I am sorry. I hadn't realized you were making a remarkable effort."

"Apology accepted," she said graciously before autocratically demanding, "Now tell me what is wrong. Why are you sneaking out of the house just as Lord Deverill is coming to propose?"

"He isn't coming here to propose," she said quietly.

As vain as ever, despite her newfound perception, Evelyn immediately thought of herself. "It's because of me, isn't it?" she asked. "You are afraid of hurting me further so you have chosen not to let Deverill propose." She leaned in and gave her sister a hug. "You are a dear, sweet friend, and I must insist that you don't let your feelings for me get in the way of your future happiness." The arms holding Catherine tightened, and she was again amazed by her seemingly fragile sister's strength. "Yes, of course I was upset at first. That you would step in like that and steal my beau struck me as patently unfair, and my behavior was somewhat extreme. I apologize for that. But now I can accept that Deverill and I were never meant to be. I see the way you and he get along together, and it is sweet in an old people sort of way. He and I never had very much in common, probably because I haven't lived nearly as long as he. It was only my pride that was hurt by his desertion. Now that I've realized that, I am very happy for the two of you and also very proud. After all, I clearly brought the two of you together."

Catherine listened to this remarkable speech, at once amazed and amused that her sister could demonstrate an unprecedented level of maturity while at the same time revealing herself to be as fascinated with herself as ever.

"I appreciate your apology," she said, gently extricating herself from her sister's fierce grip, "and I assure you that my running away has nothing to do with you. I should like to be on my way now."

But Evelyn wasn't done being generous yet. "Would that I could believe that," she announced, her hand to her forehead.

Catherine knew she could think of a convincing lie to appease her sister's conscience, but she realized she didn't want to make the effort. The truth was the truth and she might as well admit to it now, for Evelyn would find out eventually.

"Then do. Deverill is not coming here to propose. He never had any interest in me at all. It's too much to explain now, but suffice to say he was spending time with me only as a joke. You were right all along," she admitted, successfully keeping the bitterness out of her voice. Indeed, she made it sound as if it didn't bother her a bit.

"No, Catherine, don't say that," Evelyn cried, genuinely distressed by the notion. "I know I said something like that, but I was angry and being spiteful. You know how I can get sometimes when my temper runs away with me, but I never meant it and it's not true. You're a wonderful person, and if Lord Deverill cannot see that, then the devil with him. And if he thinks he can come here this afternoon and tease you in your own home, he'll learn his lesson." Her eyes grew distant as she began to scheme. "Yes, I think it is best that you go out. Don't worry about a thing here. I'll take care it of. I'll show him that you can't toy with the affections of *my* sister without paying the price."

Catherine was extremely touched by Evelyn's obvious concern and loyalty, two traits she had rarely demonstrated before, but she was also terrified of what she might do. "On second thought, perhaps I should stay."

But Evelyn would have none of it. "No, you were right. You must leave. I'm on the case now. Besides, if nothing else, I owe you for saving me from that horrid Mr. Finchly last night," she said shuddering. "I find that man thoroughly unnerving. It's his hands, you see. You think they're in one place and then all of a sudden you discover they are in another." She opened the door a crack, peeked out and sighed with relief. "Go quickly while it is safe. There's no one out there."

Catherine stood there looking at her for one more moment, silently considering her will-o'-the-wisp sister who suddenly seemed made of steel. She laid a kiss on her cheek. "You are a dear sister," she said before slipping out into the hallway, down the stairs and out of the house.

Unused to being on the streets of London without her maid, Catherine decided to go straight to the lending library after all. It was a route she was familiar with, and as much as she longed to explore the city, she knew it wasn't safe for a woman alone, even in the middle of the day.

She had been looking through the stacks for twenty minutes when she heard a voice say, "Why, there's my new friend, Miss Fellingham. Come along, Cecilia, you simply must meet her."

Recognizing the musical trill of the beautiful Clarise Menton, Catherine turned around with a ready smile on her face. "Hello," she said, happy to have a distraction. As she browsed through the books, she had contemplated running home and confronting Deverill, an impulse she knew she'd regret should she indulge it.

"What do you have there?" Miss Menton asked, looking at the novel in Catherine's hand. "*The Mysteries of Udolpho*. Really, my dear, I must insist that you put that right back. Atrocious book."

"I liked it," said the woman next to her. She had blond hair and brown eyes in direct contrast with her sister's appearance, but they looked enough alike that one could tell they had the same parentage. "And I think you should read it, Miss Fellingham."

Miss Menton took the book from Catherine's grasp. "Don't listen to my sister. She positively adores the gothics. The silly thing loves being frightened by ladies hiding under ethereal veils of lace."

"Oh, pooh, you're going to give away the whole book."

Catherine listened to this interchange with a growing sense of amusement. The two sisters had the easy affection that she and Melissa shared. "I think I shall leave the book for now since I still have *The Italian* at home."

The younger Miss Menton cheered. "There, you see, Clarise, she has taste after all. I knew I would like you from the moment I laid eyes on you. You have such pretty hair. We haven't been introduced, but I am Cecilia. It is very nice to meet you."

Catherine assured her that the pleasure was likewise hers and asked them what they were doing there.

"We just stopped in on the way to the milliner. We are going to buy Cecilia a new bonnet by a Madame Claude, I believe she's called. To be honest, I am not quite sure where we are going. I just follow Cecilia around. All our shopping excursions consist of my following Cecilia around," Clarise explained amiably. "Though I don't know why she needs a new bonnet. I could have sworn she already has a million."

This drew a laugh from Catherine. "I know. My sister is exactly the same." Thinking of Evelyn and being more in charity with her than she'd been in years, possibly ever, she asked if she may come along.

"That would be delightful," Clarise said.

"It shall be like a party," added her sister. "I do so love shopping parties."

"Well, if Catherine is ready..." Clarise looked at her inquiringly.

"Oh, yes, I am not taking any books."

"And your abigail?" Clarise asked.

Catherine blushed and confessed in a whisper, "I didn't bring one."

"Good for you," applauded her new friend. "I hate having to bring one everywhere, and as soon as I can unload this piece of baggage on some unsuspecting young man, I am going to stop. I maintain the proprieties only for Cecy's sake."

"That's very good of you," said her sister good-naturedly as they climbed into the carriage. "I know how trying this must be for you, to go to parties and balls and picnics in the park."

"My sister thinks I'm a curmudgeon," Clarise said.

Cecelia shook her head in denial. "Not curmudgeon, a misanthrope."

Once they arrived at the milliner, Catherine watched with amusement as the two sisters bickered happily about gaily colored hats. After Cecilia had picked an assortment and Clarise agreed to choose one for herself, Catherine asked for their help in selecting an ostrich-plumed bonnet for Evelyn.

The two women had impeccable taste, and Catherine left with a crowned bonnet in the Coburg style, adorned with jonquil-colored ostrich plumes that she thought Evelyn would adore. She paid for the hat with her pin money and collected her package.

On the way out to the carriage, Clarise said, "Catherine, why don't you let our footman drop the hat off at your house and you come for tea at ours?"

Catherine fell in with the plan wholeheartedly, causing Cecilia to cheer. "Oh, what a perfect day it has been. I've got several new hats that make me look ravishing, and our new friend has agreed to have tea with us."

Catherine gave over her direction and the packages to an eager footman and climbed into the carriage.

"I noticed, my dear," said Clarise, "that you paid for the hat out of your pin money. It is not safe for a woman to walk around with such a large sum, especially if she is unaccompanied."

"I realize that, of course, but I forgot I had so much with me," she said before explaining the origins of her ill-gotten gains. "I won it gambling, you see."

To Cecilia, her confession was the best of all things wonderful. "How marvelous. I've never gambled. I've only played whist for ha'penny a point, but that's such a trivial amount it might as well be nothing. Clarise, however, is a great gambler."

Catherine looked at the pretty woman, shocked by the idea of her frequenting gambling dens like the hell she went to. "You are?"

Clarise laughed. "I assure you, it's not what you think. I'm an investor. I buy stocks in companies on the 'Change— that is, the London Stock Exchange—and when they do well, we get paid dividends. I tell Cecy that it's like gambling."

Although she had thought Clarise was interesting before, Catherine now found her fascinating. She had never before met a lady who was capable of creating her own income.

Indeed, she didn't know that such a marvelous thing was possible. "How do you do it?"

"When I find a company that interests me, I ask my solicitor to gather as much information on it as possible," Clarise explained. "Then I read through the materials, and if I decide the company's policies are sound, I go to the man at the bank in the City and have him transfer the funds."

Catherine was agog at how easy she made it sound and could scarcely credit that anyone, let alone a gently bred female like Clarise, could effortlessly pull off such an arrangement. "And this is how you supplement your income?" The question, of course, was decidedly unbred, and if Lady Fellingham were in the carriage, she would be appalled by her daughter's lack of etiquette. At the same time, she would lean in to hear the answer and shush anyone who impeding her listening.

"Not really supplement," Clarise said. "By and large, it is our income."

"Clarise is so very good at it," Cecilia said proudly.

To Catherine, the independence provided by the successful purchase and sale of stocks seemed fantastical. She could not imagine attempting such a scheme, and yet she couldn't imagine *not* attempting it either. "Do you think you could teach me how to buy stocks?"

Clarise nodded her head. "Of course. It is naught but a trifle to buy them. The challenging part is selecting the right companies to invest in. It requires a copious amount of research and a lot of dreary reading, but in my experience, the reward of picking correctly more than makes up for the drudgery. It does take some practice, however, to get a feeling for which companies are good and which are bad," she cautioned. "I made some rather egregious mistakes in the beginning and brought us very close to Dun territory."

Considering how close her family already was to Dun

territory, Catherine was not much alarmed by Clarise's warning and thought that the 'Change might be the answer to all their problems. If she could make enough money trading stocks to compensate for her father's losses at the gambling table, then her mother could stop worrying and she could save for her own establishment.

These happy thoughts were almost enough to banish Deverill from her mind completely and, much diverted, Catherine went to tea with the Menton sisters.

Lady Fellingham had been keeping watch at the drawing room window, so it was no surprise that she met her daughter in the hall the second she crossed the threshold. Catherine had barely a moment to remove her pelisse before she was dragged into the parlor by her irate mother. Although she knew a long tirade was forthcoming—indeed, she couldn't remember seeing her mother so angry before—she kept to her original plan and professed complete ignorance.

"But, Mama, what can the matter be?" she asked as she watched her devoted parent pace agitatedly back and forth. "Is something wrong with Melissa or Evelyn? Freddy hasn't gotten into one of his scrapes again?" She took a seat, tilted her head and waited for an answer.

Lady Fellingham looked at her daughter for a long moment, seemingly incapable of coherent speech, then resumed her pacing and muttering under her breath. At one point she raised a fist into the air as if trying to plant a facer on an imaginary opponent. At least Catherine hoped it was an imaginary opponent and not she.

"Speak up, Mama," she said. "I can't hear you."

"You ungrateful child," her mother screeched, finally abandoning her frenzied movements and throwing herself on the divan with a hefty sigh. "I was asking God why I must be so afflicted with such ungrateful daughters."

Catherine considered her mother's pose for several

seconds while thinking of what to say. Of course she didn't want to distress her mother further—Lady Fellingham had been through a trying and no doubt tragic day—but she could not alter reality to appease her mama, as much as she wished she could. She therefore stayed with the course of action already begun. "Please, tell me what has happened."

Lady Fellingham snorted. "As if you don't know!" she cried, tears starting to form in the corners of her eyes. "As if you don't know." Her tone was more wretched than angry.

"Really, Mama, I am all at sea." She sat down next to her on the divan, patted her shoulder in comfort and held out a handkerchief. "Please dry your eyes and we will talk about this. I am sure whatever Evelyn has done, it can't be that bad."

"Evelyn?" Lady Fellingham applied the kerchief to her tears. "Why, that girl was a perfect angel. I won't have you saying one word against her."

Now Catherine was terribly curious about what had transpired in her absence. "Very well then, tell me what has happened."

"Lord Deverill happened," said her mother angrily, "just as he said he would. Imagine my surprise and horrified dismay when Caruthers told me you were nowhere to be found. That you must have gone out without telling anybody." She threw her hands into the air as if pleading with God again to explain her misfortune. "Gone out. You wretched, wretched child. What could you have gone out for?"

"Lord Deverill," Catherine asked quizzically, impressed by her own skill as a thespian. One would never know she'd spent the entire afternoon dreading this conversation. "Lord Deverill was here today?"

"Well, of course he was," her parent snapped. "He said he would come last night. How can you not remember? He returned you to my side after you danced, and he expressly said that he would see you tomorrow. I don't know what to do—"

"Where is she?" Melissa burst into the room with no regard for her mother's nerves. "Caruthers said she was— Oh, there you are, Cathy." Her bright eyes found her on the divan. Melissa grabbed her sister's hand and dragged her to the door. "Come, we must talk."

"You are not taking your sister anywhere." Lady Fellingham rose swiftly to her feet and planted herself in front of her daughters. "She and I are not done talking."

Melissa's lips pursed in disgust at having to wait for her conversation with Catherine, but she ceased her tugging and dropped onto the settee.

Witnessing this display, Lady Fellingham, her patience already worn thin, said sharply, "Melissa, a lady does not toss herself around as if she were a rag doll. It is unbred."

"I'm sorry," she said sweetly, then made a face as soon as her mother's back was turned.

Catherine hid a smile, then straightened as her mother launched into another lecture about disobedient daughters who don't stay where they are put. Lady Fellingham was in the middle of reciting for the third time the awful moment when Caruthers had made her understand that Catherine was gone when Catherine reached the end of her tether. She simply couldn't listen to the narration yet again.

"Mama, I am so very sorry that I forgot Lord Deverill was calling today. Somehow it completely slipped my mind." She wrapped her arms around her mother, enveloping her in a hug. "Please don't be cross with me. I didn't mean to cause you such distress."

But Lady Fellingham wasn't having any of it. She remained rigid in her daughter's embrace and refused to unbend even the slightest. "I'm afraid that's paltry and inadequate, and we shall stay here until you provide an explanation that satisfies me."

That her mother would hold her ground so staunchly was an unexpected development. The kindhearted lady was usually swayed easily by shows of contrition and affection. She'd rant and rail, of course, and howl like the roof had come off the building, but show her a little love and all was instantly forgiven. Catherine had seen Freddy do it a hundred times. "Very well," she said, releasing her mother and sitting down next to Melissa. "But I have no explanation other than Lord Deverill's visit slipped my mind, as I said. You aren't usually so untrusting of me." She directed her eyes to the floor in an attempt to look repentant but peeked at her mother out of the corner of her eye. Was she beginning to relent just a tiny bit?

"That may be so, my dear, but if I could only understand how you could have forgotten what could possibly have been the most important meeting of your life. You might have been a marchioness, my dear. A marchioness." At these words Lady Fellingham dissolved into a fit of tears.

Catherine found that she actually wanted to explain her odd behavior to her mother, but she knew it would be of no use. Lady Fellingham would not believe her or would assume she had misunderstood the situation or would insist that even if her understanding of the situation had been accurate at one time that surely was no longer the case. Her mother would simply not be able to believe that all her hopes and fine dreams would come to naught.

She was still considering her next words when the drawing room doors opened again, this time to admit Evelyn.

"You are returned," she said, smiling at Catherine. "Lord Deverill called in your absence, but we explained to him that you had gone out for the afternoon." Then she winked. Melissa saw this and broke into a fit of giggles.

"If you would just tell me what was so important that you had to go out today of all days," Lady Fellingham pleaded, with a disapproving look at her youngest daughter for her inappropriate display of humor. As if anything could be humorous on a day like today! "You who spends all her days sitting in her father's study. The one day I come to look for you and you are gone."

"I went shopping," she explained to the group at large.

Even Melissa and Evelyn, who were aware of her scheme, were shocked by this statement.

"Shopping?" her mother echoed. "What on earth for?"

"I bought the most darling— Wait, I'll show it to you." And she opened the doors and called into the foyer. "Caruthers. Caruthers. Where is he? Ah, there you are, my good man. Could you please get me my package? It was dropped off earlier."

"Very good, Miss Catherine."

Caruthers disappeared for a moment, and while he was gone, Lady Fellingham said, "Evelyn, did she really say shopping?"

"I believe so, Mama."

The butler returned with the tall box, and Catherine took it from him with a thank-you before shutting the door behind her. She presented the case to Evelyn with an elegant flourish. "I don't quite understand it myself, Mama. For some reason I woke up this morning with one thought in my head. I know I am not given to impetuous behavior the way you and Evelyn are, but you will forgive me, won't you just this once, for being so weak as to follow an impulse."

Now Lady Fellingham's resolve to stay angry at Catherine began to weaken. Nobody knew better than she how unimpulsive her oldest daughter was. Perhaps the errand had been too important to delay. "But why must it have been today of all days. Why today?" she asked again.

Her children were no longer listening to her. Melissa and Evelyn were looking at the box in amazement. "Go on, open it," Catherine said.

Evelyn eagerly untied the pretty pink ribbon, pulled off the top and she shrieked, "It's my bonnet. It's my bonnet!" She leaped up and hugged Catherine with so much force that Catherine had to anchor herself against the settee lest they both tumble to the floor. "It is a Madame Claude original and quite the most beautiful one I have ever laid eyes on. And yellow! You dear sweet thing, yellow is quite my favorite color for a bonnet."

"Let me see," Melissa pleaded.

Freeing the bonnet from its box, Evelyn placed it carefully on the top of her head, as if it were made of eggshells, and tied the ribbons under her chin. "How does it look?" she asked, swiveling her head this way and that. "Do say it looks splendid."

Catherine looked fondly at Evelyn in the ostrich-plumed confection. "It looks splendid."

"I want to try it." Melissa tried to grab the bonnet, but Evelyn danced away before she could establish a grip.

Lady Fellingham also showed an interest. "Come here, dear, let me take a look at you." She fluffed Evelyn's curls that were revealed by the bonnet. "You do look splendid. How thoughtful of Catherine to have bought you such a becoming present."

"Cathy, tell Evelyn that it's my turn to try the hat now," Melissa said, determined to have her chance.

But Catherine had no intention of disturbing her mother's tête-à-tête with Evelyn. "Let's us retire to the study and have a chat," she said, causing her sister to clap her hands in delight. "Don't. Make no loud noises and no sudden movements. Back out of the room very slowly. Here, I'll get the door."

Melissa complied with her instructions, though she had to cover her mouth to stop from giggling, so funny was it to her the notion of stealing out of the room under the nose of her mother.

Once they were alone in the large dark room, Melissa said, "Oh, Cathy, you should have seen it. Evelyn was magnificent. I had no idea she could be such an out-and-outer."

Neither had Catherine and even hearing the claim from her sensible youngest sister, she could scarcely credit it. "Tell me what happened."

Melissa needed no further inducement and she pulled her legs under her in the big armchair as she launched into her tale. "As instructed, Caruthers sent a boy up to inform me that Lord Deverill had arrived and I came down directly. Poor Mama, she really had no idea what to do. She kept insisting to poor Caruthers that you were in the study and that he must have overlooked you. Examine all the chairs, she ordered, and check behind the curtains. Every time he came back to tell her you weren't in the study, she sent him back again. I can't recall how many times he walked back and forth between the drawing room and the study. She was completely baffled and had no real understanding of what was happening and finally left the drawing room to check the study herself. When she came back, she was terribly pale and explained to Julian that you had caught the headache and had retired to your room for a rest. He was very polite about it and said he'd be on his way, but Mama insisted that he stay. I suspect she thought you might walk through the door at any moment. And when she noticed that he had forgotten to bring his drawings with him, she insisted that he send a footman to fetch them. Nothing he could say would dissuade her, even his sworn statements that he didn't have any drawings, and a footman was dispatched posthaste regardless."

Although she knew it was unkind, Catherine could not

help but smile at the picture her sister painted. Poor Caruthers, sent to inspect an empty room over and over again. The study was large, but there were few places to hide, as she knew from personal experience. Once she had concealed herself behind the heavy red drapes—it had been the morning of her come-out and she simply wanted a few moments of peace and quiet after so many weeks of frenzied preparation—and her mother had found her with little difficulty.

"Julian was still trying to make his excuses when Evelyn came in," Melissa said. "Oh, she was something. She came in and sat down and started talking to Julian about the most boring subjects. She devoted twenty minutes to women's hairbands alone. I have never seen anyone talk so and about such inconsequential things. By the end of the two hours, he looked like he was ready to strangle someone. Oh, it was fun. 'Tis a shame you couldn't be here to witness it. Afterward I said to Evelyn that I didn't know why you had done him such a rotten turn, and she told me that he had treated you poorly and had made you sad. I thought he was a very nice gentleman, but if he's going to hurt you then he's not a gentleman at all, and I'm glad Evelyn bored him to flinders."

Evelyn entered the room still wearing her new bonnet despite the fact that it didn't match her afternoon dress.

"Evelyn," Melissa cried excitedly, "tell Cathy what you told Julian about evening gowns."

"I simply explained how the newest designs from Paris have lower waistlines." She smiled. "Nothing to get excited about, dear."

"Oh, but she didn't," she told Catherine earnestly before turning back to Evelyn. "You really didn't. You went on and on about it, meticulously detailing every time in the last two decades that the waistline has moved more than a half inch in either direction. She was marvelous, I tell you. Simply marvelous."

Evelyn, unused to being admired by anyone in the family, much less Melissa, who so clearly preferred Catherine to her, blushed with pleasure. "Well, he is such a scion of fashion, I thought he'd want to know."

All three sisters dissolved into delighted laughter. Catherine felt tears forming in her eyes, and she grasped her stomach in pain. "I need to stop," she said, trying to breathe deeply and failing miserably. "I've got a painful stitch."

But the laughter continued for several minutes longer. Only the entrance of Caruthers with the announcement that dinner would be served in one half hour silenced them.

"I better go dress," Catherine said regretfully. It was the first time since they were children that she was reluctant to end an interview with Evelyn. "I don't want to anger Mama further."

"She has calmed down quite a bit. The bonnet was a brilliant stroke," Evelyn assured her.

"It seems to have worked like a charm, but I would not have you think me calculating, my dear. I bought the hat on a whim, with no intention of smoothing mother's ruffled feather. Indeed, if I'd been so clever, I would have bought *her* the Madame Claude original," Catherine said, smiling. "Now I really must change."

At the door, Evelyn put her hand on her shoulder and said with surprising gentleness, "You do realize, darling, that Lord Deverill is not going to give up. And after today's escapade, he might not be in such a pleasant mood."

At the mention of Deverill, Catherine tensed, clutching the bronze knob with white fingers. "No, I don't suppose he will."

Evelyn's brows drew together sympathetically. "He assured

me that he looks forward to seeing you tomorrow night at Lady Rivington's ball."

"Must I go?" Catherine asked.

"Yes, I don't think you have sufficient funds to buy Mama enough bonnets to wrangle free of the engagement," Evelyn said.

Catherine knew this was true. Her mother, who had abandoned all hope of seeing her matrimonially unsuitable daughter wed years ago, was now unable to accept that Catherine would not marry a personage so exalted as a marquess. If the irony of the situation weren't so tragic, she would have laughed.

"Very well then, I shall go," she conceded. At least at a glittering function surrounded by the *ton,* there would be little opportunity for a tête-à-tête.

"And you will be beautiful," promised Evelyn, "and you will flirt with all the young bucks and you will have a grand time and you will show the Marquess of Deverill that you do not need his condescension and you will come home victorious and then, if you still want to, you can cry in my arms."

Melissa, who was clever enough to fill in the details, even if no one explained them to her, said, "You can cry in my arms, too, if you want."

Catherine was much moved by these displays of sympathy and released the doorknob to give her sisters a hug. As she wrapped her arms around Evelyn, she thought that perhaps the situation wasn't all terrible. If she could hold her sister, with whom she'd been at odds for years, with so much affection, then perhaps Deverill hadn't done her an entirely bad turn.

Chapter Ten

Betsy *was putting* the finishing touches on Catherine's hair when Evelyn entered the room.

"Mama says we will be leaving in— No, you can't possibly wear that," she said, interrupting herself midsentence when she saw her sister's dress.

Catherine, trying to keep her head still for the maid, asked Evelyn what she found wanting. "This gown just arrived from the dressmaker this very morning."

"But the color, darling," said Evelyn, looking stunning as usual in a white silk gown in the Grecian style decorated with pink rosettes. "You can't possibly wear that shade."

Careless of Betsy's efforts, Catherine looked down at the dress. "What's wrong with yellow? Yesterday, you said jonquil is one of your favorite colors."

"Well, it is, though seeing it upon you, I'm no longer quite so sure." Evelyn shook her head. "There's nothing *wrong* with yellow on a woman of different coloring, but on you, dear, it looks wretched. Or rather you look wretched." Evelyn went to the wardrobe and examined her sister's dresses. "Surely there is something here that's appropriate, if not becoming."

"But Mama picked out this dress," Catherine protested. "She said it went with my eyes."

Evelyn laughed. "I don't see how it could. You don't have yellow eyes." She made a moue of disgust as she contemplated her choices, which were limited to varying shades of pink and light blue with the odd pistache tossed in. "No wonder you haven't gotten married. All these years we thought it was you and your sullen nature, and now we discover at the eleventh hour that it was Mama's fault all along. You can't wear that dress or indeed any of these dresses." She took out a pink afternoon dress and waved it in the air distastefully. "These are completely unsuitable. You look like a dead fish in pastels. Your complexion is too sallow. I wonder why I have never noticed before." As she put yet another pink dress back on the rack, a red ball gown caught her eye, and she considered it carefully.

"Please, Evelyn, don't tease yourself about it. I assure you that a few pastels are not all that's standing between me and holy matrimony." Catherine looked at herself in the beveled glass, admiring Betsy's handiwork, particularly the strand of pearls that she had weaved in among the ringlets. As for the dress... She knew that it did not show her to the best advantage but neither did she know what her best advantage was. "What do you suggest?" she asked, realizing this was her sister's specialty.

"I've never seen this one before." Evelyn carried the red gown over to the dressing table. High-waisted with Spanish slashed sleeves of white satin, it was made of gossamer silk and trimmed with bands of lace, satin buttons and rosettes.

"That just arrived this morning as well. Do you like it?" Catherine asked with a glow in her eyes as she looked at the red silk gown. "Isn't it gorgeous? I don't think I've ever owned anything quite so beautiful. I confess I manipulated poor Mama to gain her permission. It cost a handsome sum, and she would have said no unless I had told her some whisker about red being Deverill's favorite color." She laughed as she recalled how quickly her mother's opinion had changed. "Then she insisted that I must have it."

"Well, then, why aren't you wearing it tonight?" Evelyn asked.

"You will think me terribly poor spirited, but I was not in the mood to wear such a vibrant color," she explained.

"Pooh," exclaimed her sister. "That's precisely the time to wear a vibrant color. Here"—she handed the dress to Betsy—"help her change gowns and I shall go down and warn Mama that it will be a few minutes more before you're ready to depart."

Betsy, who agreed with Evelyn's assessment of Catherine's wardrobe and had thought the same thing privately for years, immediately began unbuttoning the dress. Catherine submitted to this treatment with a reluctant sigh, for as much as she wanted to blend into the wallpaper tonight, she knew there was no way she could wear the yellow dress now. She would be more self-conscious in the simple gown than she would in the flamboyant one.

Evelyn returned to check on matters just as Betsy was fastening the last few buttons. "Heavens, darling," she cried out, "you look magnificent." She laughed happily and skipped over to her sister. "Turn around." Catherine complied with this command with so little animation that her sister said, "My darling, someday we really need to teach you how to twirl."

Catherine said nothing as she studied her appearance in the mirror, noting that her cheeks, for the first time, had that cherubic rosy glow that she found so attractive in Evelyn. It wasn't only her complexion that benefited: Her eyes seemed to shimmer like topaz and her hair took on a rich, chocolate-brown cast. A practical woman, Catherine could scarcely believe that so meager a change as the color of a dress could make such a profound improvement.

"I like this much better," she said softly, trying to bite back a huge grin. For some reason, she felt that showing her true delight would be intemperate and immodest.

"Of course you do, darling. Nobody *likes* looking like a dead fish," Evelyn said, tilting her head to the side as she inspected her sister.

"You don't think the neckline is a little low?" Catherine asked, noting the look. "I think it's a little low."

"Pooh, that neckline is all the crack. But it does need something. Perhaps..." Her speech trailed off as she ran out of the room, returning a few moments later with a necklace in her hand. "Here, this is what you need."

Catherine looked on in amazement as Evelyn fastened the pearl-and-ruby strand—quite her most precious possession, jealously guarded and worn on only very special occasions—around her neck. Overcome by the magnitude of the gesture, she swallowed a lump in her throat and pressed a kiss against her sister's cheek. "Thank you very much."

Evelyn smiled, clearly enjoying the sensation of bestowing her largesse, and said with satisfaction, "There, doesn't she look perfect, Betsy?"

"That she does, miss," agreed the maid.

Catherine indulged one last look in the mirror before saying shortly, "Very well, then, what are we waiting for? Betsy, could you hand me my pelisse? Evelyn, I expect Mama is pacing impatiently downstairs. Shall we go?" She offered her arm.

"Yes, darling," she said, taking it. Then, in perfect sympathy, the two sisters went downstairs to find their mother.

Upon their arrival at Lady Rivington's ball, Evelyn stayed close instead of wandering off as she usually did, much to Catherine's surprise. "I am going to be right here, darling," she said, laying a comforting hand on her sister's elbow, "the entire night so if there is anything you need, you just let me know. And if I see you-know-who barreling down upon you, I shall simply intercede and discuss sleeve lengths ad nauseam if I must. Don't worry about a thing. We'll get through this together and show him in the process that he can't toy with the Misses Fellingham and get away with it."

Listening to this speech, with its touch of high drama, Catherine had to hide a smile. Her sister certainly relished playing the part of Lady Savior, but her concern was sincere and Catherine could not fault her for her histrionics. The way she had responded so readily to her need made Catherine wonder if perhaps she, as well as Freddy and Melissa, had underestimated Evelyn. Maybe she behaved so poorly because she knew none of them held her in high esteem. If she could never get their good opinion, there was no reason to try to earn it.

Catherine gave this theory several more minutes' consideration as she surveyed the room to see if Deverill had arrived yet. They themselves were frightfully late, and the flood of people arriving had slowed to a trickle. Mayhap he wouldn't come after all.

These optimistic thoughts were interrupted by Evelyn, who wanted to introduce her to a tall man in an olive waistcoat. He had a vaguely familiar look about him, and Catherine didn't doubt that she had met him previously, as she had most members of the *ton*. She simply couldn't say when or where.

"Catherine, may I present Lord Claire," Evelyn said at her most gracious.

Although she knew she looked well in the red dress, Catherine still felt like her usual awkward and insecure self and wanted to demur whenever Evelyn introduced her to someone new. But her sister was trying so hard to ensure her enjoyment and she couldn't bear to disappoint her, so she made a particular effort to laugh and flirt.

"It's a pleasure to meet you," she said cheerfully, offering her hand and smiling when he kissed her gloved fingers.

"Lord Claire has simply the most divine pair of matched chestnuts in all of London, and I am dying to take them for a ride," Evelyn explained, batting her eyelashes with such practiced ease that Catherine despaired of ever having her sister's grace and poise.

"I am at your disposal," he said with a bow. "Name the day and I shall take you for a drive in the park. It would be my absolute pleasure."

Evelyn pouted charmingly, her lower lip pronounced. "Pooh, Lord Claire, I didn't mean as a passenger."

"My sister is an admirable whip," offered Catherine, grateful to have something to add to the conversation.

"Is she? And what about you, Miss Fellingham?" he asked.

"Who do you think taught her?" she answered boldly.

Lord Claire laughed and asked Catherine for the next dance. She accepted happily, and when the orchestra struck up a minuet, she went out on the dance floor on the arm of the handsome lord.

Despite her anxiety about Lord Deverill's appearance, Catherine found herself having an enjoyable time. Whether by her sister's design or Lady Courtland's machinations, she was quite in fashion that evening. Her dance card was quickly filled, and although she recognized quite a few names as beaux of her sister, others she knew were not.

She shared one dance with Lord Winter, who approached her this time. "My dear Miss Fellingham, you look enchanting this evening," he said as he led her out onto the dance floor.

Catherine blushed with pleasure. Lord Winter wasn't as handsome or accomplished as Deverill, but he was friendly and pleasant company and he seemed genuinely to like her.

Catherine thought he would do very well as a suitor and quite possibly as a husband if it came to that. They talked throughout the dance, and Catherine marveled at how comfortable she felt with him. It was easy, she realized, to like everyone when it felt as if everyone liked you.

Catherine tried to remember the last time she had enjoyed herself so much at a social function and came up blank. For years, going to balls, even the most glittering ones, had been a dreary obligation. Perhaps had she been more outgoing and not so insecure during her come-out, her first season could have been like this.

"Catherine," said Evelyn excitedly, "you look splendid on the dance floor. I swear you are the most beautiful woman here tonight."

She laughed at her sister's obvious ploy. "Doing it a bit brown, aren't you?"

"I would never condescend to you with overflattery," Evelyn promised before plying her with more compliments. "Truly, I need to watch over my beaux more carefully lest you steal one from me." Seeing that this statement reminded Catherine of Deverill, she quickly added, "Unless, of course, we are speaking of Mr. Oscar Finchly. In which case, pray tell me how I can help you arrange the theft."

Catherine laughed at this quip, as she herself wished someone would come and secret away the oily Mr. Finchly. "Your generosity overwhelms me, my dear."

"Of course it does," she said, her smile dimming as she spotted the gentleman in question. "Speak of him and the devil appears."

Turning her head, Catherine saw Finchly approach and resolved to return her sister's goodness with a charitable act of her own. "I'll handle him," she announced. "Since I shall be otherwise engaged, could you please relate my regrets to Mr. Figston for missing our dance?"

Before Evelyn had a chance to respond, Catherine dashed over to Mr. Finchly, displaying an undue amount of haste to anyone watching. Utilizing the charms she had seen Evelyn employ earlier, she batted her eyelashes in what she hoped was a coquettish fashion and smiled. "Good evening, sir."

Finchly greeted her politely, but his expression remained blank and she could tell that he had no idea who she was. "I believe we've met before but perhaps you don't remember me. I am the other Miss Fellingham. I believe you're acquainted with my sister Evelyn."

Now he smiled and a calculating look entered his eye. "Yes, of course I remember you. You're as lovely as your sister. Beauty clearly runs in the Fellingham line. Where is that sweet child? Pray would you lead me to her so I can make my hellos to her as well?"

Although the request was worded as a question, his tone made it seem like a command, and for a moment, Catherine felt outmaneuvered, as she was fairly certain that he knew not only where her sister was but that she knew it as well. At that moment, the music began and she decided to brazen it out, no matter how unpleasant. "I would love to lead you to my sister but first you simply must dance with me. They are playing a cotillion, which is quite my favorite, and I would be wretched if I had nobody with whom to dance it. Would you please be so kind?" She fluttered her eyelashes again, feeling utterly ridiculous and fully expecting someone to come over and ask if she had something in her eye.

Catherine could tell that Finchly wanted to deny her, but whatever manners he had came to the fore and he reluctantly, if not graciously, consented to be her partner. She would have sent a conspiratorial smile to her sister, who was just then being led onto the floor by Mr. Figston, but she feared she would start giggling if she made eye contact.

The dance with Mr. Finchly was equal parts uneventful

and unpleasant. He didn't talk much and neither did she, but she found that he had the unfortunate habit of breathing heavily in her ear, as if from considerable exertion. There was also the rather indecent way he examined her décolletage, staring down at her neckline and telling her that her "jewels" were "splendid" with a sly smile. When he rudely left her on the edge of the dance floor, rather than escorting her back to her mama, she felt only relief at being out of his presence.

"Finally, my dear, you are free."

Catherine jumped at the sound of Deverill's voice and twirled around to find him standing directly behind her, looking extremely intimidating and handsome in a black cutaway-style coat over black breeches and a white waistcoat. For a seemingly endless moment her mind went absolutely blank and she could think of nothing to say—no clever rejoinder, no pithy remark. She couldn't even pull together enough words to excuse herself from his presence. All she could do was stare up at his attractive face, annoyed that he was as devastating as always. She didn't think it was unreasonable to have hoped he had grown grotesque overnight.

Aware that she had to get hold of herself, she closed her eyes for a trice and took a deep, calming breath. When she opened them again, Deverill was still there and he was still looking grim.

"Indeed I am not free, my lord," she said, pleased that her voice sounded cool and calm, as if her heart weren't pounding painfully in her chest. "I am committed for the next dance. It seems you are wrong again." With that dismissal, she brushed by him with every intention of hiding behind Evelyn for the rest of the evening. It was an act of shameful cowardliness, but she was happy to admit she was a milksop if it saved her from further humiliation.

Deverill had other ideas, however, and as she tried to pass, he clutched her arm. "I'm afraid you'll have to disappoint your next partner, for I have prior claim on you. I believe you owe me a conversation from yesterday."

He spoke quietly but forcefully and if Catherine couldn't tell from his tone that he was angry, she could tell from his grasp, which was quite strong. Feeling trapped, Catherine looked around the ballroom for someone to come to her rescue, but she knew she could not call attention to herself.

"Let go of my arm, Deverill," she said softly, though she wanted to scream it.

"I am not letting you go," he said, his expression resolute. "You can provide fodder for the gossipmongers by struggling to get away from me. That's your prerogative, of course. Or you can come with me to the balcony, where we will have our talk. You decide." His fingers tightened. "I'll wait."

He made it sound as though she had a choice, but Catherine knew the only option available to her was acquiescence. Even their standing together so closely at the edge of the dance floor would start tongues wagging soon. "Very well, my lord."

With his hand on her elbow, he escorted her to the balcony, which was quiet and empty save for a few dozen flickering candles. It was a cool night, and although the servants had opened the doors to let fresh air into the ballroom, nobody seemed inclined to seek it out.

Catherine shivered and walked over to the ornate railing, which overlooked gardens lit by lanterns and moonlight. It was a beautiful sight, dreamy and romantic, and she felt a renewed sense of melancholy that she would never have anyone with whom to stroll through a garden. *Damn him for doing this to me.*

Since Deverill had yet to speak, she decided that she must initiate conversation. The sooner their business began, the sooner it would conclude. "I am here, my lord," she said, without turning around. If she could, she'd have the entire exchange without looking at him once.

The sound of his footstep signaled movement, and Catherine felt his approach as much as heard it. Stopping directly behind her, he ran his hands gently over her bare arms and whispered softly, "You are exquisite tonight."

Catherine closed her eyes as if absorbing a great blow. She didn't know which was worse—his touch or his words. She pulled her shoulders forward, effectively breaking the contact, and coldly thanked him for his compliment. "Was there something else, my lord?"

With a groan he spun her around. Suddenly she was in his arms and he was laying heated kisses along her neck. "Do you know what it has done to me, watching you in that dress going from one young man's arms to another's, fluttering your eyelashes like an accomplished flirt? You are ravishing in red. You should always wear it."

Catherine's breathing became labored, and she realized that she was well out of her depth. These feelings—she didn't know how to handle them. And he made her feel so much. "Lord Deverill," she said, her voice thin and uneven, "I fear this is highly improper. Pray excuse me."

But he didn't excuse her; he didn't even let her go. He simply traced a trail of kisses up her neck and along her cheek. "I don't think that is possible, my dear." His voice wasn't quite steady either. "I don't think I can do that at all," he reaffirmed before laying his lips on hers.

Catherine knew that she should not be on the balcony kissing Julian Haverford, Marquess of Deverill, for several reasons, the least of which was the potential scandal. Most important, she needed to protect her own well-being. If things continued like this, she might never recover. As it was, she would wear the willow for him for months to come.

But she didn't fight the kiss. Indeed, she melted into the

marquess, wrapping her hands around his neck and playing with the soft hair on the back of his head. She knew the kiss would end soon enough, and when that happened, she would turn and walk away from him. She would leave him alone on the balcony and not look back. She couldn't look back. It would hurt too much. She couldn't imagine why he would do this to her—toy so ruthlessly with her emotions—but maybe that just was what sophisticated gentlemen of the *ton* did.

His hold on her slackened and he released her lips. Tilting his head back, he ran a gentle hand through her curls without saying anything. He simply held her like that for a while, staring down at her with green eyes.

The moment lingered sweetly, and Catherine felt a sense of connection, as if they were linked on a fundamental level. But she knew it was a trick of her own romantical mind—what green girl didn't imagine she was fated for a handsome lord?—and that the more experienced Deverill wasn't suscep-tible to such starry-eyed nonsense. The thought that this overwhelming feeling was one-sided humiliated her even more, and she took a step back, breaking the contact.

"Is that all?" she asked, her voice steely. Her heart was racing at a bruising pace, but he would never know it from looking at her. If she had her way, he would never, ever know what he had done to her with only a single kiss. She would not be that weak, not Catherine Fellingham, veriest quiz.

Her words—or rather her tone—had the desired effect, and he dropped his arms to his side. "Catherine," he began, a little hesitantly, "I know you're angry—"

"Angry, my lord?" Catherine laughed bitterly before real-izing that it would be much better if there were no emotion in her voice at all. She took a deep breath and said almost calmly, "No, my lord, I am not angry that you and Lady Courtland were using me to relieve your ennui. Perhaps if I hadn't overheard your conversation, I would've been susceptible to your charms and surely then I would be heartbroken right now. However, as they say, forewarned is forearmed. I wasn't at all taken in. Indeed, to be completely candid, I was using you, as well. I have never been fashionable, and I welcomed the opportunity you provided for me to meet other, more interesting men. It was my pleasure to fall in with your scheme. In fact, I have been meaning to thank you."

The determination, which had been present in his face from the moment he confronted her in the ballroom until now, seemed simply to sap away. "I see, Miss Fellingham," he said, his voice and countenance suddenly indifferent. "Thank you for explaining the matter to me. Good evening," he said with a bow. Then he walked across the balcony, into the ballroom and disappeared into the glittering crowd.

Entirely alone on the balcony, Catherine felt the emotions she'd smothered for so long overwhelm her, and it took all her strength not to fall to her knees and weep like an infant. Determination alone kept her back straight and her head high, and when Freddy found her still standing there looking at the gardens twenty minutes later, she seemed completely composed.

The carriage ride home was quiet, with neither she nor Evelyn inclined toward conversation. Lady Fellingham launched into a monologue of chatter—can you believe what the Duchess of Trent did? Did you see Lord Bromley's waistcoat?—but finding no corresponding enthusiasm to encourage her gossip, quickly fell silent. For her part, Catherine was grateful for the respite and was too immersed in her own misery to wonder about Evelyn's muteness.

It was only after they got home that she realized something was terribly wrong with her sister. Evelyn's face was pale, unnaturally so, her lips were drawn into a tight line, and she had a distracted air that quite rivaled anything that Catherine, in all the years of knowing her somewhat selfish sister, had ever seen. It wasn't merely exhaustion, for she had seen Evelyn stay out much later than this and dance many more sets than she had tonight and remain so full of energy that they had practically to drag her to bed. This evening, she climbed the stairs listlessly and disappeared into her room without saying good night to anyone.

Catherine tried to go to sleep, but her sister's face haunted her to such an extent it even overcame her preoccupation with her own sorrows, and she climbed out of bed, lit a candle and walked down the hall. The house was very quiet because everyone was sleeping, and as she stood in front of Evelyn's door she could clearly hear sobs from the other side. She knocked gently, and when her sister didn't answer, she tried again.

After a few moments, Evelyn's blotchy, red face appeared at the door. "Yes?" she said, wiping tears from her eyes and trying to pretend that she hadn't been crying.

Catherine pushed her aside and stepped into the room. She sat on the bed, pulling her sister down next to her. "What's wrong?" she asked softly.

"Nothing." She sniffled pathetically. "Why"—hiccup—"do you ask?"

"Oh, Evelyn," Catherine said, running her hands through her sister's hair, "if you could see your face right now, then you'd really have something to cry about."

Catherine had been teasing—she wanted only to draw a smile from Evelyn—but her words upset her more. She jumped off the bed and cried, "Don't say that. It's not true. I care about other things. I am not selfish. I'm not." She dissolved into a fresh batch of tears. "I'm not." And much in the way that Catherine had wanted to earlier on the balcony, she curled up into a ball and began weeping like a baby.

"Oh, dear, dear." Catherine bent to her knees and hugged Evelyn as the sobs racked her body. "Please stop crying. If you don't stop crying I'm going to start myself and then we'll be in real trouble. The way I feel right now, I could cry a small ocean."

After five or so minutes, the crying subsided and Catherine held her until it stopped completely. Then she made Evelyn stand up. "Come, let's sit on the bed. You'll tell me all about it, and it won't be nearly as bad as you think it is. Come," she said again when her sister resisted.

"No, Catherine, I can't. It really is that bad," she insisted. "But all will be well. I just need to get used to...it." Wiping her eyes with the sleeve of her nightgown, she straightened her shoulders and said with a calm that frightened her sister. "I'm fine now, thank you, darling. Go back to sleep."

Catherine marveled at how composed her sister appeared. But she knew that it was only a façade, and there was no way she was leaving the room until she found out what was the matter. "You cannot gammon me, Evelyn. I can tell something is dreadfully wrong, and I'm going to stay here until you tell me what it is."

Evelyn sighed deeply, turned her back toward Catherine and said, "Very well, on the morrow I will announce my engagement to Mr. Oscar Finchly. You're the first to know and can now be the first to congratulate me."

"Don't be ridiculous," Catherine exclaimed.

Throwing back her shoulders, Evelyn said, "We are engaged, and I'll thank you not to ridicule my fiancé."

Catherine grabbed Evelyn's arm and swung her around. "What insanity is this? I know you dislike the man intensely. What would compel you to act in such a fashion?"

"Nothing compels me. I do it of my own free will. I...I love him with all my heart and am very happy with our engagement," she said, wiping away a stray tear.

Catherine didn't know the last time she had heard such errant nonsense. Perhaps it was earlier that evening when she told Deverill that her heart wasn't broken. "You don't love him," she insisted. "You can't love him."

"Nothing compels me," she repeated. "I'm marrying him of my own free will. Congratulate me. I'm the happiest woman in the world."

At the word *happiest,* her face dissolved into a fresh spate of tears, but to her credit and Catherine's surprise, the smile on her face didn't waver. Nevertheless, there was something in the way Evelyn made the statement that provided Catherine with the missing piece of the puzzle. "He *is* compelling you! How is he making you do this?"

Evelyn stood there stiffly, refusing to answer or even acknowledge the question.

"You must tell me, my dear," Catherine insisted. "I cannot help you if you don't tell me."

"Nobody can help me," she said simply, with none of the histrionics in which she usually indulged.

Her strength amazed Catherine, who, for so many years, thought her sister nothing but a hen-witted piece of fluff. "You must tell me. I can help you. I can, Evelyn. I swear it. You are my younger sister, and I love you. I would never let that man hurt you."

With this declaration, Evelyn started crying again. Not the loud racking sobs of earlier but gentle quiet tears that trailed slow paths down her cheeks. It appeared to Catherine as if her sister was weakening. After a while, Evelyn said, "He's blackmailing me."

Catherine wasn't surprised by the answer, for she had known it had to be something like that. There was no other way Evelyn would have agreed to such a repugnant proposal. "How? With what?"

"If I don't marry him, he will tell everyone that Mama was selling commissions in the army. They will send her to jail; I know they will. She'll rot in some prison without water or food or...or her maid and they will make her work in some horrible factory, like the mines or cleaning chimneys. They will make her wear horrible itchy clothing that will give her skin rashes. And she'll never see the sunlight ever again." Evelyn grew more agitated as she contemplated her mother's dismal future, and her hands started to shake. "Mama wouldn't survive it. She is too soft, too spoiled. You know that, she would die in her cell and the awful guards would go down there one day and they'd find her lying there on her rodent-infested straw mattress on the ground wearing horribly ugly clothing with a horribly ugly rash all over her and she will be dead. Horribly *dead*. And it will be all my fault."

Catherine listened in silence as she rattled off this bleak fate for her mother, grateful that her sister had found some drama in her great well of dignity. Odd, but the thought of dealing with familiar, overreacting Evelyn was far more encouraging than dealing with brave, martyr-ish Evelyn.

"Oh, you poor dear," she said, enveloping her in a hug. "Is that what you've been torturing yourself with? They're not sending Mama to Newgate."

"But 'twas you who said they would."

"I was angry, Evelyn, and spoke without thinking," she explained, regretting now her harsh words. "I only wanted to make Mama understand the seriousness of her crime so that she would stop doing it. I never meant it. It's not true, dear, and I never meant to frighten you."

Evelyn digested this information, and while she clearly wanted to be swayed by her sister's words, she understood how grave the situation was. "Thank you, darling," she said, squeezing Catherine's hand, "for trying to make this seem a little less bleak. However, I am not so ignorant as you suppose. I am well aware of the wretched scandal this would cause if anybody knew. That must not happen. There is the family honor to think about for one, and you and Melissa for another. How will you make a match if the Fellinghams are infamous?"

Catherine knew that her making a match should be the least of her sister's considerations, but she didn't remark on it. The point was the same whether it included her or not. The Fellinghams *would* be infamous, and she had little doubt that the family would be able to weather the storm. They were respectable, of course, and one of the oldest families in the kingdom, but they didn't have the clout or the conse-quence. And it would take a significant amount of clout and consequence to brazen out something like this.

"There is nothing for it," said Evelyn, brushing away tears, "but for me to marry him for his silence."

"You shall not marry him." Catherine's voice was hard and forceful. "I'll not allow it."

Her sister laughed sadly. "Thank you, darling. Your support means the world to me. But there's nothing you can do. I'm sure I'll be fine. Please don't tease yourself about it."

"Stop being absurd," Catherine ordered. "You and I will think of something else, and if we can't, then fine, the Felling-hams will return to Dorset in disgrace, and Mama will learn an extremely unpleasant lesson about having to accept the consequences of one's actions. And I, for one, won't mind. As you know, I never really enjoyed London that much anyway."

Evelyn smiled at these words, for the whole family knew that Catherine never really enjoyed London all that much. "No, Cathy, that won't do. Of course there's nothing I would rather do than run away to Dorset and hide until this all goes away. But I can't. I won't. I don't want to be selfish anymore. Don't you think that I know what you and Freddy say about me? I know you both think I am a horrid person. And...and maybe I have been horrid in the past but not anymore. I want to be good like you. You can't stop me. I will marry the horrible Mr. Finchly and...and be happy with my noble sacrifice for the rest of my life." With that, her control broke and she threw herself onto the bed as yet another bout of tears overcame her. "Now, please leave me alone."

Poor waterlogged Evelyn, Catherine thought, much distressed by her sister's speech. She and Freddy had no idea the damage they had done with their careless words. "No, dear, I won't leave you alone, so you can save your arguing for Mr. Finchly. We will scrape through this contretemps together. I will not leave you alone to your fate. Don't worry, my dear. I will think of something that will save you *and* the family name. There will be no need for your beautiful, noble sacrifice, though I will be forever humbled by your willingness to make it."

"Please don't make promises you can't keep. I don't want to have hope. It is better this way." Evelyn buried her face in the pillow. "We are announcing the engagement tomorrow."

Catherine rushed to the side of the bed, got down on her knees and made Evelyn sit up. "No, you mustn't," she said, grasping her shoulders tightly. "You must promise me that you'll wait a few days. I need time to think of a plan."

Evelyn's head bobbed back and forth, as if it were too much effort to sit up, but she anchored herself with her fists on the bed. "Finchly wants to post the bans right away."

"Tell him he can't. Tell him it's indecent or that your mother would like to get to know him better," she said, thinking quickly. "Surely he can't cavil at such a reasonable request. Indeed, if he is assured of your obedience through this dastardly deal, I can't see why he would mind waiting another couple of days. You'll give me a little time, won't you?"

In the candlelight, Catherine could see that her sister's heart was breaking. She knew that she was making it worse by offering hope, and she was sorry for that, but it wasn't a false hope. She *would* come up with some measure by which to thwart Finchly. She simply needed time to organize her thoughts and identify an approach.

"Yes, darling, I'll give you some time. I'll talk to Finchly tomorrow when he comes to ask Papa for my hand," she said in a tone of voice that led Catherine to conclude that her sister was trying to comfort *her*.

"Indeed, we might not have anything to worry about, considering the unlikelihood of Finchly finding Sir Vincent at home," Catherine said with a laugh that sounded hollow and had no real humor.

Her sister smiled blankly in return. "That's true. Now, darling, it has been a long day and I must get some rest. You should go to sleep as well." She pulled back the covers, slid underneath and laid her head on the pillow. "You look tired. I know I never asked how your meeting with Deverill went. I saw that you and he had a tête-à-tête on the balcony. Perhaps we can discuss it in the morning."

Catherine tucked the covers around her sister as if she were a small child. "Yes, in the morning I can tell you all about my encounter with Deverill. I assure you, my predicament is a mere bagatelle and the details will give you much-needed amusement."

"Please don't, darling," she said. "He broke your heart and you mustn't pretend that doesn't matter, for it does, hugely."

Her frivolous sister's deep understanding and sincere concern moved Catherine greatly, and she leaned forward to press a kiss against Evelyn's soft cheek. "I love you," she said and as she spoke the words she realized she hadn't uttered them to her sister in a very long time—certainly not in the past six years, perhaps not since they were in the schoolroom together. She would do better, she promised. When this nightmare was over, she would treat her sister as a friend and confidante and a conspirator.

Evelyn smiled sleepily and her eyes fluttered shut. "I love you, too, Cathy," she murmured before dropping off.

Worry she wouldn't let her sister see clouded Catherine's face as she blew out the candle, shut the door and returned to her room. She climbed into bed and closed her eyes, but it was many hours before she fell asleep.

Chapter Eleven

After only two hours' sleep, Catherine awoke and rang for Betsy. She would have liked to lie in bed for several more hours—indeed, from the way she felt, she would have opted to spend several more days not only in bed but hiding under the covers—but she could not. She had to save Evelyn and send Finchly packing, and she would do so by any means at her disposal. Even if she had to dress up as a man, arrange a duel and shoot him herself, Mr. Oscar Finchly would not marry Miss Evelyn Fellingham. Her first preference, of course, was for a resolution that didn't require bloodshed, but if that was what the situation demanded, then she would have no choice but to oblige. *C'est la guerre*.

As Betsy entered the room, Catherine reflected on the ironical fact that Evelyn's troubles had sent her own scurrying. Compared with the monumental task of freeing her sister from the clutches of a dastardly blackmailer, unrequited love seemed rather inconsequential. Once the crisis had passed, she knew, the pain would start again, and she would have to find a way to live with a broken heart. But for now, at least, she had been given a reprieve. The Marquess of Deverill could walk into her father's office today and ask for her hand and she would give it no more thought than she would her morning chocolate. There were other things in the world more important than love—such as family and loyalty and her sister's happiness and thwarting evil.

Catherine bid her maid an unenthusiastic good morning and climbed out of bed, confident that if she gave the matter enough thought, she could find a solution. Her optimism carried her to the breakfast parlor, which she was much relieved to find empty. She was not up for the effort of small talk, especially when it centered on Deverill, for if Evelyn had seen her go off with Deverill, then in all likelihood her mother had, too.

Caruthers handed her the newspaper and asked what she required for breakfast. "I'm not very hungry this morning. I'll have some toast with jam and a cup of coffee," she said, flipping through the paper more out of habit than actual interest. The answer to the Finchly problem would not be found among a Parliamentary debate about the Coinage Act.

The logical place to start, it seemed to Catherine, was with Mr. Finchly himself. He was the problem; surely he could be the solution. Despite his behavior thus far, he was still an English gentleman, schooled in the code of proper conduct, and might need only to be made aware of how unprincipled his behavior was. Perhaps his confidence was such that he didn't understand how unpleasant his proposal was to Evelyn. She could scarcely credit that any Englishman could be so lacking in proper feeling as to coerce a young lady into marriage and began to wonder if maybe her sister had misconstrued the offer.

Yes, she thought, the entire debacle could simply be one large misunderstanding on both their parts.

This idea so encouraged Catherine, she found her appetite had returned and she ate two pieces of toast and some scrambled eggs before collecting her reticule and leaving the house. Nine o'clock was an improper time for house calls but since visiting a bachelor's residence was somewhat more improper, she didn't scruple about the time. Her course of action required her to perform unconventional feats and she would not balk. She would execute her duty boldly and bravely, though it wouldn't do to be too bold, she thought, pulling up the hood on her pelisse.

She found a hack with ease and directed the driver to Upper Seymour Street, where her mother had mentioned Finchly lived. His man reluctantly allowed her entry but made her wait in the foyer alcove instead of the parlor. Catherine wanted to cavil at the treatment, for it implied that the butler thought she was a lightskirt, at worst, or a fast woman, at best, but she knew it was exactly what her unconventional behavior deserved. Respectable women did not call upon bachelors at all, and certainly not without their maids.

Despite the indecently early hour, Finchly was awake and prepared to receive her visit. He stepped out of the breakfast parlor with a quizzical look on his face, which was quickly replaced with a smile—a calculating smile that sent shivers down Catherine's spine. "Ah, Miss Fellingham or shall I call you Catherine or perhaps just 'dear sister'? No doubt you are here to congratulate me on my good fortune in securing your sister as my bride." He turned to his man. "Bigelow, let's have some tea for the young lady, and I will have my coffee in the drawing room."

Catherine followed him into the drawing room, which was decorated in a respectable if not lavish style, and took a seat in a wingback chair several paces removed from the settee he'd indicated with a flourish of his hand. She didn't want to open herself up to the possibility of sharing a cushion.

"Pray tell me, my dear, to what do I owe the pleasure?" He smiled again, but he didn't seem the least bit pleased.

Well, neither was Catherine. "Mr. Finchly, I—"

"Come now," he interrupted with a raised hand, "we are to be family quite soon. You may call me Oscar."

The last thing Catherine wanted was to be on familiar terms with the gentleman, but she saw no reason to provoke him. "Oscar, then, I was talking to my sister last night and she informed me of your...ah"—she struggled for the proper word —"compact."

"Did she?" he asked, raising the coffee cup to his lips. "Dear sweet child. She will make me very happy."

The fact that he wasn't the least bit perturbed by her knowing the truth of his arrangement with Evelyn did not bode well for the future of the conversation, but Catherine soldiered on. It was possible that she'd been too subtle in her explanation. "I know, Mr. Finch...Oscar, about the sword you held over my sister's head."

He took a sip of coffee and dabbed at his lips with a linen. "Of course you do," he said calmly. "I expect you girls talk about everything."

At these words, Catherine realized that her mission to clear up a misunderstanding had been futile. Finchly knew exactly what he'd been doing and Evelyn's interpretation of the events had been accurate. Nevertheless, she made one last attempt. "Perhaps then you don't realize how reluctant Evelyn is to marry a man she hardly knows," Catherine suggested tactfully.

"Indeed I do, Catherine. Why else do you think I had to blackmail her?" he said, boldly admitting to his crime like the callous villain he was. "If I had believed that Evelyn would have welcomed my suit, then of course I would have proposed in the usual way, but she is clearly a young fanciful girl whose head is filled with images of romantic heroes. I thought it best not to coddle her. I am not a romantic hero, and I have no intentions of indulging my wife in such nonsense." His smile disappeared into the coffee cup, and she was confronted with his beady black eyes.

"But why do you want to marry a woman who is reluctant to marry you?" she asked, unable to grasp his motive or to understand his reasoning. "Evelyn has no great dowry. A small portion, really."

"Dear girl, rest your mind on that score. I won't have you thinking I'm a heartless fortune hunter," he said with a laugh. "I'm comfortably situated, if not extravagantly so. I need not choose a wife for the material benefits she could bring me."

"Then why coerce my sister into marriage?"

Finchly raised an eyebrow in exaggerated curiosity. "What is this? A sign of sibling rivalry? Perhaps you are too old and envious of her success to appreciate her value. Evelyn is a charming child, extremely beautiful and well-behaved. She's from a respectable—or rather respectable-seeming—family. I, of course, will not hold the sins of the mother against the daughter. Having decided it was time I married, I looked around to see who would make me a suitable wife and decided your sister, who is biddable and will give me beautiful children, is the perfect candidate."

Halfway through this appalling speech, Catherine stood up, for she could not bear to be in his company a moment longer. "I see that talking to you will get me nowhere. I had come here with the intention of appealing to your finer nature, but I realize now that you are singularly lacking in any proper feeling." She collected her things and went to the door. "Very well," she said, delivering the words in a dry clipped tone that in no way reflected the anger that was bubbling over inside her, "consider yourself warned. You will not marry my sister. I will do everything in my power to see that it does not happen."

Finchly laughed again, and although he seemed outwardly affable, Catherine observed the squinty eyes and an odd facial tick that revealed his annoyance. "Power?" he dismissed scornfully. "I wasn't aware that you wielded any power. Please feel free to do whatever you can. I shall enjoy watching your meager efforts."

Catherine's anger grew so that she could barely contain it, and she trembled slightly as she thought of this horrid, detestable man married to her sister. "And I shall enjoy watching your face once you realize that your ambitions have been well and truly thwarted by a woman with no power. It will be all the more satisfying."

Finchly cackled with amusement. "My dear, you must stop tormenting me with your passions. I must remain faithful to my beloved—for a little while, at least. Perhaps you should return in a few months after the first blush of wedded bliss fades. I would be very happy to entertain your offer again," he said with a leer, and all of a sudden Catherine felt stripped bare, as if she were still wearing a gown with a low neckline.

"You are reprehensible," she said coldly.

"Compliments will get you everywhere," he assured her as he escorted her to the door and held it open for her. He grabbed her hand as she passed, holding on despite her attempts to tug free, and kissed her palm. "It has been a great pleasure. And do remember what I said. There is no reason why we can't be *très* intimate friends."

Unable to remember when she had been so repulsed or so angry, Catherine turned away and marched down the path to the street. As she looked for a hack, she thought about how much she would enjoy shooting Finchly or stabbing him or drowning him in the Thames. All manner of painful death occurred to her as she looked down the road for approaching vehicles. She could bring him to a glassworks, tie him to a rod and throw him in the—

"Good morning, Miss Fellingham."

Catherine spun around and was confronted by the very

horribly unwelcome sight of Julian Haverford walking toward her from across the road. *Oh, God, not now.*

She took a deep breath and ordered herself to remain calm. "Hello, Deverill."

"Out for a morning stroll?" he asked disingenuously. He knew that she was much too far from home to have walked there—and that she would have taken an abigail with her if she had.

"Uh, no, I was out visiting a...friend," she lied poorly.

"Indeed?" He raised an arrogant eyebrow and examined her somewhat contemptuously from his superior height. "A very good friend, I trust, if you can call this early."

"Uh, yes. A good friend." She knew he was implying something with his seemingly mild comments, but she lacked the inclination or the presence of mind to figure it out. She was far too unsettled by the awful conversation with Finchly to stand on the street sparring with Deverill. Seeing him like this—bright and handsome, dressed for a morning drive— made her ache for all the things that would never be, and she didn't have the time to indulge in her own tragedy, for, compared with Evelyn's, it was no tragedy at all. "If you'll excuse me, I am in a rush to get home."

She moved to step around him, but he wouldn't let her. "If you are truly in a great hurry, please let me escort you in my carriage. It would be much easier and more comfortable than taking a hack."

Catherine knew he spoke the truth, but although the ride might be quicker, it would feel ten times longer as she sat in the enclosed space with him. "I thank you, but a hack will be fine."

"I must insist, Miss Fellingham, that you allow me to do this for you." He put a hand around her waist and directed her toward the carriage. "Please."

The interview with Finchly had taken a lot out of Catherine, and she really just wanted to get home in the fastest way possible. Realizing Deverill would not take no for an answer, she gave in. "Very well, thank you." She stepped into the carriage, sat across from him and examined her gloved hands with intense fascination to avoid his gaze.

They drove for a while in silence, and Catherine was glad of it because she had no desire to trade pleasantries. His offer to drive her home was mere courtesy—he'd proven time and time again that if nothing else, he could be extremely gallant when he devoted himself to the task—and after the things she had said last night, he was probably even less inclined to talk than she.

"What's this between you and Finchly?" he growled suddenly.

Her eyes flew to his. "What?" She was so surprised that she almost laughed, but something in Deverill's intimidating countenance warned her that laughing wouldn't be wise.

"Come, Miss Fellingham," he said coldly, his shoulders stiff against the back of the seat, "when a man sees a woman leaving a bachelor's quarters without her maid at nine-thirty in the morning, he must draw certain conclusions."

Catherine was appalled that he could think such a thing. Her anger was of a kind that she could barely speak, and she chose not to defend herself. It was none of his business what she did and, besides, she hadn't done anything that *needed* defending. Furthermore, if he could think such horrible, hurtful thoughts about her, well, then, he didn't deserve to know the truth. "My relationship with Finchly is none of your concern," she stated just as coldly, turning to look out the window.

"Isn't it?" He reached over and took her gloved hand. His voice was angry, but his touch was remarkably gentle. "Surely if I am responsible for your meeting, then I have some small concern. I saw you flirting outrageously with him last night.

Is he one of the men you thanked me for introducing you to? Perhaps you expect him to make you an offer? If that's true, my dear, I think you should hold out for a better proposal. Even Pearson, who has been living in your pocket these many weeks, is more acceptable. I know it's not quite the thing for a woman of your considerable years to marry someone so much your junior, but you have always been unconventional and an ape leader like yourself can hardly be choosy."

Her outrage at the very idea of this charge was immediately crushed by anguish. How could he say such cruel things to her? First to suggest that she had set up a dalliance with Finchly! Then to imply that she was trying to entrap her brother's friend in an unsuitable connection! The pain was so intense, she had no answer at first. She just continued to stare out the window, refusing to let him see the hurt on her face. Then she pulled her hand away and said quietly, "As I said, my lord, I'm not accountable to you for my behavior. Now I beg of you, leave off questioning me."

Catherine expected him to persist, but much to her surprise, he sat back and remained quiet for the rest of the short journey.

When they arrived at her address, Deverill insisted on escorting her to the door, even though she declared it was quite unnecessary. Not only did she want to get away from his unnerving presence as quickly as possible, she also didn't want her mother to see them together and jump to more impossible conclusions.

At the door, he put a hand on her arm. "Miss Fellingham, I've warned you before about Finchly," he said more reasonably, even though his tone was cold and indifferent. "He's a cheat and a liar, with not a scrap of honor. You would be wise to keep your distance."

"I assure you, Deverill, I know all about Finchly's honor," she said with a cynical laugh.

Abruptly, his expression changed and he said, "What has he—"

"Thank you," she said firmly, opening the door and stepping inside before he could finish his thought. "Goodbye, my lord."

Catherine shut the door firmly behind her and rested her shoulders against it, too overcome by the scene in the carriage to do anything but review it over and over. His opinion of her, which she'd always known was not great, was far worse than she'd ever expected. To believe for a moment that she would have anything to do with Finchly, a cheat and a liar to be sure...

But as his warning echoed in her ear, she realized that in all her panic to come up with a solution to their problem, she never figured Finchly's reputation as a card cheat into the equation. Surely, if the Marquess of Deverill suspected he played his fellow gamblers false, others must wonder about it as well. That, she thought with growing excitement, could be her ace in the hole. If she caught Finchly cheating at cards, then she could threaten to expose him to the *ton* just as he had done to her family. She could trade her silence for his.

It was a solid plan, she knew it. She simply had to figure out how to execute it. A game must be arranged, that much was obvious, but how? She would need a conspirator who knew more about gambling than she.

"Catherine dear," her mother called as she traipsed down the stairs in a simple afternoon dress, "if you're going to go driving with Deverill, I do wish you'd tell me. Not that I mind, of course, although a gentleman could come in and say hello to your family."

Engrossed in her new scheme, Catherine was quite surprised to find herself still standing in the front hall and even more surprised that her mother knew she had been out with Deverill. The only way she could know was if she had posted herself by a window and saw him drop her off.

"I was very cross when Caruthers told me you'd gone out alone," Lady Fellingham continued, "and I could have sworn he said you took a hack. But, la, everything is all right. I am so glad that Deverill has forgiven the horrid mix-up of the other day. How atrocious it was at the time—I positively cringe at the memory—but now that it's come out all right, I'm so relieved. I told Sir Vincent that he should expect an offer any day now. He scoffed, which wasn't at all appropriate. Just because you're old, doesn't mean you're not attractive to an experienced man like Deverill. Sir Vincent doesn't like him, of course, for he's convinced his interest cannot be serious and must have some nefarious cause, but he won't withhold consent. I'm sure of it. He's just a concerned papa, as is right, so don't tease yourself on that point."

As her mother prattled on, her eyes glowing with the false promises of the future, Catherine decided she would get no help from that quarter. She considered her father next. He certainly knew his way around a gaming table and the rascally reputation that Lady Bedford alluded to indicated that he had schemed a time or two himself. But Sir Vincent always preferred to submit to the easiest path and giving in to Finchly's demands might, in his opinion, require less effort than engineering a card game. That left Freddy but even as she thought about him she knew he would never do. He was still getting into scrapes himself and relied on Catherine's help to get out of them. If he got involved, he would no doubt do something hare-brained that somehow made the situation worse.

No, it seemed that there was not one family member whom she could ask to help her entrap Finchly. She could not seek advice outside her family, for to do so would require a confession of her mother's scandalous behavior. She would not compound the problem by spreading the tale.

As Catherine despaired of ever saving Evelyn, her mother continued to chatter about her future with Deverill. "The old marchioness doesn't go about much in society anymore, but I'm sure she will make a special effort for the ball. How could she not, if it's in honor of her own son's wedding?"

Unable to bear any more, she snapped, "Stop, Mama, stop. Lord Deverill will not now nor ever ask for my hand in marriage. It simply won't happen so please stop talking about it."

Her mother looked at her with surprise and then disdain. "Ungrateful child! I did not raise you to be an old maid and I'll thank you to remember that the next time a handsome, titled, wealthy man starts dancing attendance upon you."

Catherine knew there would be no next time. "Agreed, Mama. Now can we find a new topic to discuss."

Her mother was so taken aback by her daughter's rudeness, she didn't know how to respond and stared at her as if meeting a stranger. Finally, she said, "I don't know what my dear friend was about, thinking she could marry you off by the end of the season. You are the most impertinent girl without proper feeling for your mother or your father."

At the mention of her mother's co-conspirator, Catherine perked up. Of course, Lady Courtland! Why hadn't she thought of her before? Swiveling in the hallway, Catherine reached for her pelisse, realized she was still wearing it, and called for Caruthers to bring around the carriage.

"You are going out again?" Lady Fellingham asked, more mystified than angry at this additional proof of her daughter's peculiarity. "But you've only just returned."

"I have an errand," she explained, eager to be gone. She strode to the door, even though it would be a few minutes before the carriage appeared. "Have you seen Evelyn today?"

The change in subject, though abrupt, did not confuse Lady Fellingham, who expected interest to be shown in her middle and favorite child at any given moment, and she launched into a lengthy discussion of Evelyn's condition (languid, pale, no appetite) that lasted for several minutes.

When the carriage finally appeared, Catherine heaved a sigh of relief, grateful for the opportunity to advance her plan, of course, but also thankful not to have to listen to any more of her mother's inane monologue.

"Of course, she could be coming down with something," Lady Fellingham continued. "The dear thing doesn't have quite your stout composition and—"Cour

"I'll be off, then," Catherine said, opening the door. "Please tell Evelyn I haven't forgotten my promise and that I'm working on a plan.

"What promise?" her mother called after her, surprised that her daughters could have any dealings that didn't involve her. "What plan?"

On the ride to Arabella's, Catherine thought about how much more she'd rather take the lady to task for breaking her heart than ask for help. But she was not a fool and would never let her sister suffer because she was weak and gullible.

Catherine was confident her mother's friend would agree to lend her assistance, as her ladyship seemed always on the lookout for a distraction. She had almost said as much to Deverill when she was so coarsely—and very publicly—arranging Catherine's future. She didn't doubt that the challenge of besting an opponent would appeal to her more than the moral imperative of rescuing an innocent girl, which was fine with Catherine. Lady Courtland's motives didn't concern her, as long as they aligned with her requirements.

And they had better align, thought Catherine with a touch of despair, for if this plan didn't work, it would be pistols at dawn for her and Finchly.

Chapter Twelve

W*hen the dour-faced* Perth opened the door and saw that it was Lady Fellingham's daughter, he quickly stepped aside. "Please, miss, why don't you wait in the drawing room. I will get her ladyship presently."

Catherine, trying not to be offended by the butler's easy admittance—had she really been that forceful the last time she came?—followed him into the drawing room to wait.

Lady Courtland didn't tarry long, and minutes later she entered the room and immediately enveloped Catherine in a lavender-scented embrace. "You poor dear," she crooned in her ear. "Come, sit and tell me all about it."

Flabbergasted, Catherine sat down on the settee next to her mother's closest friend, wondering how she could possibly know what had transpired. Had Finchly spoken about it? To whom would he confess such a dastardly deed?

"I must admit, Lady Courtland," she said slowly, her hands still enveloped in the older woman's grasp, "to being surprised that you already know."

She smiled understandingly and squeezed Catherine's

hand, as if to give comfort. "Lord Deverill was just here looking miserable, and you must call me Arabella."

The admittance of Deverill into the conversation at once embarrassed, confused and annoyed Catherine. For goodness' sake, she thought peevishly, why must everything be about him? "I don't understand. How does Deverill know about Finchly's blackmailing scheme?"

"Well, the man is clearly besotted and— Did you say Finchly's blackmailing scheme?" Arabella asked, shocked.

Catherine nodded vigorously. "Yes, that horrid Mr. Finchly is threatening to tell the beau monde about my mother's indiscretion lest Evelyn refuse to marry him," she said and watched in amazement as a series of emotions darted across her ladyship's lovely face.

"Oh, dear. That's quite an unexpected development. 'Tis a pity we can't foresee *all* the possible snags with our plans when we originally conceive them," she said, sounding deeply disappointed by her inability to predict the future. "But I can't say that I'm entirely surprised by Mr. Finchly. I didn't feel entirely right about offering him our assistance. You see, I knew his mama and there wasn't a more conniving peeress among the *ton*. She died some years ago in a carriage accident. Good riddance, I said. But one does want to give everyone the benefit of the doubt, and Finchly did seem respectable. I see now, however, that the apple doesn't fall far from the tree." Arabella released Catherine's hands and stood up. "Your sister must be frantic. Don't worry, we'll thwart his scheme."

The relief Catherine felt at these words was incalculable and she took her first easy breath in hours. "You have no idea how happy I am to hear you say that. I've come up with a plan, but I need your assistance to bring it off."

"Of course you have. I'd expect nothing less," Arabella said admiringly. "Tell me, what do you need me to do?"

"Help me arrange a card game at which Finchly will be caught cheating," Catherine explained.

"Brilliant. Then we can ensure his silence by promising ours. You are very clever to make use of his weakness against him. Have no fear, I know exactly how to do it. Now," she said, matter-of-factly, "on to more important matters."

Catherine, who could think of nothing more vital than thwarting that wretched cad who would destroy her sister's happiness, looked at Lady Courtland quizzically. "What's more important?"

"Deverill, of course," Arabella said.

Catherine snapped to attention, her newfound calm deserting her. "I do not know what you mean," she said coldly.

"He'll be relieved that Finchly is only blackmailing your sister," she said calmly, either insensible of the upset she caused Catherine or indifferent to it. "He came here this morning in a frenzy, begging me to gain your confidence and find out what it was between you and Finchly. He said he saw you coming out of his apartments this morning without your maid and drew all sorts of horrible conclusions. Ordinarily I would not excuse such ungallant behavior in a gentleman, but given the circumstance, it's forgivable. No man wants to see the woman he loves coming out of another man's apartments without her maid at nine-thirty in the morning."

As she listened to this speech, Catherine felt herself growing agitated, and she had to take several long, deep steadying breaths. Deverill love her? No, the idea was too ludicrous to indulge, and yet she reveled in hearing it said. "I think you mistake the matter. Deverill does not love me," she said with surprising composure.

"Pooh," Arabella said with a wave of dismissal. "You are in love with him and he you. I know it for a fact since I arranged the whole thing myself."

"Deverill does not love me." Her tone was more forceful this time. "Nor I him," she added and then marveled with disgust at how thoroughly her words could lack conviction. She very much feared that her heart was sewn quite plainly on her sleeve.

Lady Courtland laughed with amusement. "That's right, Julian Haverford, Marquess of Deverill, the most sought-after lord in all of society, is mooning after you like a puppy in the first throes of calf love because he has nothing better to do."

Catherine dipped her head with a jerk. "Precisely."

"Ridiculous."

"'Twas you who said it," Catherine insisted, feeling sick as she recalled the conversation that had led to so much misery. "I heard you say it. You can't deny it."

"Of course I said it," Lady Courtland admitted, eyes wide and innocent. "The surest way to scotch a matchmaking plan is to admit it exists."

This simple statement quite took the wind out of Catherine's sails and she stared at her ladyship, bewildered and aghast. "Wh...what?"

"My dear girl, one can't just go up to a man like Deverill and announce that you've found him the perfect mate," she said slowly, as if explaining a simple mathematical equation to a child. "You need a ruse to give him the opportunity to get to know the girl without feeling threatened by matrimonial prospects. I assure you, I know of what I speak. I've arranged several very successful matches. The Earl and Countess of Shrewsbury, that appallingly happy couple that live in each other's pockets? One of mine."

Catherine shook her head, unable to believe that Arabella had orchestrated far more than she had known. Seeing her confusion, Lady Courtland sat again on the settee and took Catherine's hands in her own.

"I knew from the moment you barged into my drawing

room, overwhelming poor Perth, that you would be perfect for Julian. The respectable girls he courts—Incomparables all —are simpering misses like your sister, and they bore him to distraction, though, like all men, he's not sensible enough to admit it. Instead, he feels an enduring sense of dissatisfaction and can't conceive of its cause. It's the same with his mistresses," she stated forthrightly, causing Catherine to startle, then blush at the appalling indelicacy of the topic. "They are all stunningly perfect creatures with nothing but looks to recommend them. But you are something out of the ordinary. You're clever and well informed and forthright and daring. For goodness' sake, my dear, you read *journals*. Who among our acquaintance does anything as shocking? I knew right away the match would take and so it has. We simply need to sort out this misunderstanding about Mr. Finchly first," she said happily.

Catherine pulled her hands free and stood up. Her disquiet was so great, she needed to move around. Sitting still felt intolerable. "Bringing about a match might have been your true purpose, but it was not Deverill's. He fell in line with the assignment, not your intentions," she said, determined to remain sensible, despite the provocation to believe the unbelievable. "He doesn't love me. I'm an ape leader, the veriest quiz."

"Pooh," her ladyship said dismissively. "You are a lovely young woman with spirit and backbone, if lacking *a little* in confidence. Why else do you think I made sure you heard my conversation with Deverill?"

This revelation shocked her as much as the last, and she dropped into an armchair by the fireplace. "You *meant* for me to hear that?"

Arabella smiled. "My dear girl, I am the wife of a politician and have enough sense of discretion not to bandy about the name of my good friend's gently bred daughter in public.

When I saw you there, standing with your mother with a bored expression your face—you were clearly woolgathering —I recognized an opportunity and took it. Fortunately, Deverill obliged by following me to the exact spot where I knew you would overhear. I don't think anyone else did. We were positioned in an alcove that had no neighbor."

Catherine could scarcely credit her story, though Arabella's look of triumph seemed to confirm it. "But you said such cruel things."

Now Arabella's lips turned down in an exaggerated frown. "I know, my dear, and I'm sure that was horrible of me, but I thought it only fair that you have the same information as Deverill. It would not be sporting to give him the advantage. Furthermore, I knew the shock of hearing the words out loud would do you good."

"Do me good?" Catherine echoed, wondering if her mother's friend had become completely unhinged. How could hearing something that awful do anyone good?

"Why, yes. The words I used might have been harsh, but I didn't say anything to Deverill that your own mother didn't say to me here in this very room," she stated boldly and, Catherine had to concede, accurately. "It was clear to me that she had quite given up on you and you, in return, had given up on yourself. But I knew if you heard the words spoken by someone else, you would hear them for what they are: ugly, nasty lies. And it worked beautifully. You rose to the challenge and Deverill was enchanted and now you shall be married and I can add another match to my roster of success stories."

Arabella finished her remarkable speech with another triumphant grin, and Catherine shook her head, unable to comprehend such Machiavellian scheming, the depth of play of which exceeded anything she'd encountered before. She wanted to believe her—oh, what a lovely tale she weaved of two fated souls—but Catherine was too practical to be taken in by a pretty yarn. She could accept that her intention in wanting to shock her out of her own pitiful opinion of herself had been good. That part of the plan worked exactly as its architect had intended, and for that she could be grateful, if not glad.

"Thank you for the interest you have taken in my life and I appreciate the good you tried to do," Catherine said with far more graciousness than she was feeling. Indeed, her thoughts were in a jumble and she wanted nothing more than to run home and hide in her father's dark study until she could make sense of them. "However, I came here to discuss my sister's happiness, not my own."

"But your happiness is so much more interesting to me," Arabella declared. "What is your issue with Deverill? Tell me, does he not meet your requirements for a future husband? I assure you, I have complied with your request."

Catherine could not recall making any requests, and she stared at her ladyship in amazement. "I recollect no requirements."

"Don't be absurd, dear. You stated right here in this room that he must be tall. And Deverill fits the bill quite nicely. You have to look up to him, do you not?"

She vaguely remembered the conversation to which Arabella referred but couldn't believe the woman had actually been serious. "Let us return to the matter of Finchly," she stated firmly, "for the matter of my future is none of your concern and, regardless, it has already been sorted to my satisfaction."

Amused, Arabella folded her arms across her chest and raised a curious eyebrow. "Has it?" she asked, mildly.

As soon as she made the claim, Catherine realized she'd overstated the matter but refused to back down. "Yes, I'm going to set up my own establishment. Nothing grand, of course, but just a little place where—"

She flinched as her hostess laughed with genuine humor. "You are a delight, dear, and I quite admire your pluck, but that will never do."

The plan still needed for its finer details to be worked out, Catherine knew that, of course, but she also knew it had merit, and as she told Lady Courtland about it, she became more and more convinced of its feasibility. "It will do very nicely," she insisted with surprising vehemence. "I'll find some doddering old female relation in want of a position—surely we have one knocking about on some branch of the family tree— and have her as my companion, for respectability's sake. And I will be completely self-sufficient and live on my earnings."

"Your earnings?"

Catherine nodded emphatically. "Yes. I shall be a lady investor."

"A lady investor?" Arabella asked with more wonder than derision.

"My dear friend Miss Clarise Menton assures me it's quite the easiest thing to earn a sufficient amount," she explained. "I'm good with figures. Not brilliant like my sister Melissa but tolerably useful."

"You know, my dear, as many fortunes have been lost in silver mines as they have at the faro tables."

In fact, Catherine did not know this, and the excitement that had been mounting since she first proposed the scheme began to wane. "I...uh, will not be investing in silver mines. I shall follow the suggestions of my friend."

"Fustian!" dismissed her ladyship. "You will marry Deverill and have children and make your mama happy. Now, come, tell me what is wrong between you and Deverill, and we will sort it all out together. There is no need to be shy, my dear. I have only your best interest at heart. And your mother, pea-goose though she is, is one of my oldest and dearest friends. I wouldn't have offered her my help if I didn't regard her so highly."

Realizing that they would never return to the matter of Finchly until Arabella had her pound of flesh, Catherine decided to stop avoiding the topic and answer honestly and openly. "There's nothing to sort out," she said in what she hoped was a flat, detached tone. "He courted me as a favor to you, and despite my knowledge of the prank, I found myself growing more attached than was wise. I therefore made it clear to Deverill that there was no reason to continue the charade and that far from being taken in, I had been using the connection with him to further my own ends."

"Oh, dear, you have made quite a muddle of it, haven't you?" Arabella asked. "No wonder poor Deverill was in here earlier looking very much the worse for wear and muttering some nonsense about how you were just using him to meet other men. I could scarcely credit it."

Catherine stared at her ladyship in wonder, afraid to believe her. What if she was still trying to mastermind a match with half lies and overstated facts?

"I did tell him that," she admitted. "And it was partly the truth. You see, after I overhead your conversation, I resolved to take advantage of my would-be popularity because I knew how fleeting these things are. And if I happened to meet a gentleman whom I could admire as much as Deverill... I told him of my thoughts because I was angry and humiliated and I didn't want him to know how much I—how I felt about him."

"Well, no bother," said Arabella airily. "The next time you see him, you must simply tell him you love him and all will be right."

"What?" Catherine shrieked, sounding alarmingly like

Evelyn when denied an ostrich-plumed hat. "No, I couldn't possibly."

Her ladyship considered Catherine silently for a long moment, then shook her head sadly. "Then you are not half the girl I thought you were and undeserving of him anyway. Now, regarding your plan for Finchly," she said brusquely, sitting down at the writing table, which was situated near the window, and locating a sheet of paper.

Now? Catherine thought, nearly hysterical. *Now* she wanted to talk of Finchly, after saying such remarkable things and throwing her entire being into turmoil? Tell Deverill she loved him! She couldn't possibly do something so bold and terrifying and potentially humiliating. He wouldn't laugh, of course, he was too much of a gentleman for that, but he would be embarrassed for her and try to extricate himself as gently—and quickly—as possible.

No, she wouldn't do it.

And yet, to be not half the girl Lady Courtland supposed her! How could that statement affect her so much? The woman was a born manipulator and no doubt carefully chose her words with maximum calculation to get the effect she wanted. Even knowing that, Catherine found that she very much wanted to be the girl Lady Courtland supposed her. Her ladyship had a better opinion of her than her own mother and, apparently, than she herself.

Not half the girl I thought you were.

How was she to talk about Finchly with that thought rattling about in her head?

She would simply have to try. "Yes, thank you. Please tell me how you think we may execute it," she said in what she thought was a reasonably calm tone.

Scribbling wildly, Lady Courtland rang for a servant. "I am just dashing off a note to—" The doors opened, and the footman entered the room. "Ah, there you are, Perth. I'm finishing this note that I want you to deliver. You do not need to wait for a response." She folded the missive and slid it into an envelope. "Here you are, my good man. Do be quick about it. And on your way out will you tell Mrs. Taylor that we'd like some tea."

Catherine stared in wonder as the footman bowed and left. Dashing a note off to whom? she thought, wondering if in her emotional tumult she had lost track of the conversation.

Misinterpreting the look on her young visitor's face, Arabella said, "You poor dear, you look quite parched. Tea will be here in a moment. We'll have to wait for a little while, at least, and nothing quite passes the time like a pot of tea and a little gossip."

"Wait for what?" Catherine asked, still trying to figure out if she had missed something or if her ladyship had failed to explain.

"The response to my note."

"But you told the footman not to tarry."

"There was no need," she explained. "If he's at home, Deverill will come directly here. He has never been one to refuse a damsel in distress."

Her ladyship could not have said anything that would have struck more terror in Miss Fellingham's heart, and the poor girl did not have the composure to hide it. "Deverill is coming here?" she squawked, jumping to her feet and walking to the window, as if to see him arriving at that very moment.

"I understand your concern," Arabella said reasonably, "but you have no cause for fear. I will not pester you to make a confession of love, and Deverill is far too well bred to trouble a lady with his emotions. We will simply discuss a plan for Finchly."

Her assurances did little to quiet Catherine's mind, and unable to be so close to the window, where he might see her when he arrived, she walked to the other side of the room. "I cannot believe you would tell Deverill about my sister's trouble and my mother's indecent scheme."

"He's an honorable gentleman," Arabella promised her, "and can be counted on for his discretion."

Catherine shook her head and strode to the window again to peek out. "These are family matters," she explained logically. "I cannot approve and must insist that you send a second letter telling him not to come."

Arabella dismissed this suggestion with a wave of her hand. "He'll be family soon enough, you'll see."

Catherine, who somehow found this statement more unsettling than all the other unsettling statements made by her ladyship that morning, begged her to please not say things like that.

"Yes, yes, of course. It is *I* who have misread the situation. You're charming dear. Very well," she said, throwing up her hands in defeat, "I will accept that I am wrong—Deverill isn't in the least bit besotted with you; there, are you happy now? —if you will sit down and stop that incessant pacing. You are making me anxious."

Just then a footman entered carrying a silver tray, and Catherine thought about darting through the open door to escape. But she knew that that sort of behavior wouldn't solve anything and she was sensible enough to admit that Deverill was just the person who could bring about Finchly's disgrace. If matters between them hadn't devolved to such a wretched state, she most likely would have brought the plan to him herself. "Very well," she said, submitting.

"Thank you," agreed Arabella, gracefully filling a teacup. "Now do sit down. You are frightfully tall, and I am getting a crick in my neck from looking up at you."

Catherine sat in the armchair adjacent to the sofa and accepted the cup of tea. From there, she had a view of the window but could keep her back turned so as not to indulge it.

True to her word, her ladyship talked of inconsequential things, gossiping with the same enthusiasm as her mother but without the same level of spite. Some of her stories were quite amusing and Catherine smiled to be polite, but nothing she heard could take her mind off the fact that in a few minutes the Marquess of Deverill would be there. Her anxiety slowly increased until she could barely contain her nerves and it was all she could do to remain seated, politely drinking tea.

When Deverill did arrive, she knew the exact moment, for she'd turned her head to the window when the clop-clop of horses stopped in front of the house.

"Deverill," Arabella said, standing to greet her new guest. "Your prompt reply is extremely gratifying."

Deverill, whose eyes had been trained on Catherine from the moment the doors had opened and revealed her to his sight, turned his head slowly toward his hostess. "My dear," he said, bowing over her hand, "I came over as soon as I got your note. Please tell me how I may be of assistance." He turned to Catherine. "Miss Fellingham, I'm happy to say you look much improved from earlier today."

Catherine, unprepared for his presence despite the ample warning, muttered an unintelligible reply. Her hand holding the cup was shaking, and she had to put it down lest she spill tea all over her dress.

"Please join us, Deverill," said Arabella, holding out a cup of tea. "I was just telling Miss Fellingham here about Mr. Benchley's kerfuffle yesterday in the Serpentine, but she's too distracted by her troubles to appreciate the humor of a overly large gentleman splashing around in a pond looking for his spectacles."

"Understandable, of course." He accepted the tea and

looked at Catherine. "I'm yours to command. How may I help?"

Catherine blushed at this gallantry but saw nothing of the besotted lover in his behavior. Indeed, he seemed more distant than ever—his civility, while flattering, felt like mere obligation—and that made her even less inclined to confide in him. But confide she must and she wouldn't be a ninny-hammer about it, pussyfooting around the details of her mother's disgrace to save the Fellingham honor. No, she would simply state the matter in a calm, indifferent tone, as if discussing a mundane business matter with an associate.

"To help my mother supplement our income, Lady Court-land devised a scheme wherein they would sell commissions in the king's army," she explained, determined to parcel as much of the blame as possible on Arabella's shoulders. "The scheme went on for a while without our family knowing it until a friend of Freddy's kindly informed us of it. As soon as I found out, I put a stop to it immediately. However, one of the men my mother helped was not so honorable and now he's threatening to expose our family to the scandal if my sister doesn't agree to marry him."

"Finchly!" Deverill exclaimed suddenly. "He is black-mailing your sister."

Catherine sighed, relieved that he had figured it out for himself, for it meant that he understood now why she had been at his apartments earlier this morning. "Yes, he is. I thought I could reason with him, but he is a true villain and would not be swayed by morality or common decency. I've come up with a plan to thwart him, but I can't carry it out on my own and that's why I called on Lady Courtland."

Her ladyship nodded. "And that's why I called on you, Deverill. As you know, Finchly is widely suspected of cheating at cards, although nothing has ever been proven."

"That's quite true," Deverill confirmed, looking at Catherine. "Won't play with him myself. He's a slippery eel."

"I'm very much afraid you are wrong, Julian. You'll be playing cards with Finchly tonight at your club." Arabella patted prettily at her lips with a serviette.

"I shall?" he asked, as though he had a small idea of where his friend was headed. "And I suppose he will cheat?"

"Of course," she said. "And even if he doesn't cheat, you shall make it look as if he has."

Deverill nodded thoughtfully, and Catherine waited anxiously for him to speak. It was one thing to grasp quickly what was being asked of him; it was quite another to agree. He knew Finchly to be a villain and could not condone his treatment of poor Evelyn, but that did not mean he would agree to behave in a manner that was potentially dishonorable. If Finchly didn't cheat, then perhaps the marquess could not consent to making it look as if he had.

After a long moment, he turned to Catherine. "You thought of this plan?"

Catherine nodded and examined his handsome face, trying to find some indication of how he truly felt about her, but he gave away nothing. His green eyes, usually so expressive, were oddly flat, and he wore an expression of polite curiosity. "We must trade our silence for his silence," she explained. "It's the only way to make sure the sordid tale does not get out."

"It's a good plan, Miss Fellingham," he said quietly. "I did not realize you could be so diabolical."

The second the word was out of his mouth, Catherine felt herself blushing to the roots of her hair, for he did indeed know just how diabolical she could be. She had told him so herself only the night before. "I...I don't...I didn't..." she stammered, not sure if she was trying to defend herself or apologize. Then she ordered herself to gather her wits and murmured a polite thank you, as if he had offered her a compliment.

If Deverill noticed anything strange in her behavior, he did not refine upon it. Indeed, Catherine was despondent to note that his behavior was everything that was correct, proper and aloof. Arabella was wrong. He felt nothing for her, not even disgust. He consented to help with mild indifference, as if agreeing to wear a fawn-colored waistcoat instead of a taupe-colored one.

Despite his coolness, Catherine smiled warmly at him, grateful for his assistance. He didn't have to be effusive with her as long as he saved Evelyn. "I thank you, my lord, on behalf of my whole family."

"Very good," Arabella said approvingly. "Now, Deverill, the details. We must decide when, where and who."

"The who is easy enough. I will invite Bainbridge, Martindale and Halsey to play," Deverill said, casually rattling off a list of the beau monde's most sought-after Corinthians. "They're all good men with impeccable reputations. Finchly knows that they're not given to idle gossip and should he become the subject of talk, society would be inclined to believe them over him."

"Excellent choices." Arabella nodded approvingly. "I understand that Halsey has just returned from the Continent. You'll do it tonight, of course, before Lord Raines's ball. At your club, I presume?"

"No," he answered consideringly. "I would rather not dirty my own pen. I have a gambling hell in mind that would serve us much better. For one thing, Finchly is a regular and I should be able to find him there easily enough. And for another, the owner, Marlowe, owes me a favor. I helped his establishment avoid a rather embarrassing situation recently."

At this oblique reference to their earlier escapade, Deverill kept his eyes trained on the peeress and didn't so much as glance in Catherine's direction, another indication, she felt, of his indifference toward her.

"Splendid!" Arabella said. "I knew you were just the man for this problem. Now what about—" she broke off as the doors to the drawing room opened to admit her butler. "Yes, Perth?"

"A missive marked urgent has arrived for milady," he said, holding out a white slip of paper.

Lady Courtland apologized to her guests whilst retrieving the note from the hand of her servant. After a quick perusal, she said, "You're going to have to excuse me. There's a matter I have to take care of. I shall return presently. Catherine, isn't there something you wanted to discuss with the marquess?" With these distressing words, which she had *promised* not to utter, she left the two of them alone.

Not entirely surprised by her ladyship's betrayal, Catherine stared down at her own clasped fingers and wondered if she had the nerve to look up at him.

"Yes, Miss Fellingham?" he prompted.

At his polite tone, she raised her head and saw him looking at her with curiosity. There was no affection in either his look or tone, and she knew again that Arabella was wrong. He didn't love her. It seemed to her right now that he barely even liked her. "Her ladyship overstated the case. I imagine she knows how grateful I am for your help and assumed I wanted another opportunity to thank you for the service you do my family. We are extremely grateful."

"I assure you, Miss Fellingham, as a gentleman, I am honor bound to help your sister out of this distressing circumstance," he explained, making it clear to her that his willingness to help had nothing to do with his affection for her. "I do not doubt that marriage to Finchly would be intolerable to anyone, no matter how delicate her sensibilities."

Catherine nodded and returned her attention to her

clasped hands, thinking of Arabella's departing words and the declaration she expected of her.

Would she say it? *Could* she say it? The very idea seemed preposterous and yet something inside her wouldn't let the matter rest. Arabella's insistence that Deverill loved her had wormed its way into her heart, creating an unbearable burden of hope, and Catherine knew a declaration was the only sure way to put an end to it once and for all.

The very thought of making a confession terrified her to the point where she could barely breathe, for it would be the single biggest risk she'd ever taken in her life, and Miss Catherine Fellingham was not the sort of girl who took risks. She recalled all those years she sat in her father's study, reading books and newspapers and journals, happy to be left alone and yet, she could admit now, not quite happy. She'd told herself she was choosing independence and freedom from frivolity, but in truth she was merely hiding from all the things that scared her and intimidated her and made her feel like she was half the person she thought she was.

Six years later, she was older and wiser and more alone than ever.

Catherine closed her eyes, counted to ten and took deep, measured breaths in an attempt to calm herself down. She could do this. All she had to do was open her mouth and speak three measly words. It was daunting, yes, but surely Miss Catherine Fellingham had some small amount of courage.

"Lord Deverill," she said, clutching the teacup, for she had to do something with her hands or they would curl into tight fists, "over the last few days we seem to have had a series of misunderstandings and I just wanted to say that I... that I—" But here she faltered and despite her best intentions the words wouldn't come out. She tried again. "I just wanted to say that I...um...I—"

Seeing her struggle, Deverill interrupted her. "Miss Fellingham, the hour grows late, and I am sure that your mother must be wondering where you are. No doubt you didn't mean to be gone for so long. Your sister will be anxious to learn of the good news. Not to mention that you've kept the coachman waiting."

Catherine listened with a growing sense of devastation as he rattled off this list of reasons why she should leave. He knew, she thought. He knew exactly what she was trying to say and was sparing her the humiliation. Absurd misses like her must fall in love with him all the time.

Feeling an unexpected well of loneliness, she took a deep breath and said, "You are right, my lord. How inconsiderate of me not to have thought of my sister sooner." Suddenly she wanted nothing else than to be out of his presence and back in the safety of her father's study. She put the teacup down, rose to her feet and smiled with all the civility she could muster. "Please make my apologies to Lady Courtland."

Deverill stood and bowed over her hand. "Of course."

Catherine nodded and walked to the door. She had her hand on the knob when she turned around to look at him one last time. "Goodbye, Julian," she said softly, the finality of it weighing heavy on her heart. After tonight, she would make sure she never dealt with him again.

Something of her distress must have conveyed itself to him for he suddenly was at her side and holding her arm. "Miss Fellingham...Catherine...my dear, we must talk," he stammered, losing some of his detached air.

Catherine didn't know what lay behind his change of heart, but she did know that she couldn't bear any more. Looking at him—so dear, so handsome—she realized that she would never marry. How foolish to think she could find another man she loved as well as him. That would never happen, and she knew now that she would follow the plan outlined to Lady Courtland: invest on the 'Change, set up her own establishment, maybe host a few small parties and be happy in her independence. If any good had come out of the Deverill affair, it was the realization that she could hold her own socially, and if she chose not to go among the *ton* it was because she didn't want to, not because it had rejected her that first season.

"There's no need," Catherine said, determined to avoid further conversation. Her moment of boldness had passed to be replaced by the same old Catherine everyone knew—shy, awkward, dumb. It was still early in the afternoon, but she felt as though she had been awake for days. She was exhausted and overwrought and fearful that she might fall off her feet if forced to stand on them for much longer. No, she could not bear any more. "Please do me the consideration of letting me return home. As you have pointed out, my sister will be worried."

Deverill dropped her arm and stepped back. "By all means, go. I didn't mean to add to your distress."

His said this last piece with a trace of bitterness, and Catherine wondered at the cause. Surely she hadn't done anything to put his nose out of joint. After all, *she* wasn't the one who had toyed with *his* feelings. "Of course not," she said, more gently than she had meant to. "And I thank you again for the service you do my family. I assure you, we'll not soon forget it."

"I'm relying on that," he murmured so quietly she wasn't quite sure whether she'd heard him correctly.

"Yes, well..." She couldn't think of anything else to say. "Until later, then."

"I trust you will be at Lord Raines's ball?"

"In all likelihood."

"Then I can assure you of the happy conclusion of this

affair at that time. Perhaps you will save me a waltz?" he asked, the familiar teasing glint returning to his eyes.

Unable to stand the way that familiar look made her feel, she nodded abruptly—which was not, she told herself, agreement to his request—and left the room. No, she would not be saving a waltz for the charming Lord Deverill, nor would she wait for his arrival at Lord Raines's ball to learn of her sister's fate. She would go the gambling hell and witness the scene for herself. She wanted to be there when Deverill wiped that smug smile from Finchly's face. With her hopes of requited love dashed, there was very little satisfaction left to her and she would not be deprived of what small amount remained. She would be there to demonstrate to the awful cad that she had some small amount of power after all.

Despite her misgivings, Catherine knew she would need Freddy's help, so upon arriving home, she asked Caruthers if her brother was in.

"Yes, miss," he said, relieving her of her reticule and pelisse, "I believe he's in the study."

Catherine nodded at this unexpected development and proceeded to her father's study, wondering as she went what in the world Freddy was doing there, for he never had any use for books. She found him behind the large oak desk, a candle next to him and a quill in his hand.

He looked up when she entered. "Ah, there you are, Cathy, I was just wondering which you would prefer—my pocket watch or my signet ring," he asked, as he put down the pen and rubbed his eyes. "Don't worry. I have you down for my books. Not a remarkable collection, of course, but my tutors at Oxford will make me read literature occasionally and I have a fair number of Greek classics. They're a particular favorite of yours, are they not?"

The sight of Freddy behind a desk looking studious was so shocking to Catherine that his words barely registered.

"What are you doing?" she asked, rather than express her preference, which was for the signet ring. Freddy's pocket watch kept deplorable time.

"I am making out my last will and testament, of course," he said as if stating the obvious. Then he yawned and stretched his arms over his head. "Been doing it for hours."

Catherine sat down in a leather chair across from Freddy and picked up the parchment. She read silently for several minutes before breaking out into gales of laughter.

Affronted, Freddy grabbed the document from her. "I don't see what's so funny. A fellow's will is serious business."

"Of course," she said, trying to give the matter the respect her brother clearly felt it deserved. "But I don't understand why you're giving Mama your snuff box."

The question made him blush slightly, and he answered stiffly, "It is only a memento. A token, really, to comfort her in her grief."

Catherine, duplicating her brother's solemnity, considered him for a moment. "All right, Freddy, what's the game? Why are you making out your will? I hadn't realized your demise was imminent."

He sat up straighter in the tall wingback chair, and Catherine noticed for the first time how much he looked like their father. "I'm afraid I can't tell you everything," he announced in a voice that was unusually calm and mature. Then he added, a little defensively, "It is men's business and should be left to men. Why don't you get ready for Lord Raines's ball? And see to it that Evelyn gets dressed as well."

"Get ready now? Why, it's not even lunch— Evelyn!" she exclaimed as the scene in the study suddenly became clear. "Do you know about this business with Finchly?"

Freddy's flush deepened as he realized Catherine knew about it, too. "Yes. Pearson heard they were engaged from his brother Morgan, who heard it from Micklesby, who heard it from Barthes, who heard it from Finchly, who told him to expect an announcement soon. Of course, I told Pearson it was a bag of moonshine, but then Evelyn told me it was true and promptly turned into a watering pot. My coat is still wet!" he said with disgust, almost as if this were the greater offense. "I intend to call him out, of course. His behavior is despicable, to prey on an innocent young lady like that. I don't care if it does ruin the family. He won't get away with it."

Catherine thought this was a fine speech, and it warmed her heart to see him passionate about something other than the state of his cravat. At the same time, the thought of Freddy with a pistol aimed at another human being was terrifying. "You mustn't call him out. It won't do any good. You will be dead, and he will still tell everyone the truth about Mama. The only advantage as far as I can see is that there will be one less Fellingham alive to blush," she said, dampingly. "But do not despair. I'm working on a solution, and a happy resolution is within our grasp."

Freddy narrowed his eyes, suspicious of her intent. "I won't be fobbed off with a fairy story while you go out and challenge him to a duel yourself."

Although Catherine had considered that very thing, hearing her brother say it out loud made it sound ridiculous and she laughed at the absurdity. "No fairy stories, I promise. Indeed, I've arranged with Lady Courtland for Finchly to be caught cheating at cards. Once he is caught, we will trade our silence for his. It happens tonight and was the very reason I sought you out this afternoon. I would like to attend the event, and I would be grateful if you would accompany me."

"Cheating at cards, eh?" he said consideringly. "That is an inventive plan, as there have certainly been rumors about Finchly's infernal luck. He never loses, you know. You say

Lady Courtland arranged it? You brought our sister's predicament to her attention?"

Catherine nodded. "I believe it's only fair that she extricate us from this mess, as she is the one who got us into it."

Freddy could not cavil at this logic, for it was true enough. Their mother had more hair than sense and would always follow the dictates of her much more clever friend. "You are right. I should be there. It is the Fellingham honor that's at stake. Thank you for telling me," he said, folding up his last will and testament and slipping it in the top drawer of the desk.

It was obvious he had no intention of taking Catherine along, and his sister let him enjoy that misconception for a few moments before disabusing him. "Very good. And where are you going?"

He seemed not to immediately grasp her point, for he opened his mouth to speak and his jaw flapped several times before he realized he didn't have the answer to that question. "You are not coming," he said, his voice tight with resolution. "In the absence of our father, I'm the man of the house and it's my responsibility to see this matter through."

At this, Catherine smiled. "Our father is not absent. He's down the hall in the drawing room."

Annoyed, he said, "I meant figuratively absent, not literally."

"It won't wash, Freddy," she said, although, in truth, she had a little sympathy for his situation. "Finchly is wholly repugnant and I simply must be there when Deverill wipes—"

"Deverill!" Freddy said in surprise. "He has a hand in this?"

"Yes. He's arranging the game," she explained. "He will invite some of his friends who are known to be entirely trustworthy to witness Finchly's humiliation."

"Well, you certainly can't come if Deverill is there. I don't want him cuffing me on the ear and calling me a coxcomb again," he said, the indignity still fresh. "Besides, I promised him that I wouldn't take you to another hell."

"Who is Deverill to tell you what to do?" she asked, knowing full well the fascination her brother had with the older, more accomplished peer. "You are the man of this family. You even have a last will and testament. You're not so easily intimidated."

"Cut line, Cathy," he said, much offended by her tact. "A gentleman has to keep his promises. It's a matter of honor."

"Very well, then," she said, realizing it was futile and returning to her original strategy. "I trust you and your honor will represent the family well at whichever gaming hell you wind up at. I only hope it's the right one."

He paused for a long moment, no doubt trying to figure out a solution to the conundrum that didn't include threatening to tell on her to their mother. Like breaking promises, tattling didn't fall under the purview of proper gentlemanly behavior. "Fine," he said petulantly.

"And you'll lend me breeches?" she asked.

Freddy heaved such an oppressed-sounding sigh his sister could easily imagine him scratching her name out of his will. "Yes. But this time we have to do a better job with the cravat. I can't go around with a fellow wearing such an abysmally tied knot. Embarrassed me last time."

Not minding the criticism, Catherine gave him a big kiss on the cheek and a wholehearted thank you before going to Evelyn's room to assure her sister that she had everything well in hand.

Chapter Thirteen

E ven in the hack, Catherine refused to tell Freddy
where they were going.

"We're on our way. What harm can it do now?"
He looked out the window and observed the passing streets,
trying to figure out their route.

"Well, after I tell you, you could bind my wrists, order the
driver to stop, hand me over to your confederates in the hack
that has been following us since we left the house and force
me to dance at Lord Raines's ball while you go on by yourself," she said with what she thought was apparent logic.

Freddy's eyes opened wide, and he stuck his head out the
window to see who was behind them.

Catherine smiled. "Nobody is following us, you coxcomb."

"But you just said—"

"I made it up," she said brightly. "I was just outlining the
possibilities as I see them."

Her brother stared at her. "When did this happen?"

"What?" She looked down at her clothes expecting something to be horribly wrong, but her black breeches were
clean, her white shirt was pressed and her cravat tied in a

semirespectable fashion. The wig on her head was heavy and it itched, but by all accounts, it was straight and properly centered.

"This—your personality," he explained with a loose hand gesture. "You used to be so placid. Now you are given to odd fits."

Not sure how one responded to such a comment, she simply said, "Oh."

"Maybe it's Deverill. You females get all queer over men like Deverill. Of course, you never have before. It's usually chits like Evelyn who lose their heads," he said and then laughed.

At the mention of Deverill, her cheeks began to flush and she was grateful for the gloom of the carriage, which hid her face. "What is funny?" she asked, wondering if he was laughing at her. Had she been acting that queer over Deverill?

"Just imagining Mama's face when she finds out about this evening," he explained. "You'll have a devil of a time convincing her that Deverill isn't about to make an offer."

Catherine knew he spoke the truth, but she also knew their mother was so stubborn and impervious to reality that the only thing that would eventually convince her was time. In a week, when Deverill had stopped dancing attendance on her, she would begin to grasp the truth. In a few months, she would be unable to deny it.

"I think it's best for all parties concerned if we don't tell Mama about this night's work," she said, thinking more of Evelyn than herself.

Freddy assured her she wouldn't hear it from him. "It's Lady Courtland you should be concerned about. She and Mama are bosom friends. They tell each other everything."

Catherine acknowledged the truth of the statement and hoped she could prevail on Lady Courtland to keep this adventure to herself. As grateful as she was for her help, she cringed at the thought of having another conversation with her ladyship, as none of their previous ones had turned out the way she'd wanted. No doubt, she had dropped many encouraging hints in her mother's ear, assuring Lady Fellingham and herself—mistakenly, of course—that her scheme was going exactly according to plan. Catherine was so lost in these thoughts that she hadn't noticed that the hack had stopped until Freddy said, "Damnation!"

She jumped in her seat. "What is amiss?"

"You've taken me to my own hell," he said accusingly. "Of all the curst— Of course this is it. It's the only one you know. I should've figured it out."

Catherine leaned forward and patted him on the knee. "Don't tease yourself about it. If I hadn't come with you, I would have come in the hack following you."

Freddy sighed resignedly and climbed down to the street. Then he politely offered her a hand.

"No, silly. Gentlemen don't help gentlemen down from their carriages," she said, reminding him of her disguise, although she couldn't imagine how he could forget. It was as plain as the whiskers on her face—the glued-on whiskers that tickled her nose and made her want to sneeze. "Do you really think this is necessary?" she asked of the added camouflage.

"Yes, I don't want Deverill recognizing you and giving me another tongue lashing," he said. "Now remember, act masculine."

Catherine found this direction vague, but she nodded affirmatively and followed her brother inside. Although it was still early in the evening, the gambling hell was more crowded than it had been last time. She marveled about this to Freddy.

"Well, of course it is. Think what day it is." At her baffled look, he added, "The beginning of the quarter. People are always flush at the beginning of the quarter."

This explanation sounded reasonable to Catherine, and

she fleetingly wished her father would take the same sensible approach: play when you're flush and stop when you aren't.

Upon entering the establishment, they found an unoccupied corner by the faro table and Freddy surveyed the room. "Are you sure this is the place?" he asked. "I don't see Deverill or Finchly."

"I'm sure this is the place." She craned her head to look above the crowd, but she was a few inches shorter than her brother and had an imperfect view. "Perhaps we are early. Oh, there's—" Without warning, she turned toward the wall and started examining her shoes. "Is he gone?"

"Who?" asked Freddy, mystified by her strange behavior.

"Marlowe," she said softly. "The proprietor of this fine establishment. The man who wanted to throw me out last time because his dealer was cheating and that was somehow my fault."

"Oh, him." He raised his head and looked around. "Must be gone. I don't see him. Oh, wait a minute. There's Deverill."

"Where?" she asked, her head swiveling as she tried to stand on tippy-toes to get a better view. But she was wearing Freddy's shoes, which were several sizes too big, and she immediately lost her balance. She flailed for a moment, then pressed her hand against the wall to steady herself.

"I said, act masculine," Freddy growled, aghast at her antics. "Deverill is over there, by that door. No, he just went through it."

Stable now, Catherine followed his gaze. There were three doors. "Which one?"

"The one that the large man with the scar over his right eye so enormous that I can see it clearly from twenty paces is standing in front of," Freddy said in disgust. "That door, of course."

Catherine examined the gentleman in question, his scar as

huge as Freddy described, and considered their options, which were limited to only two: going through the door and not going through the door. She knew which route she would take, of course, but first she would have to convince her brother to distract the guard.

"Distract *him*?" he said, appalled by the part he was to play in the plan. "You mean, let the large, frightening man beat me to a bloody pulp so you can stroll right in? I don't think so."

"Think of it logically," she said. "One of us has to get into the room and I'm the better choice, for if it's a small group, Finchly will surely recognize you as soon as you enter. Otherwise, I would distract the guard and let you sneak by."

"You'd do it?" he asked, even more appalled by the alternate plan. "That would be a huge success with Deverill. I'd rather confront the oversized, scar-faced Cyclops than Deverill any day."

"Oh, Freddy, you're a sweetheart. Go on then, get over there." She gave him a little push. "I suggest you wobble uncertainly as if foxed and then spill a drink on him. That is always a reliable method for getting someone's attention, though do be careful not to get any bruises. You know how Mama finds them frightfully unbred."

"Wait a minute. I'm still thinking about this." He raised a hand to his chin. "How come I'd be recognized by Finchly in a minute and you wouldn't?"

"Because I'm incognito," she said.

"Deverill easily saw through that last time."

"Ah, but thanks to you, I've got this very clever mustache this time," she said, screwing up her face in emphasis. "Furthermore, Deverill cited the fact that I was with you as the reason he was able to deduce my presence. Neither he nor Finchly will be privy to that vital piece of information."

Freddy looked far from convinced but conceded with a

reluctant sigh. "I'll do it. But I wish Mama were right about Deverill offering for you and taking you off our hands. You are a menace, and I don't want to be responsible for you anymore."

He sounded so churlish, Catherine forgot herself enough to laugh in her natural vocal register. As soon as she realized what she'd done, she clamped her mouth shut and looked around. When it was clear that nobody noticed, she said in a soft voice, "Freddy dear, you're my younger brother. You've never been responsible for me. I've always been responsible for you."

"Some responsible," he muttered as he went to find a drink to spill on the behemoth at the door, "sending me off to get thrashed within an inch of my life."

Catherine waited until Freddy was a few feet from the man, then scurried around to the far side of the door. Her brother obligingly spilled his glass of whiskey, and while the guard with the scar was wiping his shirt and cursing at Freddy, she slipped through the door.

Immediately, she turned and was confronted by five pairs of surprised eyes staring at her. Deverill, Finchly and three other men she didn't recognize were sitting at a round table playing a card game she couldn't identify. She knew it wasn't whist or faro from the number of participants and the type of table they played on. Perhaps this was loo—another indulgence of her father's.

Examining the situation, she noted that each man had a fair amount of counters in front of him and a fresh drink. Finchly, who was handling the cards, halted in midshuffle, raised an eyebrow and looked at her expectantly. Returning his gaze, Catherine felt a shiver of hatred run up her spine. It wasn't good, she thought, to despise someone this much. Afraid that she might give something away despite her brilliant disguise, she turned her attention to the other men at the table.

A blond gentleman in a bright-blue waistcoat—Bainbridge? Martindale? Halsey?—took an elegant pinch of snuff and said, while staring blankly at her, "Can we help you?"

Remembering to lower her voice, she said, "I'm looking for a game of..." She trailed off when she realized she didn't quite know what game that was. Then she said with more conviction, "A game of cards."

With a grim countenance and flashing green eyes, Deverill said through a clenched jaw, "Surely you can find a game of cards out there."

Of course he had recognized her. She had known he would and only argued otherwise to appease Freddy's concerns.

"Nonsense, my lord," dismissed Finchly, jovial and flushed and perhaps a trifle disguised, "we're just beginning a new hand and the more the merrier. Where's that man Marlowe? Let's have him bring in a chair for the gentleman."

Catherine didn't want Marlowe to come in and recognize her so she grabbed a chair she had noticed in the corner of the room. "No need to bother him." Unwilling to make eye contact with Deverill, she placed her chair next to his so she wouldn't have to look at him.

Finchly nodded approvingly and resumed shuffling, an act he did with a surprising amount of skill and speed. Indeed, Catherine marveled that a man with so little to recommend him in all manner of deportment as Finchly could do anything with such grace. When he was satisfied with the shuffle, he placed a turned-down card in front of each player at the table. Catherine stared at hers for several seconds before she realized that everyone else had picked up his card and she quickly followed suit. She had a ten of hearts. While she was trying to decide if that was good or bad, she felt a hand at her knee. Her eyes flew to Deverill's. What was he doing? Surely he didn't think that just because she was—

He pressed counters into her hand. Of course, an ante. She saw that the others had already tossed some counters into the middle of the table. Thank God Deverill had the presence of mind to give her a stack. She had foolishly forgotten to exchange her money when she had come in. It was a grave oversight but one she wasn't entirely responsible for, as her numskull brother should have reminded her to.

As she counted the chips Deverill gave her, she realized that the coins in her pocket would not be enough to repay him. The play was deep indeed. Feeling unusually grateful for Deverill's consideration, she touched his knee in an informal thank you and quickly pulled her hand away as a prickle of awareness shot up her spine.

To regain her composure, Catherine examined the other players. The man sitting directly to her right had a swarthy complexion and long, dark hair tied in the back with a leather strap. His cravat was arranged in an elaborate confection, but aside from that his dress was simple: unadorned waistcoat, pantaloons, Hessians. He was clearly not going to Lord Raines's ball after this evening's play. By contrast, the thin-lipped blond man next to him was dressed in full evening regalia, much in the same way Deverill was. Finchly was next at the table. He, too, was dressed simply, if not a little slop-pily. His cravat seemed almost undone, and she marveled that a gentleman would look so disheveled in public. She hoped, though, that this was a good sign. Perhaps he was suffering great losses and would soon begin cheating. The last man at the table was so handsome that Catherine had to remind herself not to stare. Dark hair cut à la Caesar, a chiseled jaw that seemed modeled out of marble, soft blue eyes... She wondered why she had never seen him before or why Evelyn hadn't gone into raptures over this fine specimen. Surely he was more beautiful than Deverill—in an effete sort of way, of course. Maybe this was Halsey, the one Arabella declared had recently returned from the Continent.

Deverill kicked her under the table, and Catherine realized that it was her turn to do something. Fiddlesticks! She should have been watching the way the game was played, rather than examining the players. Recalling all that she knew of gaming, which was really only that her father lost huge amounts of money when he did it, she decided one could not go wrong by tossing a few counters into the pot. From Deverill's absent nod, she concluded that she hadn't done anything to embarrass herself.

Finchly dealt her a second card: a king of spades. Not knowing what else to do, she simply threw even more of Deverill's blunt into the middle. After an awkward moment— and a kick in the shin from Deverill—she realized she had won the hand. She quickly turned her little squeal of delight into a cough. Finchly and the beautiful Halsey looked at her oddly. The other two didn't seem to notice anything was amiss.

Finchly placed the deck in front of her and said, "Your deal, Mr...."

"Lewis, sir, Lawrence Lewis," she said, using the name she had invented for her previous gambling expedition—a combination of her mother's maiden name and her father's middle name. She touched the cards gingerly, unsure of what to do with them. Should she shuffle them as Finchly had done? What if she dropped them and they scattered all over the table and into everyone's laps? Deverill, impatient with her inactivity, squeezed her knee again and she cut the deck. The cards didn't flutter nicely and she feared she might tear them, but in the end, she did a decent enough job of shuffling. At least she thought so. From the scowl on Deverill's face, she concluded that her performance was far from impressive.

The hand was played without any great upsets, and Catherine believed she had a good understanding of the crux of the game. All one had to do was gather as many cards as possible without their total equaling more than one-and-twenty. Her only serious faux pas occurred when she was dealt one-and-twenty at the onset—a natural vingt-et-un, explained Deverill—and didn't say anything. Apparently one was supposed to announce such a development immediately.

Catherine tried to enjoy herself, but her impatience was getting the better of her while the counters in front of her were depleting rapidly. She wanted this episode to be over and Evelyn's future secure—all without her owing Deverill a pile of money her family did not have. When she was sure no one was looking, she tapped Deverill on the knee and sent him a speaking glance. He made an almost imperceptible shake of the head. She sighed loudly. Again Finchly and Halsey looked at her. What, she asked herself, annoyed by their glances, didn't men sigh?

After another half hour, she decided she'd had enough. Deverill needed to put an end to this charade before she lost more money than she would ever be able to pay back. A close examination of Finchly had revealed nothing of his methods. He was now winning steadily and had amassed a tidy fortune in front of him, but she didn't have a clue as to how he did it. She looked around the table to see if anyone else was concerned, but none of the men seemed at all put out by their losses.

While Catherine was deciding how to play her cards, the door opened and the large man with the scar stepped in. He sent a confused look her way, clearly wondering how she had gotten in there without his knowing. She could see the faint discoloration of the whiskey on his otherwise pristine white shirt.

He took drink orders and left again. Catherine requested

a gin not because she liked the taste, but because it was what Deverill had bespoken and she couldn't think of a spirit other than sherry at that moment.

When her drink came, she took a large sip, primarily because the room was warm and she was very thirsty. It tasted like water. "Why, this isn't—" Her exclamation was summarily cut off by Deverill's booted foot stomping on hers. She realized that she had been about to make an egregious error and recovered the best she could. "...at all the kind of quality gin I am used to. Where is that man? I would like another one but the good stuff this time."

"Not quality gin?" asked Finchly. "Here, let us have a taste." He reached over to pick up her glass and Catherine panicked. She picked up her drink and swallowed the water in one giant gulp. Then she started coughing violently. Deverill slapped her on the back, ostensibly to help, but he did it harder than necessary and it didn't help at all.

She noticed Finchly—and the others—were staring at her oddly. "I...uh...didn't want to judge prematurely. It suddenly occurred to me that I should at least try another sip, and upon reconsideration, it was just the thing. Now, where is that man?" She looked around the room rather uselessly. "I should like a refill."

Finishing his drink, Finchly said, "I believe I shall join Mr. Lewis in another." He got up and went through the door for a moment. In the few moments that he was gone, Halsey leaned over and whispered something into Deverill's ear.

Finchly returned to his seat and the guard brought in two drinks. He had to lean over Finchly in order to retrieve the empty glass and lay down the full one. As he was doing so, he lost his balance for a moment and knocked Finchly. He blushed faintly and apologized. Catherine wasn't surprised. In her experience, large men tended to be clumsy. Next, he placed a glass in front of her without mishap. Hesitantly,

Catherine tasted hers, and quickly realizing it was the real stuff this time, limited herself to shallow sips.

The card playing resumed. Worried now that she might throw everything off with her carelessness, Catherine made sure her behavior was circumspect. She resolved to wait patiently and to allow Deverill to follow his original plan with no further disturbances from her.

Her patience was rewarded. With the very next hand, Martindale—the blond man sporting the teal waistcoat, she had discovered—asked, "I say, Finchly, what's that?"

Finchly looked up from his cards, surprised by the question. "What's what?"

"Bainbridge, my good man," Martindale said laconically, "would you be so kind as to examine Finchly's cuff and tell me what I am seeing. It looks to me like a card, but I would loath to make a premature accusation."

Finchly, in the act of taking a sip of his gin, paled considerably and dropped his glass. Hitting the table, it tumbled over and rolled onto the floor, spilling its contents along the way. He pushed his seat back and stood up to get out of the gin's path and in the process, a card fell out of his sleeve: an ace of clubs. They all saw it happen, Finchly especially, and he stared at it for a long time. The confusion was written plainly on his face—as well as the guilt.

Watching, Catherine tried to make sense of his expression. Her original assumption was that Finchly had been set up. After all, it was what they had come here to do. But then why did he look so guilty? Had he in fact been cheating? Or was he such an inveterate double-dealer that he didn't know anymore when he was doing it and when he wasn't?

Very quietly, Martindale said, "Finchly, I would ordinarily demand an explanation, but the situation seems quite evident. Given your reputation, I can't even say that I am surprised."

Finchly looked around the table at the austere faces and considered his defense. "This isn't...I don't know...I'm innocent," he insisted. "I...I have never cheated at cards." This last was said with so little conviction it seemed that not even Finchly believed it.

"Come, Finchly," said Bainbridge, "spare us your empty protestations of innocence. Have a little dignity, man."

Speechless, Finchly opened and closed his mouth several times, his lips flapping ridiculously. After a few moments of staring dumbly, he said, "Gentlemen, you have my word of honor that—"

"Think carefully, Finchly, about what you say before you say it," Halsey warned. "You don't want to sully your honor any more than you already have."

Finchly's helpless look was almost comical, and Mr. Lewis had to hide an inappropriately gleeful smile. Thinking again of their conversation earlier, Catherine didn't feel one whit of sympathy for him. Maybe if he hadn't said those despicable things about her, she wouldn't relish his misfortune but... He was a horrid toad who had tried to destroy her sister's life and deserved all that he got.

Deverill let him stew for a full minute more before saying, "Martindale, Bainbridge, Halsey, why don't you let me have a moment alone with Finchly. Perhaps if there isn't such a crowd, he'll be able to explain himself better."

"What about Lewis?" Bainbridge asked.

"I don't think Mr. Lewis's presence will bother Finchly. Come on, gentlemen," said Halsey, who seemed to have a better sense of what was going on than the others, "I find I'm suddenly in need of fresh air."

Finchly watched them leave with something akin to regret written on his face, and Catherine wondered at it. Did he think they would go straight to Brook's to spread the tale?

Calmer now and with a better grip on himself, Finchly

turned to Deverill and said, "Thank you, my lord, for giving me the opportunity to defend myself. Sadly, I fear the others"—he looked at the door through which they had just passed—"have already judged me."

"Save it, Finchly," said the marquess crushingly.

"But, my lord, you said—" Finchly clenched his fists.

"I don't care if you are guilty or innocent. Considering all I know of you, I very much doubt that you are innocent. But, as I said, that is neither here nor there," Deverill announced coldly, showing more interest in straightening his shirt cuff than he did in Finchly.

Finchly seemed prepared to defend himself again in righteous anger, but to Catherine's relief, he wisely held back. She was tired of listening to meager protestations. She supposed Deverill was as well.

"Very well, then," he said, sitting back down in his chair and leaning his arms against the table, careful of the spilled gin, "what do you care about?"

Deverill smiled thinly. "What do I care about? Yes, that seems to be the question, doesn't it?" He pushed his chair back and stood up. He was already a fair number of inches taller than Finchly and now he towered above him. "I am prepared to convince Martindale, Bainbridge and Halsey that what happened here tonight was all a simple misunderstanding."

"And how do you propose to do that?" he asked, hope creeping into his voice and color into his face.

"Don't let that bother you," said Deverill mysteriously. "The point is, I am willing to save your worthless reputation...for a price, of course."

Finchly nodded as if he had expected this development. "Of course. But what can I do for the exalted Marquess of Deverill?"

Catherine, watching the proceedings quietly from her

chair, marveled that there wasn't a trace of irony in Finchly's voice. He sounded completely resigned. Perhaps that was what persistent cheating did to a man, she thought. It prepared him for the inevitable worst.

"Nothing much," the marquess said coolly. "Simply release Miss Evelyn Fellingham from your—shall we say agreement—and I will ensure that nobody hears about your transgression."

Finchly stared at the marquess for several seconds, then fixed his glare on Catherine. His eyes blazed with sudden recognition, and he showed none of the resignation from moments before. "It's you, isn't it?" he sneered angrily, his nostrils flaring slightly. "I knew something wasn't quite right. ..." His voice trailed off as he realized that he had walked right into a trap.

Sitting very stiffly and holding in a smile of relief, Catherine said calmly, "I warned you, Mr. Finchly. I told you that you would be thwarted by a woman with no power, but you didn't have the sense to believe me. I believe now I've proven my point."

Finchly's face curled into a hideous snarl. "Why, you conniving little—"

In a flash he was up, his chair overturning behind him as he leaped across the table to tackle Catherine. The force of his weight knocked her over, and she tumbled to the floor just as his open palm struck her cheek. She cried out, feeling the pain before she understood its cause, and thrashed her arms and legs to break free of the mass that was now pressing on her chest. And then just as quickly, the weight was gone and Finchly was across the room, clutching a bloody nose. Lord Deverill stood over him, grim and fierce and as terrifying as any avenging angel.

Struggling to regain her breath, Catherine sat up and stared at Deverill as she began to fill in the gaps in her understanding. Her cheek throbbed and she knew a welt would soon form, ensuring she would not be going to Lord Raines's ball tonight or anywhere else in the immediate future. Her clothes were disheveled, her shirt ripped from her trousers, the top button torn, her cravat thoroughly unraveled. So much for Freddy's hard work, she thought, somewhat hysterically as she felt laughter rise in her throat. She pushed the hysteria back, unwilling to lose her wits now that the danger had passed.

Deverill, flushed and also breathing hard, was determined to give her time to recover, and although the look he gave her was searching and concerned, he didn't say anything. He was waiting for her to signal that all was well.

She gave her pulse a few moments more to steady, then said with a calmness she didn't quite yet feel, "Thank you, my lord, for your assistance. I fear if it weren't for your quick intervention, it would be me with a bloody nose."

"Catherine, my dear, how many times do I have to tell you that 'Julian' will suffice?" he asked with a sort of chiding good humor that belied his grim expression. "And there's really no need to thank me. I'm gratified to learn that dozens of useless hours spent sparring with Gentleman Jackson have some purpose after all."

His handkerchief soaking with blood, Finchly listened to this exchange and growled in disgust. "I see it all now," he said, his voice nasal from the blow to his nose. "Your sister came crying to you, and you went crying to Deverill. How cozy for you all." He repositioned the cloth, trying to find a clean patch to apply to the bleeding appendage. "Your sister mentioned something about Deverill courting you, but I told her not to be ridiculous. Why would a nonesuch even look at an on-the-shelf spinster with no conversation?"

It occurred to Catherine that Finchly had no idea that he was imperiling himself further with talk like this. He seemed completely oblivious to the marquess's clenched fingers or the way his nostrils flared.

"I told her the very idea was preposterous," he continued. "Indeed, her form is nothing to scoff at with that pair of luscious—"

Deverill had the other man on his feet and by the collar so quickly, Catherine hadn't even seen him move. "I don't think you are in a position to be disrespectful to a lady," he said with quiet menace.

With Deverill tugging so abruptly at his shirt, Finchly was forced to abandon his nose and balance himself with both hands. As Catherine watched the blood dribble down his chin, she decided that she had seen enough. Her intention was for Finchly to be humiliated. Well, he had been humiliated, and seeing it afforded her little of the satisfaction she had anticipated. It merely gave her an additional disgust of him.

"Deverill, let him be," she said, suddenly exhausted. She wanted the whole episode over and done with. "And do give him a fresh handkerchief. All that blood is becoming tiresome."

The marquess complied, releasing Finchly with a jerk of his hand that sent the other man tumbling backward. He took a white square from his waistcoat and threw it at him.

"Am I to assume that we are agreed," asked Deverill, seemingly picking the conversation up where it had been left before the violent interruption. "My silence for your silence?"

Finchly, his pugnacious little face pulled tight, clearly wanted to argue further, but he realized the wisdom of silence and acquiesced with a nod.

"Good, then your business here is concluded," Deverill said, turning his back on the pathetic figure and striding over to where Catherine sat on the floor. "Would you be so good as to send in the others? I would like to have a word with them."

"But I can't go out there looking like this," Finchly protested, appalled by the notion of being exposed to his peers with his nose dripping blood.

Deverill waved an indifferent hand as he got down on his haunches to examine Catherine's face. "It's really no concern of mine what you can and can't do. But I see no reason why you can't go out there looking like that. We are in a gaming hell, not White's or Brook's. The level of decorum is not as high."

This wasn't altogether true—bloody noses were not de rigueur in any venue save the boxing ring—but Finchly was smart enough not to belabor the point. Instead, he simply stood up, held on to a chair for a few seconds to assure his balance and then walked to the door.

"Oh, Finchly," Catherine called as he was about to leave, "do be a dear and send in my brother, Freddy. He's out there somewhere."

He slammed the door behind him with a crack.

"Freddy!" exclaimed Deverill. "Is that cawker here as well? I thought I told him with sufficient menace never to bring you here again."

Catherine laughed weakly. "Poor Freddy. But you mustn't take it out on him. He's no match for me."

At the sound of her laughter, Deverill froze. He stared at her for a long time, long enough for her to become aware of how ridiculous she must look. First the mustache, then the ugly welt on her cheek, then her tumbledown neckcloth. She tore off the mustache, the pain of which was minimal compared with her cheek, and sought to break the tension. "Another Roman Ruin ruined," she said, lifting one end of the cravat.

The marquess smiled, as she had intended, and gently ran a finger along her cheek. "That must hurt."

She nodded slowly, her eyes trained on his, suddenly so close.

"I'm afraid there will be no hiding the bruise," he said, pressing a kiss so gently against her cheek she could barely feel it.

She nodded again, her heart quivering at the contact.

"You'll have to keep a low profile for a while." He laid a kiss along her jawline. "Your coterie of admirers will be disappointed," he added, inching another kiss nearer to her mouth.

"Will you?" she murmured, though the ability to make coherent speech was rapidly leaving.

"That depends," he said, finally capturing her lips in a searing kiss that shook her to the core and left her more breathless than ever. "No, I don't think I will mind greatly if your suitors are denied the pleasure of your company." He was about to kiss her again when a discreet cough from the doorway brought them to their senses.

"Ah, Halsey," he said, seemingly unperturbed by the fact he'd been caught kissing a gentleman of their acquaintance. "Good of you to wait. Aside from a slight alteration or two, everything proceeded as planned."

Halsey smiled. "I saw Finchly's nose."

"Yes, well, we can't have him offending a lady. But, of course, you haven't met Miss Fellingham," he said, rising to his feet and gently helping Catherine to hers. "Please let me do the honor. Miss Catherine Fellingham, may I present to you Eric Peters, Earl of Halsey."

Catherine, feeling sillier than ever in her disguise and thoroughly embarrassed at being discovered in Deverill's arms, curtsied. "My pleasure, sir. I thank you very much for your participation in tonight's proceedings. It means a great deal to me and my family."

He bowed in return. "Not at all. I can always rely on Deverill to make things interesting." He looked at the marquess. "If that is all, I'm going to leave. I have to make an appearance at Lord Raines's ball." At the door, he paused. "By the by, Martindale and Bainbridge were too caught up in a game of faro to be interrupted, but I'll assure them all is well on my way out."

Just then the door opened and in walked Freddy. "Hallo, Catherine, Deverill." He didn't recognize Halsey so he just nodded at him as the other man passed through the door. "What the devil happened to—" He broke off as he saw the bright red mark on her cheek. "Did Finchly do that?" he growled.

Fearful that her brother would storm out after the villain and create a scene, Catherine said, "Yes, he did, and Julian has already planted him a facer, so you needn't tackle him as well."

"Did you, sir?" he asked Deverill. "A hook or an uppercut?"

"Never mind all that," Catherine said impatiently. "The important thing is, it's all over. Finchly has agreed to withdraw his suit and not to say a thing about Mama."

"That's jolly good, of course. But I want to hear more about the fight. Did he put up a defense?"

"But that's not important," she insisted.

"Not important?" he repeated in disgust. "Catherine, I just spent the last hour fetching drinks for that house with a scar so that he wouldn't beat me to a bloody pulp for spilling whiskey on him. I deserve some reward." As if realizing that his sister simply couldn't understand this reasoning, he applied directly to Deverill. "Surely, my lord, you think the hit is important."

Before Deverill could answer, Catherine hooked her arm through Freddy's and led him from the room. "Come, we must go home and tell Evelyn the good news. She must be crawling the walls by now." She looked behind her to make sure Deverill was following.

Freddy shook free of her grasp. "Don't do that. I can't be seen linking arms with another man."

"Oh, I forgot," she said with a laugh before realizing the motion hurt her cheek. She raised a hand to quiet the throbbing and Deverill disappeared for a few minutes to fetch a towel with ice.

"Try this," he said, once they were settled in his carriage. "The cold should help reduce the swelling."

Although he was sympathetic to his sister's pain, Freddy was dying to hear the details and impatiently insisted that someone tell him all that had transpired before the sun came up.

When he was assured of Catherine's comfort, the marquess said, "Everything went according to plan. Halsey, Martindale, Bainbridge and I asked Finchly if he wanted to join us in a game in the back room. He was so flattered by the invitation that it didn't occur to him to wonder at it. I had arranged the room with the owner beforehand, and he told Munson—the man you call a 'house with a scar'—to serve us watered-down drinks and Finchly the real stuff. I wanted him to be a trifle foxed and not thinking clearly. I hoped that he would cheat on his own, but his losses were minimal and I could not detect anything suspicious. Then your sister showed up and practically gave the whole thing away—several times, I might add."

Catherine sputtered and tried to interrupt, but Deverill would not let her.

"Don't deny it. You *did* almost ruin everything," he insisted. "For one thing, you cough like a lady."

She had never heard anything so ridiculous. As if ladies coughed any differently than gentlemen. "That is so—"

"Once your sister arrived and upset the cart," continued Deverill as if Catherine had not spoken, "I decided to put an end to the whole charade. I made a gesture to Munson that indicated it was time. He then pretended to bump into Finchly, all the while planting the incriminating card on him. Munson used to be the finest pickpocket in Piccadilly before he grew too large to be invisible, although he still moves with enviable speed."

"Good show, sir," cried Freddy admiringly. "I'm sorry that my sister nearly toppled your scheme. I tried to keep her out of it, my lord, but I'm afraid she coerced me."

"Think nothing of it, my boy," Deverill said, surprising both Freddy and Catherine with his good humor. "I know how convincing she can be when she wants something."

Freddy smiled, relieved that he wasn't going to be taken to task for his sister's behavior. The rest of the ride home was consumed with his questions, and when they arrived at the Fellingham town house, Freddy said, "Are you sure you don't know who Halsey's tailor is? I don't think I've ever seen a coat cut finer."

"Don't be silly, scapegrace," his sister scolded. "How would Julian know a thing like that?"

"He might not know, but he could find out," Freddy said, looking embarrassed and hopeful at the same time.

Again, to the surprise of both Fellinghams, Deverill laughed. "I shall devote myself to solving the mystery first thing in the morning."

Freddy smiled hugely. "Thank you, my lord. You're a regular out-and-outer." Just then, the driver opened the door and Freddy shook hands with Deverill before climbing out. "We are greatly in your debt, and if there is ever anything the Fellinghams can do for you, it would be our pleasure."

"Actually, I have something in mind," he said, "but I'll take it up with your father."

As Catherine moved to climb out of the curricle, an arm snaked around her waist and pulled her back against the seat. She looked at Deverill in amazement, but he only grinned widely at her and told Freddy that they would both be in in a few minutes. And then her blasted brother shut the curricle door and left her alone with him.

"My lord, I don't think—"

Before she could say anything more, she was pushed back against the cushions and ruthlessly kissed. She thought about protesting, but the sensations were far too enjoyable and she just sank deeper and deeper into the web of desire he was weaving.

After several minutes, he pulled back slightly, although his body was still pressed against hers. As soon as her lips were free, she resumed her sentence from earlier "—that you should—"

He cut her off with another kiss, and when he released her this time, he placed a finger over her lips to keep her from speaking. "No, not this time. You're *not* going to do that to me again."

She stared up at him, baffled. Since his finger did little to impede speech, she asked, her voice not quite steady, "Do what to you?"

He looked at her from beneath hooded eyes glinting with desire. "Ask me if that is all in that cold, indifferent voice you used last night. Because this time I can feel you trembling in my arms and because this time I won't believe that you feel nothing at all. And I won't walk off in a huff and resolve never to speak to you again. I know better now."

Recalling the scene at the Rivington ball, Catherine closed her eyes as the humiliation washed over her anew. How could this have happened again? Why did she have to dissolve uselessly every time he came within two feet of her?

Deverill felt her tense in his arms and shook her quite

violently. "Open your eyes," he demanded, "and look at me, damn you."

She complied, responding reluctantly to the anger she heard in his voice.

"We're going to have this out once and for all," he said, tightening his hold on her, "and neither one of us is leaving this carriage until we are well and truly engaged."

Catherine was so shocked by this announcement that she would later swear that her heart stopped beating for an entire minute. "Engaged?" she whispered. "But that's madness."

"I don't care. We will stay here all night if we have to. Of course," he said, considering his plan, "such a development would leave you horribly compromised and you'd have to marry me anyway, but if you agree now, you will at least be able to pass a comfortable night in your own bed." He pressed himself against her. "Not that this is such an awful alternative."

Catherine's body responded to this closeness of his, but she refused to let desire cloud her thinking. "I don't want to marry you."

"Yes, you do. You are so in love with me that you can't bear the thought of living without me," he said confidently, "and yet you are going to give it a try because you think that *I* think that you're the veriest quiz."

This was so close to the truth that Catherine shuddered. "'Twas you who said it," she reminded him with considerable asperity.

"Stop being so damn hen-witted," he demanded. "If I did say that—and I'm not quite convinced that I did—it was months and months ago."

Amazed, she looked at him. "Months ago? My lord, it was only two weeks ago."

"Was it?" he asked unconcerned. "Well, it feels like a life-time ago, which is all that signifies. And it's completely unfair of you to hold that against me. What did I know then? *How* could I have known? I hadn't a clue that Bella's new project was the thoroughly charming woman I'd just met at the British Museum. When we did finally meet formally, in the park, if you recollect, while you were out for a drive with that puppy Pearson, I was most surprised to discover the truth. I'd already intended to pay you a call, you know. I'd given your direction to the driver and as such knew exactly where to find you."

Catherine's heart tripped as she realized that he had felt it, too—that sense of connection that had struck her so strongly at the museum, though it was a mere shadow of what she felt now.

"Really?" she asked, afraid to believe in what still felt to her like a fairy tale too wonderful to be true.

"My dear remarkable, beautiful girl, what do I have to do to convince you that I love you?" he asked gently. "I have already saved your sister from a wretched marriage and your family from public disgrace. I have asked you to marry me. I have even agreed to ask Halsey who his tailor is as a favor to your brother. Surely, if *that* isn't a sign of a besotted suitor, I don't know what is."

She laughed softly at the last, for it did strike her as a rather extreme measure, and she recalled what Lady Courtland had said about the ladies he usually courted. Perhaps in his experience, she really was remarkable. "But this afternoon when I tried to broach the subject, you interrupted me," she said, recalling the painful scene. "I screwed up my courage to declare my love for you right there in Lady Courtland's drawing room and you told me to go home."

"My love," he answered foolishly before enveloping her in another consuming kiss. "You must forgive me," he said, when at last his lips were free. "I was still smarting from the insults you had dealt me the night before, and I am afraid my pride got in the way." He hugged her tightly. "Really, to tell me that you were using me to meet other men! Neither my ego nor my heart could easily get over such a setdown. I will have to tread very carefully with you, my dear, for you are far too skilled at punishing me."

"I didn't know I could hurt you," she said, marveling that it was possible. "And what about you, my lord? What terrible things you said to me this morning. Calling me an ape leader to my face and stating outright that I should welcome an offer from Finchly. How could you believe that of me?"

"I trust you're not going to hold me accountable for the mad ravings of a jealous man. You cannot know what it's like to see the woman you love coming out of the apartments of another man at an indecently early hour," he told her, laying soft kisses along the nape of her neck until she could no longer think of a reason why he shouldn't.

Catherine thought in retrospect that it was a very likely possibility that they would have passed the entire night in the carriage after all had Evelyn not come pounding on the door. The two barely had a moment to separate before the door opened and Evelyn's blond head popped in. But even though they managed to put a respectable distance between them, what they had been doing was readily apparent from their flushed faces and labored breathing.

"Oh," said Evelyn, momentarily taken aback but then forging on carelessly. "I just couldn't wait any longer. Freddy told me the marvelous news, and I wanted to thank you both." She leaped into the carriage and threw her arms around Catherine. "You are the finest sister in the world, and I am so horribly sorry for all the mean things I've said to you."

Despite her sister's poor timing, Catherine was happy to see her. She had wanted to break the good news to Evelyn herself, but she should have known Freddy wouldn't be able to wait. "I always knew you never meant it."

Evelyn kissed her on the cheek before releasing her. "And I know that's bouncer, but thank you, dearest, for saying it." Then she gave similar treatment to Lord Deverill. At first he was stiff with surprise, but after an almost comically helpless look at Catherine, he relaxed in Evelyn's arms. After a few seconds, she let go. "I know it is not at all the thing for me to go around hugging strange lords, but since you are going to be my brother, I don't think it at all exceptional." Evelyn clapped her hands happily. "Oh, what a perfect evening. I am given an eleventh-hour pardon from a horrible life sentence—the details of which you will have to tell me yourselves since I don't think Freddy quite understands all that happened—and you, my dearest sister, are proposed to by the handsomest peer of the realm. Mama is going to be so happy. Speaking of which, you have five more minutes alone in the carriage before Freddy comes out. He's awfully worried about Catherine's reputation and he was all set to come out here, but I insisted he let me. Freddy doesn't have the deep understanding of matters of the heart that I do," she explained confidentially before jumping out of the carriage.

"Well, my lord," said Catherine once her little sister had closed the door and restored their privacy—at least temporarily.

"Well what, my love?" he asked softly, rejoining her on the cushion.

"Five minutes isn't a very large amount of time, and I am still not fully convinced that you want to marry me," she said slyly.

With a soft laugh, he gathered her close. "Don't worry. By the time Freddy gets the bottom to come out here and pull you forcefully from my arms, you will be."

About the Author

Lynn Messina is the author of more than a dozen novels, including the Beatrice Hyde-Clare mysteries, a series of cozies set in Regency-era England. Her first novel, *Fashionistas,* has been translated into sixteen languages and was briefly slated to be a movie starring Lindsay Lohan. Her essays have appeared in *Self, American Baby* and *the New York Times* Modern Love column, and she's a regular contributor to the *Times* parenting blog. She lives in New York City with her sons.

Made in the USA
Middletown, DE
21 November 2021

53087309R00161